THE RIVER'S EDGE

A Novel

Tony Hayden

authorHOUSE®

AuthorHouse™
1663 Liberty Drive
Bloomington, IN 47403
www.authorhouse.com
Phone: 1-800-839-8640

First published by AuthorHouse 4/15/2009

ISBN: 978-1-4389-7120-9 (sc)

Printed in the United States of America
Bloomington, Indiana

This book is printed on acid-free paper.

A note from the author:

Writing *The River's Edge* was an incredible voyage for me. This was my first attempt at crafting a dynamic story, with believable characters, and suspenseful plot. When I created it, I was so wrapped up in the "big" story, that I neglected some of the smaller, important stuff. Many readers were more than happy to point this out, and thankfully, I was more than happy to listen and learn from them.

In this edition of *The River's Edge*, I tried to incorporate many of the suggestions I received. Not because I wanted to pander to my readers, but because I truly felt that these recommendations had merit. If anything, this novel has been a wonderful education for me. I have learned more during the past two years than I think I ever could have, sitting in a classroom. And this is coming from a former American History teacher who values education immensely.

A special *Thank You* goes to my friend, Tony Borton, who is also a writer. His encouragement and attention to detail proved invaluable during this revision of *The River's Edge*. When his novel hits the shelves, I highly recommend you pick it up and prepare yourself for a spiritual journey.

If you are reading *The River's Edge* for the first time, I sincerely hope that you feel rewarded after you close that final page. If this is your second journey to Chiapas, Mexico, with the Iverson's, please understand that the story is still fundamentally the same, but better. I also want to personally thank you for your investment in me as a new author. I am truly honored to share this amazing experience with you.

For my father, Wayne L. Hayden
Thank you for turning my penny heads up.

*The line dividing good and evil
cuts through the heart of every man.*

Alexander Solzhenitsyn

Prologue
Chiapas, Mexico

Aldo Castillo stood at the edge of the primeval forest and looked down upon the tiny village of Ocultada. He was Chief Elder to the eighty-six *Hach Winik*, "true people," who inhabited the hidden settlement, deep in the Lacandon Jungle. Ten years earlier, Aldo had led his people away from Najá, a government enforced commune in northern Chiapas, to this roadless valley, three kilometers west of the great Usumacinta River.

Aldo smiled as he watched his people perform their daily tasks. Men, women and children, all dressed in the traditional white tunics of the Lacandon people, busied themselves with essential chores. The men, with long black hair spilling across their white robes, stood on the thatch roofs of their homes and wove fresh fronds into the coverings, while women brought large piles of firewood from the jungle. A group of small children were laughing as they took turns swinging in a brightly colored hammock, tied between two Chocho Palms.

Aldo raised his arms to the heavens and spoke in his native tongue. He chanted a muffled prayer to ask Mensabak, the God of rain and protector of the dead, to bring life sustaining water back to his remote valley. Weeks earlier, the abundant stream that followed the valley floor, past his vibrant community, had stopped flowing. Women were now carrying water from a spring high on the mountainside. The task was relentless and was rapidly fatiguing the wives assigned to the chore.

A deep rumble rose from the north. Mensabak was answering Aldo's prayer.

Rex Smith was Chief Engineer for the American led project to dam the Usumacinta River. Power generated from the four hydro-electric dams, to be built along a two-hundred mile stretch of the river, would supply enough electricity to meet the growing needs of southern and central Mexico for years to come.

Today, engineers were preparing to divert water from the Usumacinta, into an alternate river valley so workers could begin stripping loose soil from the bedrock, several feet beneath the river. Cement factories were coming on line to begin the arduous task of producing high quality concrete to construct the dam's foundation.

Rex was consulting with several explosives experts about the event scheduled to take place in less than thirty minutes.

"There will be a wall of water, fifty-feet high, traveling roughly thirty meters per second, down that valley," one of the engineers injected into the conversation.

Rex lifted his gaze from the plans on the table and searched the room for the Mexican army captain assigned to protect his workers, "Captain Marquez," he said, "Were your men able to clear the people from that village to the south?"

Captain Eduardo Marquez sat at a small table in the corner, peeling an orange, being very careful not to stain the blue ascot tied around his neck and tucked neatly into his uniform. Without raising his head, the captain mumbled, "The village has been cleared."

Captain Marquez didn't like sitting here with these arrogant American men and he wasn't about to take orders from them. If they wanted to move the people from that village then they could make the two day trek on foot to do so. Marquez and his men were not about to.

"Thank you, captain." Rex turned to his next in command, "Let's divert this river."

Aldo noticed his people below turning toward the growing roar to the north. He had heard stories from others who had witnessed great eruptions of fire and ash from mountains, and for a brief moment he considered this possibility. The ground beneath his feet began to tremble as Aldo watched children in the village below, climb trees for a better view of the approaching thunder.

The village chief cried out as a wall of white water appeared and rushed toward his unsuspecting community. The children saw it first and tried to climb higher in the trees to escape, but the trees fell like corn stalks to the scythe. He could not hear their screams for help. Seconds later, Aldo watched as the entire village of Ocultada was washed away in an angry torrent of foam and fallen logs. The screams of his people, drowned out in the deafening roar. Chief Aldo stumbled toward the rising water. Falling to his knees, he asked, "Why did you forsake us, Mensabak? What did we do to anger you?"

The water rose higher and was now swirling around Aldo's thighs. He could not stand; refused to rise. He could never run from the Rain God's wrath, and now that all his people were gone in the violent torrent of water, Aldo chose to join them. Mensabak was merciful and did not make Aldo wait for long. In less than five minutes time, the village of Ocultada and all if its inhabitants disappeared forever.

Twelve miles to the north, the cheers of the workers, engineers, and soldiers could finally be heard over the dissipating thunder of spent explosives.

One

Northwest Colorado

He could hear the low pitched buzz of the approaching snowmobile as it followed the power lines up the steep ridge to where he was working. Jim Iverson had worked for the telephone company since returning home from the first Persian Gulf War in 1992. It was a great job that offered solitude and a decent living wage for his small family. Jim was responsible for maintaining high capacity and fiber optic lines that fed remote cell towers and classified military sites located within a one-hundred mile radius of the small Colorado mountain town of Majestic.

The White River National Forest challenged Jim in ways he had never imagined. His tour in Iraq in the early nineties with the U.S. Army's Special Forces had shaped his life and set a tough physical standard for him to live by. This was the perfect job for him.

Three days earlier, Jim had been dispatched to Yellow Jacket Pass after a heavy snowfall, to repair damage to lines that monitored a remote relay site for the U.S. Air Force. The approaching snowmobile was a co-worker from Meeker who filled in for Jim while he was on well earned vacations. The engine noise grew louder as the Yamaha

VK used all of its 120 horse power to crest the south facing ridge where Jim was now standing.

"Holy Mother of God, Jim, could you have found a tougher place to get to?" This was Kevin Strickland, a long time colleague and good friend of Jim's.

"I couldn't make it too easy for you, Kevin," Jim said shaking Kevin's heavily gloved hand, "You're getting way too soft around the middle with your cushy city job."

Kevin laughed as he climbed off the now steaming snowmobile, "I'm not looking forward to covering for you for a full year while you're off soaking up the sun in Mexico. This is a young buck's job and I know my rugged good looks don't show it but damn, I'm an old man!"

Jim laughed and quietly assured himself that this "old man" could out work most men half his age. He had no doubts that his area would be in top condition when he returned from southern Mexico a year from now.

Jim's wife, Carol, was a high school teacher in nearby Glenwood Springs. She was working on a PhD in anthropology and had taken a sabbatical from her teaching to travel to Chiapas, Mexico. She planned to live with and study a small village of Indians who were in danger of losing their native land to development brought on by the free trade agreements. Jim couldn't stand the idea of being separated from his wife of twelve years so they decided to pull their ten year old son from school and make the journey as a family. Even as a teacher, Carol agreed that this experience would be every bit as educational for their son, Taylor, as a year spent in a classroom reading books and doing worksheets.

Jim joked, "Kevin, don't grow too fond of my mountains, I've pissed on every tree out here and that makes this place eternally mine."

Kevin laughed loudly and stated, "Don't you go worrying your pretty little self about that. I plan on spending most of the year working the lines near Lake Avery and having Rainbow Trout for dinner every night. Now, let's get this equipment loaded and haul our sorry butts off this mountain before the sun goes down."

Thirty minutes later, Jim led the way down the snow covered pass to the company four by four and utility trailer parked just off Highway 64. As civilization grew closer, Jim grew eager to get home to his modest cabin built on two hundred acres outside the small town of Majestic. Majestic was the perfect mountain village nestled among the towering Lodgepole Pines about thirty miles northeast of Glenwood Springs. Jim had bought the land and built the cabin with bonus money he earned while serving in the military.

He met his beautiful wife shortly after at a gas station in Rifle. As soon as he saw her, he knew that he would spend the rest of his life with her. Carol was fresh out of college in Boulder, Colorado, and full of optimism and excitement for her new career, teaching science to high school students. Her smile and radiant green eyes warmed a place in Jim's heart that he was sure had died in the desert of Iraq. Jim had resigned himself to a life of solitude to ensure that he never had to share what happened to him and his reconnaissance team over there.

Seeing Carol as she stood at the small window that separated her from the cashier, changed Jim's life forever. It was amazing. For a man of few words, he knew exactly what to say. For a man of disciplined movement and lean muscle, he knew exactly how to caress and embrace this woman who obviously shared his soul. One year later, they were married and two years after that Carol gave birth to their son, Taylor.

Jim had never dreamed his life would be so fulfilled. Everything was perfect. He was a little uneasy uprooting his family and moving to southern Mexico for a year. He always knew that Carol had sizeable goals and had set her sights on teaching anthropology at Colorado University. He always knew that one day, in order to keep her, he would have to follow her. That time had come and he was ready, albeit reluctantly, to chase her dreams for awhile.

Near the bottom of Yellow Jacket Pass, Jim and Kevin exchanged last minute advice and held an extended handshake that only true friends are comfortable with.

"You be very careful down there Jim," Kevin offered, "They don't respect human life like we do here."

Jim swallowed hard with a brief flashback to the Iraqi desert, "Thanks, Kevin. And you watch out for the mountain lion living up on Flat Top. Come spring, she'll probably think even your sorry ass would make a tasty meal."

After Kevin drove away toward his home in Meeker, Jim settled in to the toasty cab of his company truck to watch the dazzling Rocky Mountain sunset. He was well aware that this would be his last opportunity for a long time to observe the deep blue Colorado sky transform to brilliant orange then blood red before settling into a dark blanket painted brightly with millions of tiny stars.

Two

Carol Iverson stood at the kitchen window fidgeting with a dish towel as she watched the sun slip behind the snow covered mountains. Jim had been gone three days now and they were scheduled to fly out of Denver International Airport at 7:00 a.m. the next morning. He usually kept her updated by radio about when he would be home but the day had passed without word. She was a little upset that it was left to her to prepare for the trip alone but she couldn't hold a grudge. Jim's supervisor had been more than accommodating when asked for a one year leave of absence. Carol knew that the phone company's gracious behavior had been due in part because they understood how hard it would be to find another worker as selfless and dedicated as her husband.

Carol wasn't worried about Jim's safety. Through twelve years of marriage she had grown to understand that there was no situation he couldn't handle. His awareness of everything around him at all times had always provided her with a sense of ease whenever Jim had to spend time in the mountains repairing phone lines. She just wished that he wouldn't cut it this close.

An internal nagging guilt flushed over Carol as she thought about dragging her ten year old son away from his friends and the only life he had ever known. She felt a little selfish for pulling her husband away from his dream to pursue hers. Carol had always been a giving person. Every day, she immersed herself in the success of her students. Their failures were hers and she carried their hopes and fears, successes and disappointments with her everywhere she went.

Carol was endlessly devoted to her son, Taylor. After hours of grading papers and helping him with his homework, she still found time every night to read to him at bedtime. Last fall when Jim offered to take on this task, Carol flatly refused. She cherished this special time with her son, "Now if you would like to help grade research papers for me, that would be wonderful." Jim quickly found something else to occupy his time. Sometimes he just didn't get her sense of humor.

Explosions and sounds of a fierce battle filtered into the kitchen from Taylor's room. He was obviously busy defeating another alien invasion and saving planet Earth on his new video console. Carol walked to his bedroom door and stood there watching the animated character leap from rock to rock while somersaulting and blasting insect looking creatures from behind their plasma shields. When Taylor looked up from the carnage displayed on the TV, Carol said, "Fifteen minutes, bud, then I want your teeth brushed and you in your pajamas."

"Mom, it's not even seven o'clock," Taylor protested.

"I know, son, but we leave for the airport at four a.m.. Tomorrow will be a very long day for all of us, so please don't give me any grief!" Carol pleaded.

"Okay!" Taylor relented, "When's Dad coming home? Are we not going if he doesn't come home tonight?"

"He wishes," Carol joked. She ruffled Taylor's hair and in a reassuring tone said, "Your father will be home soon, Tot. He's looking forward to spending a lot of time with his best son in the whole universe."

Taylor sulked off to the bathroom to brush his teeth, "Mom, I'm his only son and please stop calling me Tot; it makes me feel like a baby!"

"I know, Tot. Sometimes I just can't help myself."

Tater Tot was a nickname she and Jim had given their son when he was a baby. It just seemed to fit and Carol was not quite ready to let that part of his childhood go. She leaned against the door and watched him as he walked down the hallway. He was so tall and extremely handsome for a ten year old. Carol just felt in her heart that someday he would do something great for this world. He loved science and anything to do with space. He often talked about being a doctor on the space station. Carol wasn't ready to think about that just yet. If she could, she would stop time now and hold on to these days forever.

Two hours later, Taylor was tucked into bed and snoring softly while Carol made her way through the spacious log home, setting timers on lights to give the appearance of an occupied house. Friends and co-workers had agreed to stop by every couple of weeks to check on things and ensure everything was in order.

Shadows danced across the dark living room as the headlights from Jim's company truck swept the front of the house. Relief passed through Carol's chest followed by a hint of frustration at Jim's failure to keep her informed on his whereabouts. Jim opened the door to the mudroom off the kitchen and made a considerable amount of noise dropping his gear to the tiled floor.

"Shhhhhhhhh!" Carol cautioned quietly as she stepped into the room and embraced the only man she had ever loved, "Taylor did not want to go to sleep tonight. He had a million and one questions about our trip tomorrow." Carol nuzzled into Jim's neck and breathed in the strong aroma of sweat, campfire and warmth. This was always the scent of her husband after his long trips to the backwoods. Jim's tang teased Carol's emotions with lust and loneliness at the same time. She took one last deep breath and whispered, "Please don't shower before you come to bed tonight."

Jim wrapped his arms around Carol's waist and sighed deeply, "It is so nice to come home to a ravenous woman, but I'm sure that when you get a whiff of the rest of me, you're going to change your mind about that shower."

Carol stepped back and smiled, "Maybe," she said, "Why didn't you call me on the radio today? You had to know that I would be worried sick about you."

Jim shrugged, "The radio's broke, angel. The handset came out of its pack and was damaged while I was working my way through, probably fifty acres of fallen timber. It's a real mess up there. I haven't seen that much snow since the first year I worked up here. We're going to end up replacing ten miles of fiber optic cable up to the Air Force site. I filled Kevin in on everything. He'll have to take care of it this summer."

Carol held her finger to Jim's lips, "No more shop talk. For the next year, mister, you are mine and nobody else's."

Jim laughed, "I can't see a one room hut in the middle of a jungle, with Taylor and Spider Monkeys watching our every move, doing much for our love life, do you?"

"Shhhhhhhhh!" Carol teased, "We'll just have to practice tonight being very quiet."

Jim stepped into the steaming shower and stood with his eyes closed as the inviting heat massaged three days worth of kinks from his neck and shoulders. He heard the faint click of the shower door and opened his eyes to the smooth curvature of his wife's graceful, ivory colored body. Their shapes melted into one and initiated a dance that only true lovers ever experience.

Later that night, Carol lay in bed with her back to Jim as he caressed her powdered skin.

Carol sighed and spoke softly, "I'm sorry that I'm pulling you away from these mountains that you love so much."

As he drifted off to sleep, Jim whispered, "I would follow you to the moon, sweetheart."

Three

One week earlier
Zapatista Camp in the Highlands
Chiapas, Mexico

S ergio Salinas sat comfortably against the fallen tree as he drew a sketch in the dirt of the latest road blocks set up by government soldiers. The members of his group had long understood not to travel on the roads of Chiapas, but it was always useful to know specific places to avoid. Life had been difficult for the Zapatista rebels since the Mexican Army had moved in and occupied the area in 1994. Experts estimated that over fifty thousand federal troops now subjugated the small state of Chiapas.

Sergio and his younger brother Cristobal had embraced the rebellion from its onset. Both had grown up among unrelenting poverty in the small village of Perdido not far from where they were now camped. The Salinas brothers felt that any uprising against those who would take their ancient lands was not only demanded by tradition, but also morally justified. The Mayan Indians had been fighting and defeating those who would steal their homes and force their people into slavery for hundreds of years. The Mexican government was just the latest monster to oppress the Mayan people in order to bring more wealth to the *cochinos* in the big cities.

The latest plan for Chiapas called for the construction of enormous hydroelectric dams along the Usumacinta River. Water behind the dams would flood much of the fertile land now farmed by Mayan people. The President of Mexico was calling for the relocation of several villages to make way for foreign investors and development. At the thought of this, Sergio spat on the map he had drawn in the dirt. In the beginning, the revolution had been glorious. The world paid attention to their demands for justice and help came from many places. The media in Europe and America told his people's story and it seemed like the Mayans would win this battle with very little bloodshed. Ah, but the *politicos* in Mexico City understood that the world would soon become bored with the plight of the Mayan Indians and find somewhere else to expend their feigned outrage.

Several years later, with the uprising mostly pacified, the Mexican government was moving ahead quickly with its plans. The Americans had turned their backs on his people with their NAFTA and CAFTA agreements. They failed to understand that Sergio's people did not want economic development. They simply wanted to live free and work the land that their ancestors had worked before them.

Cristobal approached his brother and asked to speak to him in private, "What is it you want, *hermano*?" asked Sergio.

"I have a plan that I want to discuss with you, brother," Cristobal answered in a reluctant tone.

"Be very careful what you say," Sergio cautioned, "This forest has many ears."

Cristobal took his cue and sat close to Sergio, "We need to bring the world back to our cause," he offered, "We need money to buy weapons and feed our soldiers and we need to do all of this immediately!"

Sergio cautiously looked around the camp to see if anyone was listening. Everyone seemed to be occupied with their daily tasks.

"What you are telling me brother is no secret. As long as the world remains ignorant to our cause, we are nothing but lawless rebels hiding in the jungle."

"I have a plan," Cristobal offered excitedly, "I want to kidnap an American engineer, one that is here making plans for the dams."

Sergio remained silent, never losing eye contact with his brother.

Cristobal was a little shaken by his brother's silence but decided to continue, "An American hostage will bring world attention to Chiapas and people will remember our cause. They will see that we are desperate and Mexico's plans for our land will be brought into the light again." Cristobal waited, then became angry with his brother's lack of response. He shouted, "We will demand a ransom for the American and buy explosives to destroy the hydroelectric dams while they are building them."

Sergio's eyes shared his anger at Cristobal's outburst, "You will lower your voice, *tonto!*" Sergio scolded, "Do you not believe that taking an American hostage would turn the world against our cause?"

Cristobal shook his head vigorously and said, "No, brother! People do not like America any more. They have caused wars and lied to the world. Europe is disgusted with America's arrogance and torture. They will embrace anyone who sticks a finger in America's eye."

Sergio looked away and pondered his brother's revelation. The Zapatistas were in serious trouble. Even the villagers were starting to accept defeat and their support was becoming a rarity. Cristobal was suggesting a bold new offensive and Sergio had to admit that he was somewhat intrigued by the idea. Lighting a fire in the hearts of the Mayan people was exactly what was needed right now.

The villagers and farmers knew that the American free trade agreements were the final straws that would inevitably break their backs and they were angry at the Americans for that.

"You will speak of this to no one," Sergio demanded, "Bring me a detailed plan in one week. If it is a good plan, with the blessings of our ancestors, we will take it to the Council of Elders for final approval." Sergio stood and walked into the forest to give this idea more thought.

Cristobal sat for several minutes shaking internally from the anticipation of a new uprising by the (EZLN) Zapatista National Liberation Army.

Four

Taylor Iverson stood on the platform at Denver International Airport with his parents, waiting for the underground train to approach. His inability to sleep the night before seemed to have no lasting affect as the excitement grew in Taylor's belly for his first ever flight on an airplane.

During the shuttle ride down the mountain from Eagle, his mom and dad used every minute to caution him about *this* and warn him about *that*.

"There are jaguars and poisonous snakes in the jungle," his mother shared.

"And cannibals," his father added, "Don't forget the cannibals!"

Taylor didn't fall for it. He had spent the last three months reading everything he could find on Chiapas, Mexico. Nothing he had read made any mention of cannibals. Plus, the grin on his father's face was a dead giveaway that he was having fun at Taylor's expense.

The information he had read, filled Taylor with wonder and excitement. The beautiful waterfalls, the jungles filled with every shade of green, the awesome insects and colorful birds, and especially the poisonous snakes and jaguars.

"Train's coming!" Taylor shrieked with excitement, "I want to sit by the big window in the front."

As the train approached, Carol put her arms around her son and held on to him, "Wait until all the passengers exit the other side, then you can choose where you want to sit."

For Taylor, the underground train ride was exhilarating. Propellers mounted to the tunnel walls spun in a silvery whirlwind as the cars passed. The train slowed, then sped up as it rounded bends and deposited passengers at their terminals.

"Can we ride it again?" Taylor asked as they disembarked and rode the escalator to their concourse.

"Not today, Tot," his dad replied, "We've got a plane to catch."

Taylor made a low grumble in his throat and gave his father a disapproving look, "Please don't call me Tot. I'm not a baby anymore!"

Taylor's attention was quickly diverted as they approached the gates on their concourse. Oversized windows revealed gigantic jets as they filled with passengers to shuttle them around the world.

"Is that our plane?" Taylor asked in awe, pointing to a Boeing 777 at the first gate they passed. His eyes were wide with excitement as he imagined flying in a plane as huge as the one he was looking at now.

His father chuckled, "I wish," he exclaimed, "I don't think our plane is going to be quite that large."

Taylor deflated a little but puffed back up as they approached their gate with the Mexicana Boeing 737 parked outside.

He expelled a long breath, "Cool beans!" he said. Placing his face against the cold window, he peered out at the bright white airplane sparkling in the morning sun.

Carol approached the ticket counter while Jim took a seat near Taylor, "Can I check in now?" Carol asked the young female agent.

The woman smiled and took the Iverson family's tickets. She typed on the computer and thumbed through the small booklets. A frown crossed her face as she came to Carol's ticket. The young lady looked up at Carol and with a nervous tone said, "Here are your boarding passes. I've placed you all together near the front of the plane in seats 11A, B and C. Enjoy your flight."

Carol took the passes and smiled at the odd behavior of the agent, "Thank you, Rene," she added after glancing at the young lady's name tag.

Before Carol made it back to where her husband and son were waiting, she was approached by an older, slightly overweight man in a gray camelhair blazer.

"Mrs. Iverson?" Without waiting for a reply, he continued, "I'm Geoff Baker with airport security."

Carol was a little stunned, "It's nice to meet you, Geoff. Is there something wrong?" she asked while placing the boarding passes into her purse.

"No ma'am, just some routine questions. You've been randomly selected for additional security screening. Would you mind stepping over here out of the way?" Geoff gestured to a table behind the check-in counter.

Slightly annoyed, Carol replied, "No, I don't mind. Can I take a second to tell my husband what's going on?"

"That won't be necessary," the security officer insisted, "It will only take a minute. If you don't mind," he added, gesturing again to the table.

Carol glanced at Jim who was pointing to something out the window and talking excitedly to their son.

"Well, if it won't take too long, our plane will be boarding shortly." Carol walked behind the counter and stood at the head of the table. Another man was already seated at the table with an open folder and some official looking papers off to one side.

"This is Bob Winter," Geoff introduced, "He's with the Department of Homeland Security and he'll be asking you a few questions." Geoff pulled out the chair next to Carol, "Take a seat please and we'll get you back to your family in a jiffy."

Carol quickly glanced back toward Jim and Taylor who were now engaged in their secret handshake. She let out a deep sigh and sat in the chair. Mr. Winter failed to make any eye contact with her. Instead, he sat quietly and examined several documents before him.

"Can we make this quick please, Mr. Winter? I have a plane to catch." Carol allowed the frustration to show in her voice.

"Would you mind handing your purse to Mr. Baker?" Bob finally asked, never looking up from the paper that held his attention, "He'll be conducting a thorough search while I ask you a few questions."

Carol handed her purse to the security officer and watched while he dumped the contents onto the table.

"Mrs. Iverson," Bob began, finally making eye contact, "We are a little confused about why your family purchased one-way tickets to Mexico. It's not often that we see American families traveling to such a troubled region of Mexico, without plans for a return flight. Would you mind explaining this to us?"

Carol breathed a sigh of relief, "Oh, I understand now." She looked at the gentleman with her purse disapprovingly as he used a ball point pen to separate her jewelry on the table, "I am traveling to southern Mexico to research Mayan culture for my thesis. I am pursuing a PhD in anthropology at CU in Boulder."

Mr. Winter put his hands together in a praying motion and rested his fingers against his chin in a gesture Carol considered to be overly dramatic, "I'm sorry, how does that explain the purchase of a one-way ticket?"

Carol finally let her exasperation show, "My family and I will be spending a full year in Chiapas, Mexico, so that I can complete a thorough analysis of the effects of modernization on ancient Mayan culture, Mr. Winter. When my study is complete, the University will make arrangements for our return." Carol raised her voice slightly, "Do I really fit the profile of someone you two need to worry about, or am I just here for your amusement?" Carol laughed incredulously as the security officer cautiously sniffed her powder compact and set it aside.

Bob Winter was unfazed by Carol's short outburst, "Have you made contact or attempted to make contact with any terrorist organization in southern Mexico?" he asked pointedly.

Carol responded, "If you mean the EZLN in Chiapas, everyone knows the Zapatista rebels were pacified in the late 1990's. Or are you so deranged as to suggest that I am in contact with al-Qa'ida and Usama bin Laden himself?"

Mr. Winter wrote something in his file and waited patiently for Carol to answer his question. After Carol realized what the government official was waiting for, she answered, "I have had no contact with any person in southern Mexico. The University made all the arrangements. Would you like to see a copy of my itinerary?"

The DHS agent smiled, "If you don't mind. Mr. Baker here will make a quick copy and we'll let you get back to your family."

After a brief hesitation, Bob added, "We will also need to see a copy of the temporary visas authorizing your extended stay in Mexico."

Carol picked the itinerary and visa from a stack of papers next to her now empty purse and handed them to the security officer. He took the papers and the powder compact and walked to an office marked "Airport Security". Carol asked Mr. Winter, "May I put my purse back together now?"

"Of course, please let me apologize for any inconvenience this has caused you." Mr. Winter offered with a forced smile, "You must understand that since 9/11 the government takes security very seriously."

"Oh, I understand completely, Bob," Carol quipped, "You never know when a frustrated doctoral student is going to fly another jet into a mud hut in Mexico City."

Geoff returned with Carol's papers and handed them to her with a sheepish grin, "Thank you for your cooperation, Mrs. Iverson," he said.

Carol chose not to ask about her powder case and opted instead to find her husband and son as quickly as possible.

As Carol approached, Jim recognized a hint of agitation in her features, "Hey, baby," he said soothingly, "Is everything okay? Taylor thought you went off to find a restroom."

"Everything's fine, honey," Carol paused, "There was just a mix up with our seating arrangements. It's all taken care of now."

Five

The Iverson family quickly settled into their seats on the cramped interior of the Boeing 737 for the first leg of their flight to Mexico. After a brief layover at Mexico City International Airport, Jim, Carol, and Taylor would take a short flight to Villahermosa, Tabasco, then catch a bus for the final 190 kilometer trip to the village of Tojolaba.

"You would think," Jim offered as he buckled Taylor's seat belt, "that after the amount of money we have turned over to the university, they would at least spring for first class seats."

Carol responded, "It's kind of hard to justify first class anything when you're spending research grant money."

As the plane rolled down the runway, Taylor was glued to the window. He continually worked his jaw trying to equalize the pressure in his ears, "Wow," he exclaimed as the plane lifted into the air and gained altitude quickly, "Where are the mountains, Dad? I bet we can see our house from up here."

After a quick glance out the window, Jim replied, "They're on the other side of the plane, tiger. See the sun? You're looking east."

Taylor bumped his forehead with the palm of his hand, "Duh," he said, "Maybe we can see Uncle Doug's house in Oklahoma." He looked hard toward the horizon then quickly lost interest and opted for closer objects to stare at.

Jim watched as his son peered between his thumb and forefinger while he simulated a pinching motion, "What are you squishing, Tot?" Jim asked.

"The cars on the highway look just like army ants, Dad. *Eciton hama...*" Taylor finally blurted out the scientific name, "*Eciton hamatum.* Did you know that army ants live in the jungle where we're going, Dad? And they eat things like lizards and scorpions and even birds?"

Jim smiled, "Just as long as they don't eat little boys, they can have whatever they want for dinner."

"The book I read says that army ants don't eat people," Taylor informed his father, "But if enough of them bite you, it can make you really sick."

Jim glanced at Carol as she poured over notes she had assembled for the trip, "Do you mind if I catch a nap, honey? Someone kept me up awfully late last night," he teased.

A smile spread across Carol's face as she flushed red in her cheeks, "I had to make you happy last night," she whispered, "As busy as I'm going to be, it may be awhile before we get a chance to make love again."

Jim leaned closer to Carol's ear, "According to Ranger Rick sitting there by the window, I may not be the only thing biting you during our rendezvous in the jungle."

"Settle down, Tarzan," Carol giggled, "I was never fond of the *jungle love* proposal you suggested."

Jim sat back in feigned surprise, "I remember the negotiations between you and me very well," Jim stated, "The contract specifically calls for no less than three dates in the wilderness each month."

Carol laughed quietly, "Go to sleep, monkey man. I'll wake you before we land in Mexico City."

Jim smiled and took one last glance at Taylor who was now playing with the buttons on the armrest of his seat, "Wake me if you see any *Eciton whatever they are's* trying to pinch the wing off the airplane, okay, tiger?"

Taylor smiled and rolled his eyes, *"Eciton hamatum,* Dad. I don't think army ants fly."

Jim leaned his seat back and closed his eyes. As was usually the case, his dreams were immediately filled with scenes of dust, chaos and spilled blood.

January 16, 1991
Hwy 1, twelve miles North of Baghdad, Iraq

Team 531 of Charlie Company, 5th Battalion, 10th Special Forces had been tasked to watch the highway north of Baghdad. They were looking for any movement on the road to signal Saddam Hussein might be fleeing to his home town of Tikrit. Command was literally praying for any opportunity to take out the vicious dictator of Iraq. Team 531's only mission was to dig in, stay hidden and report all official traffic moving north from the capital city of Iraq.

The six men who made up this team were close. They had worked together on missions in Central and South America, tracking down drug cartels as well as in North Africa, spotting for aerial attacks against suspected terrorist camps.

Highway 1 ran north from Baghdad through Tikrit and beyond. It was paralleled on the east by the Tigris River and on the west by a busy railroad line.

Captain Miller, the team's leader, had selected a concealed location near an abandoned water tower on the far side of the tracks to observe traffic. The team would be able to clearly identify any vehicle moving in either direction along the highway.

Their position lay among strewn debris at the bottom of the tower. There were no signs of any person coming near the rubble in quite some time and the team was well hidden from peering eyes on the trains as well as the highway.

So far, only civilian traffic and a small number of military vehicles had been spotted on the highway. The team had noted and reported a slight increase in civilian traffic leaving the city that morning.

Once Allied forces began bombardment of Baghdad early the next morning, team 531 would be extracted and re-tasked.

Sergeant Jim Iverson was well hidden as he sat near a stripped and abandoned flatbed pickup. His camouflage blended perfectly with the desert sand and rusting forty gallon drums strewn about. Jim was one of two weapons specialists on the team. He was currently securing the right flank of their position and keeping watch for approaching trains. Sergeant Iverson noticed a dark cloud of smoke working its way up the highway and immediately reported to Captain Miller that a civilian bus was approaching and was having obvious mechanical trouble. The team froze in place as the bus, loaded with passengers, ground to a noisy halt less than one hundred meters from their position.

"Keep out of sight and use extreme noise discipline," the captain's whispered voice cautioned over the secure radio channel, "Remember your rules of engagement," their leader added.

The team had been given strict rules to not engage the enemy unless it was deemed absolutely necessary for 531's survival. It was understood among elite soldiers that you rarely if ever engaged in hostilities with civilians.

Tension grew among the Special Forces soldiers as forty passengers climbed off the bus and stood watching the driver while he raised the engine access door at the back of the bus.

"Carpenter," It was the Captain's hushed voice again, "Can you make out anything the passengers are saying?"

Corporal Nathan Carpenter was the team's linguistics specialist. He spoke Arabic and Spanish fluently and understood some Kurdish.

"Nothing so far, captain. It's a little too far to make out," reported Carpenter.

Events got worse quickly as an Iraqi two-ton military truck approached and slowed. Jim held his breath and willed the desert colored vehicle to continue on its journey toward Baghdad. It didn't.

The truck pulled to a stop and six soldiers, carrying automatic weapons, slowly climbed down from the cargo area. Two more, with side-arms only, jumped from the cab of the truck.

"Sergeant Iverson, are those red cords on the Iraqi's uniforms?" Captain Miller whispered into the transmitter of his radio.

"That's affirmative. We have Republican Guard to our front," Jim replied in a serious tone.

21

The Republican Guard was Saddam Hussein's personal elite army. They were rumored to be the finest trained and best organized forces in the Middle East.

"Okay, everyone stays cool, the bus gets repaired and all Iraqis go on their merry way." The captain's voice did not reflect the optimism of his words.

The team moved and breathed less than the debris that surrounded them. Their minds screamed as a small boy of about ten years became bored with the repairs taking place at the back of the bus and turned their way. He walked slowly toward the railroad tracks, kicking a small rock ahead of him. The boy sat and used the rock to bang on the steel rail of the track for a short time. After looking back to the bus for any sign of objection, he stood and started for the abandoned water tower.

Jim woke with a start and found that he was drenched in sweat. Carol was sleeping, but Taylor was wide awake and staring at his father.

"Are you okay, Dad?" Taylor asked, "Were you having a bad dream again?"

"I'm fine, son. Just a little woozy from the flight." Jim quickly tried to change the subject, "Would you like something to drink?"

"No thanks. What were you dreaming about, Dad?"

Jim wiped the sweat from his forehead with the palm of his hand, "Oh, I don't know," Jim lied, "I can't even remember now. Are you sure you don't need to use the restroom or something, kiddo?"

"Mom took me already. She says you never tell her about your dreams either. She thinks you have bad dreams about the war in Iraq." Taylor waited, never breaking eye contact with his father, "Do you?"

Jim fidgeted nervously, "Well, I guess if I was going to have bad dreams about anything, it would be that."

"I think war would be cool!" Taylor exclaimed, "You would get to stay up all night and carry around machine guns, and when the bad guys come—" Taylor never got to finish his thought.

Jim grabbed his son's arm, a little too tightly, and brought his face close to Taylor's, "War is never cool, Taylor Paul!" he said forcefully, "Too many innocent people die in wars while the people who need killing are safe behind their desks thousands of miles away." Jim let go of Taylor's arm and took a deep breath. With giant tears in his eyes he hugged his son and whispered, "Little boys just like you die in wars, and believe me, there is *nothing* cool about that."

The transfer in Mexico City went smoothly and the Iverson family was finally landing near the location they would call home for the next twelve months. By the time stairs were rolled up to the side of the small plane they were on, the sun had already settled in the west.

Carol looked for any person standing in the small lobby of the airport holding a sign with the Iverson family name printed on it. There were only four other people in the lobby and none of them were holding signs. Carol walked to the transportation desk and was informed that their bus was not scheduled to leave until 6:00 a.m. the next morning. The friendly attendant behind the counter told Carol that the Mexican army had imposed a curfew on vehicles traveling the roads of Chiapas, after dark.

Jim and Taylor were actually relieved by the news. The thought of a four hour bus ride after a long day of flying in cramped airplanes was at best, torturous.

Jim led his family across the street to a dimly lit but well kept hotel and the Iverson's settled in for the last night of comfort they would experience for quite some time.

Six

Village of Perdido
Chiapas, Mexico

Cristobal and his older brother sat outside a shaman's home at the center of the smoky village. Their horses waited nearby, tied to the branches of a young mahogany tree. Sergio had come to the shaman as he often did, to ask for guidance from his ancestors. Cristobal was offering a bold plan for the Mayan people and Sergio was unwilling to travel his brother's new path without blessings from the ancient ones.

The supernatural elders had been quiet tonight as the shaman made his prayers. Sergio took this as a sign to proceed cautiously and to seek direction again when the full plan was revealed to him.

"Tell me what you have discovered, *hermano*."

Cristobal had looked unhappy since he arrived before sunset, "I am not sure my plan will work, Sergio. The foreign engineers are guarded very well, especially the Americans. They are surrounded by *mercenarios* wherever they go. Even to the bathroom, brother." Cristobal looked into the eyes of his older brother and saw a glimmer of hope fade away.

"It was a risky plan from the beginning, Cristobal. The foreigners sense our desperation, so they will be very cautious."

Cristobal hung his head, *"Lo siento,"* he said quietly, "I am sorry to have failed you and the elders."

Sergio touched his sibling's shoulder affectionately, "Tell me everything you witnessed. Leave no detail out. Maybe the two of us will discover a weakness in their protection."

Cristobal perked up, but just a little. Even though his plan was unworkable, he was still anxious to share his shrewdness at spying on the foreign workers.

"I drove the bus to Palenque and sat outside the foreigner's hotel," he said with a slight smile. Cristobal had been driving a shuttle bus around Chiapas for five years now. The Mexican army had stopped and questioned him repeatedly about his loyalties and considered him to be just another local trying to etch out a meager living among the growing tourism trade.

"The engineers never leave the hotel alone," Cristobal shared. "They always travel with at least three body guards. I walked into the lobby of the hotel to ask directions while they were eating dinner one afternoon. The mercenaries watched me closely and spoke to each other on their radios. They wear bullet proof vests and carry those automatic weapons like you see on the American shows about the drug enforcers. HK's I think they are called."

Sergio leaned back against the folded serape he had placed behind his back for comfort. He stared at empty space as he tried to picture the scene his brother was describing. "Do the body guards ride in the same vehicles as the engineers when they travel to the river?"

"Yes, brother. And they always travel with a military escort. One vehicle in front and one behind. Never less than twelve Mexican soldiers plus the *mercenarios*. We would be slaughtered if we tried this." Cristobal stared at his brother and tried to penetrate his thoughts, "What are you thinking, Sergio? Do you see any weakness in their defenses?"

Sergio did not answer. Instead, he fingered a small figurine, carved from jade, he had discovered when he was a small boy, among the ancient ruins of Yaxchilan. The figurine was of a jaguar warrior and was widely known to give its bearer strength and wisdom in battle.

"Do the soldiers stay with the engineers at the river?" Sergio asked.

"Yes," Cristobal answered, "The Mexican soldiers set up check points on the road leading to the river. They are never more than one kilometer away. Then they escort the engineers back to the hotel in the afternoon."

Sergio sighed deeply, "If we came from the river, could we catch them off guard?"

"I thought of that too, *hermano*. Amador Medina delivers food to the foreigners while they are working. He says that the mercenaries patrol the river in an inflatable boat with a fast motor. We would never escape in our slow canoes. Our chances of surviving would be *desolado*."

Sergio breathed in the heavy aroma of boiling corn as the Mayan women began preparations for the next day's tortillas. The wonderful smell stirred something primeval in his soul. He was captured by a vision of glorious temples and fields of corn and squash during a time of Mayan domination. In his vision, Sergio stepped to a small portal in the observatory tower of the ancient Palenque Palace. He was looking for Venus to make its first appearance on the horizon to signal the start of warfare. Venus never appeared.

Sergio stirred from his vision and looked deep into Cristobal's eyes, "The ancestors say that this is not our path, *hermano*. We will not pursue this any further."

Cristobal stood, defeat apparent in his stooped posture, "I have failed you, Sergio. I have failed the Zapatistas. I ask for your forgiveness." Without waiting for a response, Cristobal untied his chestnut gelding and walked north toward the far end of the village where his home and family waited.

Seven

The Iverson family woke early the next morning, refreshed and ready to begin a new chapter in their lives. Carol had been assured by the university that the elders of Tojolaba were expecting her and had made arrangements for her family to live in an empty shelter at the outskirts of the small village. Jim was not impressed by the word "shelter".

By 6:00 a.m. the family was fed, packed, and waiting at the airport for the bus to arrive that would take them into the hot and humid rainforest of eastern Chiapas. The growing anticipation among the family members bounced between them like the excited orb inside a busy pinball machine.

Taylor was animated and climbed onto anything that allowed easy access. Jim was cautious and maintained constant vigilance of their surroundings, and Carol fidgeted with her papers and equipment, making sure nothing was left behind.

While they waited for the overdue bus, Jim pulled Carol close and looked into her shining green eyes, "I can remember only three times in our past that your eyes have sparkled this brightly." After a brief pause, he continued, "The day I met you. The day we were married, and the day Taylor was born."

Carol smiled mischievously and giggled, "And I remember only three other times seeing you this nervous and ready to bolt like a frightened jackrabbit. The day we met. The day we were married, and the day Taylor was born." Carol laughed out loud as Jim grabbed her by the rib cage and tickled her mercilessly.

Taylor jumped from the railing he had been balancing on, "Stop it guys, I think that's our bus."

The family was surprised to see a converted school bus, painted white, pull to the curb in front of the airport. The lean driver stepped through the open door and nodded to the Iverson's as he spoke to local passengers who had gathered at the stop.

Carol judged the driver to be in his mid-twenties. He had long hair and looked uncomfortable in the uniform the shuttle company had provided for him. Carol asked in fluent Spanish, "Will this bus take us to Tojolaba?"

The driver looked at Carol with a hint of anger in his eyes and answered rudely in English, "Yes, this bus will take you to Tojolaba. But, Tojolaba is no village for tourists."

Carol was taken back by the abruptness of the driver. Until now, her family had been treated with utmost respect by every local they had encountered, "We're not tourists," she retorted, still speaking in Spanish, "We will be living in the village and have been welcomed by the elders there." Carol smiled smartly and led her son onto the bus.

The driver stared after Carol as she chose a seat near the front of the bus. Cristobal Salinas knew the day would eventually come when foreigners came to live on the lands of his people. Never in his life did he expect it to happen this soon.

Jim watched the exchange between Carol and the driver closely, "Where would you like me to put these?" Jim asked the driver with unveiled warning in his voice as he gestured to the family's abundant number of bags and trunks.

Cristobal's temper flared then quickly abated as he stared into the eyes of the arrogant woman's husband. He had witnessed this battle hardened look of untold experience and palpable danger only twice before; once, in the eyes of Marcos, the famed leader of all the Zapatistas, and again in the eyes of the *mercenarios* guarding the engineers at the hotel in Palenque. Cristobal quickly averted his eyes and directed Jim to an empty storage space located at the back of the bus.

The main road into Chiapas was well worn and riddled with potholes. As the bus bounced along the winding road, Jim, Carol, and Taylor were enamored by the colors that filled their vision. Peasants lined the roadside peddling blankets made from homespun wool and decorated with bright patterns of reds and greens and gold. Children stood beside hastily constructed tables filled with flowering red bromeliads and perfectly shaped calla lilies. All were dressed in immaculately embroidered shirts and shawls and gave glorious abstraction to the deep green background of the lush forest.

As the bus approached a premier tourist spot known as Agua Azul, the environmental magnificence of Chiapas, Mexico, became apparent. A deep blue river saturated with lime, flowed wondrously over formations made from petrified logs and deposited limestone. Local merchants carried colorful clothing and woven hats while others occupied stands that sold Coca-Cola on ice and fried breads dipped in sugar. The daunting forest, filled with shadows, acted as an ever present frame around this brilliant amalgamation of Mother Nature and mankind.

The bus pulled to a stop among wandering merchants. Air hissed as brakes were set and the doors opened with a rush of warm atmosphere replacing the cool interior air.

Cristobal spoke first in Spanish, then English to his passengers, "We will leave in thirty minutes for the village of Ocosingo." Without acknowledging any questions, Cristobal stepped off the bus and walked to a merchant peddling herbs and local remedies. They spoke briefly then watched as the Iverson's left the bus to explore the unique water source.

"I'm not sure, but I would say our driver has a case of the ass for Americans," Jim said as he walked with Carol and Taylor.

"Don't take it personally, honey," Carol offered, "These people are watching as their way of life quickly erodes out from under them. Twenty years ago, they made their living working farms and selling their products to other Mexicans. Now, this entire region is inundated with cheap produce from America and the farmers are forced to sell their land to wealthy speculators for pennies on the dollar. Now, the government is coming in and threatening to flood their remaining homes and sacred land with water to build hydroelectric dams. These people have a right to be upset. They have a right to be suspicious of foreigners."

Jim looked around and was taken in by the splendor, "I would be pretty angry too, if I was forced to share this beauty with a bunch of fat, bitchy tourists."

Carol laughed and walked over to where Taylor was dangling his bare feet in the lustrous water, "We'll make a pact right now to come back and visit this place at least once a month while we're here, okay, sport?"

Taylor splashed water with his toes, "I could live right here, Mom. This place is so cool!"

After thirty minutes, the bus slowly pulled away from the natural beauty of Agua Azul. Roadside merchants rapidly thinned out then became nonexistent as the bus traveled further into the highlands of Chiapas. At the village of Ocosingo, several passengers departed and the bus turned east toward the Lacandon jungle. It seemed to Carol as though the deepening forest was reaching in to reclaim the rural road and all those who traveled it.

A short time after leaving the village, the bus ground to a halt in the middle of the road. Jim immediately went to high alert as memories flooded back of another bus making an unexpected stop along a lonely road between two cities. Jim was sure he heard sounds of gunfire, screaming and unanticipated death. He immediately stood and furtively searched out the windows for the source of his imagined firefight.

"Sweetheart?" Carol asked as she softly touched her husband's shaking arm, "What's the matter, baby?" She stood and rubbed Jim's back lightly, "It's only a checkpoint, honey. Are you okay?"

Jim regained his composure and looked embarrassingly around the bus. The few local passengers remaining stared at him with a mixture of amusement and fear. He smiled sheepishly and followed Carol back to their seats, "I'm sorry, I thought I heard gunfire," he told Carol. Jim turned to the other passengers and spoke louder this time, "I thought I heard gunfire. I'm really sorry for frightening you."

Cristobal stepped off the bus and spoke to a lone soldier standing in the middle of the road. The two men stood and talked quietly, seemingly at ease with each other. Something Cristobal said caught the soldier's attention and he immediately spoke into his radio handset while walking toward the bus. Cristobal never budged as the soldier climbed aboard the bus and spoke quietly in Spanish to the seated passengers.

"He wants everyone to get off the bus," Carol translated. "He says that this is just a routine check and that he is sorry for any disruption."

Jim grunted and led his family onto the road behind three of the local passengers. As he passed the soldier, Jim searched his eyes and posture for any signs of malice. The young man smiled and nodded at Jim and appeared to be friendly. Cristobal followed the Iverson's and stood next to Jim, waiting further instructions from the soldier.

Sounds of a laboring vehicle reached the passenger's ears as an olive colored military truck climbed the hill from the east and stopped in the middle of the road. Cristobal sidestepped a little, trying to put some distance between himself and the Americans. Jim could sense the veiled fear behind Cristobal's eyes and pulled Taylor close for protection.

"If this situation escalates," Jim advised Carol in a hushed tone, "take Taylor and run a half mile into the forest behind us. Then turn and make your way back toward Ocosingo. Keep the sun behind you as you go."

Carol looked at Jim with a worried expression. "Jim," she insisted, "This is just routine. It happens all the time down here and nobody ever gets hurt. Please relax, honey. You're scaring Taylor and me."

Taylor held on to his father's belt loop with his head tucked close into Jim's rib cage. He chose not to speak. Like his father, he intently watched the movement of every person present.

Jim looked at Carol with fire in his eyes, "This smells bad and you need to be prepared for anything that might happen," he scolded. "Now listen! If things get stupid, don't worry about me. Just take Taylor and do what I said, okay?"

Carol nodded then shook her head as she tried to understand Jim's paranoia.

Three soldiers dressed in olive drab uniforms and carrying American made M-16 rifles, jumped from the back of the truck and raised their automatic weapons as an older man, obviously the leader, stepped from the passenger's side of the cab. He spoke loudly to the three soldiers and dismissed them with a practiced hand gesture.

Carol translated for Jim, "He told them to put their weapons away. That they were scaring us and acting like fools." She looked at Jim, "See, honey? Everything is going to be fine."

Jim relaxed a little as the leader approached with a hefty smile on his face. The man appeared to be in his mid-forties. He was lean, medium height and sported a bright blue ascot tied around his neck, tucked neatly into the *V* of his shirt.

"*Americanos?*" he asked as he approached the Iverson's.

Carol answered in Spanish, "*Si, somos americanos.*"

The soldier smiled at Carol then directed his attention toward Jim, "I speak English," he stated triumphantly, "I am Captain Eduardo Marquez of the Mexican army." He pulled a small notebook from his shirt pocket and flipped through several pages until he found a blank sheet of paper to write on, "What is your name, please?" He looked at Jim expectantly and waited patiently.

"Have we done something wrong, captain?" Jim asked without answering the question.

"Oh no, no, no, no," protested Captain Marquez, "We love *americanos* in Mexico. I am here to protect you." Gesturing with the pen and notebook, he said, "You must understand that in order to keep your family safe in this troubled region, I must know who you are and where you will be staying. Do you agree?"

Jim relented, "We are the Iverson's." He spelled the name for the slow writing captain, "This is my wife Carol, and this is my son Taylor." He spelled Taylor's name as well, "My wife can better explain the remaining details. She's the one in charge for the next year." Jim couldn't help but smile.

The captain looked confused for a brief moment then turned reluctantly to Carol. Jim could see the inner turmoil in the Mexican soldier as he tried to remain professional and only look at Carol's face. He lost the battle and his eyes slowly followed the curves down Carol's breasts, past her slender waistline to her well toned legs. The captain caught himself and glanced embarrassingly at Jim.

Carol cleared her throat to get the captain's attention, "We will be staying in the village of Tojolaba. Are you familiar with it?"

Captain Marquez stuttered, "*Si*, ah yes. I know Tojolaba. I just came from there." The captain, now unsure of himself, looked back to Jim and asked, "Do you mind if I ask what business you have in such a rural village?"

Jim smiled, shrugged and pointed back to Carol. He was pissed at the captain's leering and was enjoying how uncomfortable it was for the officer to have to speak to his wife.

Carol answered, "I am researching modern Mayan culture and will be analyzing the effects of the free trade agreements on their traditions." Carol offered more before being asked, "We will be living in Tojolaba for the next twelve months."

A long, slow whistle escaped from the captain's mouth, "*Senora*, this is a very dangerous place for such a beautiful woman and such a small child. There are rebels in these mountains who will slit your throats while you are sleeping, for no good reason."

The captain looked at Jim as if he were crazy, "*Senor* Iverson, you must not allow this. You must take your family back to America and keep them safe."

Jim frowned and nodded toward the captain's truck. The three soldiers who had accompanied the Mexican officer were now asleep in the back, "It looks like you and your highly trained *ladies* should have no trouble keeping my family safe. But if you find yourselves too busy painting your nails and can't," Jim leaned in close and slowly tugged the ascot from the captain's shirt, "rest assured that I will."

Captain Marquez felt a cold sweat spread across the back of his neck. He would not be humiliated by this condescending American. Placing his hand on the grip of his holstered sidearm, Marquez stared into Jim's eyes and tried to give a silent warning. The American was not receiving his message. Marquez concluded that this man was either very stupid or very dangerous. *Stupid*, he wrongly decided. To make his point, he turned his attention to the bus driver, "Where is your filthy rebel brother?" he yelled.

Cristobal stood stunned by the quick turn of events. He could only shake his head and shrug.

The captain stepped close to Cristobal and drew his sidearm, "When you see him next, you tell him that I am personally going to shoot him in the belly."

Jim could see the fear in the bus driver's eyes. He stepped closer to the army captain and turned to shield his wife and son from the scene.

Captain Marquez was growing more unstable by the second. He was angry at himself for feeling belittled by the American man and was determined to show the arrogant *americano* that he was not a person to tangle with. He grabbed Cristobal by his long hair and put his pistol to the driver's temple, "Maybe I will just kill you instead," he said angrily.

Through years of military training, Jim Iverson had learned to respond to violence with quick action. In one synchronized movement, he grabbed the captain's ascot and twisted it tight around the officer's neck. Pulling Marquez toward him and off balance, Jim used his left hand to turn the weapon away from the driver's head and remove it from the captain's grip.

The Mexican soldier who had stopped the bus, panicked and fumbled with his automatic rifle to remove the safety. The three soldiers in the back of the truck never woke.

Jim glared at the choking captain and said very quietly, "You will not murder this man in front of my family."

Releasing Marquez's ascot, Jim removed the magazine from the handgun and tossed it into the trees. He worked the slide and ejected a round from the chamber, then turned and tossed the empty weapon to Marquez's fumbling soldier. Signaling the driver to get back onto the bus, Jim turned and led Carol and Taylor through the open door, pushing the bewildered Mexican soldier aside as he did.

Captain Marquez caught his breath, while the passengers frantically re-boarded the bus behind the Iverson's. Cristobal dove into his seat and closed the door. The bus lurched past the idling army truck and resumed its journey down the mountain, leaving the captain standing alone in the middle of the road. Marquez was visibly outraged with himself for being caught off guard by the *americano* named Jim. He stomped back to his truck, yelling at the sleeping soldiers and screaming at his driver to take him back to his headquarters. Captain Eduardo Marquez quietly vowed not to let his humiliation go unanswered.

Eight

As the bus lumbered back up the rutted dirt road, diesel fumes belching from its overworked engine, the Iverson's stood at the entrance to the small village of Tojolaba. This tiny but active rural community sat at the base of the Sierra Norte mountains, where the forest of the highlands met the rainforest of the Lacandon jungle. Tojolaba was built around the headwaters of the important Lacandon River.

The Iverson's watched as crystal clear water magically bubbled from the side of the mountain and gave birth to a stream, abundant with life sustaining liquid. Jim, Carol, and Taylor's eyes swept over the village; their vision filled with scenes of Mayan women on their knees, with looms of colorful wool stretched before them as they weaved brightly colored clothing. Children were sweeping with brooms made from split saplings harvested from the surrounding forest. More women, dressed in beautifully embroidered, crisp white shirts, stood at the bubbling spring collecting water for their families. And several old men sat outside one hamlet at the center of the village, smoking tobacco from hand carved pipes.

Slowly, activity in the village came to a halt as its inhabitants grew curious of the gawking Americans.

"They knew we were coming, right, honey?" Jim whispered.

Carol looked toward the old men who were now gesturing and laughing, "Of course they knew, Jim," she said, slightly frustrated, "We were supposed to be greeted by a professor from the University of Arizona. He was going to introduce us to the village elders and help us get settled."

Taylor scanned the entire village one more time then offered, "I don't think any of these people are college professors, Mom."

Relief washed over Carol as she heard the sound of approaching vehicles from the direction the bus had departed. The Iverson's watched as two, relatively new Jeep Wranglers entered the village and parked among a few vehicles, obviously owned by locals.

"Hello!" said an aged and well tanned man with white hair as he climbed from behind the wheel of the first jeep, "You must be Carol Iverson."

The polite American smiled big as he approached the waiting family. He quickly offered his hand to Carol and introduced himself, "I am Professor Marcus Redding from the University of Arizona. I hope your journey down here was pleasurable." Without giving Carol a chance to respond, Professor Redding turned to Jim and offered his hand, "I can't tell you how wonderful it is that your whole family will take part in this experience. The wealth of information that will be gained from your interface with the indigenous population of this settlement will be immeasurable." The professor ruffled Taylor's hair and stood smiling at the Iverson's.

Carol introduced her family, "It's very nice to meet you Dr. Redding. This is my husband James and my son Taylor. I can't tell you how happy we are to see you."

"Yes," responded the professor, "I waited for you yesterday afternoon and when you didn't arrive, I went back to Ocosingo and made arrangements to spend the night. I saw your bus go through this morning and got here as quickly as possible. That damn soldier at the checkpoint actually made me point out on a map, every place I have been while in Mexico. Astonishing!" he concluded.

Carol waved toward the village, "We were supposed to arrive late yesterday, but they told us the busses can't run after dark in Chiapas.

So we spent the night in Villahermosa and took the first bus out this morning."

The professor herded the Iverson's toward his Jeep, "Of course," he offered, "The Zapatistas are growing more active in the highlands with construction starting on these new dams and a new Central American highway. There has been no bloodshed yet, but the Mexican Army is intent on wiping out the rebels before they gain support from the people again."

The four Americans stopped at the Wrangler loaded with supplies, "These are for you," reported Dr. Redding, "I've taken the liberty of stocking you up with canned foods, dried meats and lots of other essentials. We can't have you starving your first month here. There are also some bedrolls in here with wool blankets. Believe it or not, it can get quite chilly here at night."

Jim expressed his gratitude and started unloading the supplies.

"Oh, don't bother with that right now, Mr. Iverson," the professor exclaimed, "The Jeep is yours as well, while your family is in Chiapas, of course."

"Cool beans!" Taylor exclaimed, "Now we really can go back to that awesome waterfall we were at today." Taylor climbed behind the wheel and pretended to drive the Jeep.

"Let's get you properly introduced to the village elders," offered Dr. Redding. "Then, if it is alright with you, James, I will take Carol and discuss proper protocols and record keeping. Unfortunately, it's a lot of boring stuff that wouldn't excite you or Taylor very much. Shall we?" The professor gestured toward the group of old men who were now standing and waiting patiently.

After brief introductions with the elders standing outside the town hall, Jim and Taylor were shown to their new home on the western edge of the village while Carol and the professor walked to the Jeep to discuss "proper protocols".

"This is where we're going to live?" asked Taylor with a sour look on his face.

Jim walked around the outside of the one room hut made from mud packed around an array of carefully placed logs from the forest. The roof was made from thatch and appeared to have been recently patched and in good shape. The entrance was a framed hole in the east facing wall with no door. A large rooster stood at the threshold and challenged Taylor as he tried to enter.

"Dad, I don't think this chicken is going to let us live here," Taylor explained as his father rounded the corner with a look of pure amusement on his face.

"That's not a chicken, old McDonald. That's a rooster," Jim chided, "How is it that you can recite the scientific name of every insect in this jungle but you can't tell the difference between a rooster and a chicken?"

"I must have been sick the day my class visited the farm," Taylor offered with a serious look on his face, "Is he going to bite me?"

"Nah," Jim replied as he grabbed a stick from the ground and chased the loudly clucking bird from its roost, "Roosters don't have teeth."

Taylor and Jim peered into the dark recesses of the mud hut. Cracks in the wall emitted sunlight that danced playfully with the dusty interior. Bags of grain lined walls papered with flattened Corona boxes and a dark stain of ash marked the center of the dirt floor where fires were built to cook and warm the shelter.

"Son, you and I have a lot of work to do before we can call this home," Jim mused after a long sigh, "Let's start by bringing our bags over and then you and I can unload that Jeep. What do you say, champ?"

Carol and Dr. Redding walked to the waiting Jeep with a hired driver behind the wheel.

"Of course, we would like you to keep a daily journal of your experiences here in Tojolaba," the professor instructed, "It would be very helpful if you convinced your husband and son to do the same."

"We've discussed that already and both are willing to contribute their thoughts," Carol replied, "Taylor is quite an artist so he asked if he could include drawings in his journal."

"That would be wonderful, Carol. We might even include some of them in our final publication of this critical study."

Carol smiled and remained quiet while the professor continued.

"We expect you to come to San Cristobal once every two weeks to pick up supplies and report to us on your findings so we can correlate them with other studies taking place here. Bring your initial survey of village population, social organization and mortality statistics. Include a rough outline of the predominate clan structure of Tojolaba as well. We will also make copies of your journals so please be sure to include them in your portfolio. San Cristobal is a wonderful city to visit. With this curfew in place, plan on spending the night while you are there. Consider it a rejuvenation period. This experience will be quite taxing on you and your family."

The professor hesitated for a second before continuing, "I know that you were very active as an undergraduate student in supporting the Zapatista uprising."

Carol was taken back by Dr. Redding's knowledge of her past. "During my senior year, I organized some rallies and raised some funds for them, but it never went further than the Boulder campus," she replied defensively.

"You raised and sent exactly two hundred and twelve thousand dollars for their movement, Carol. That was a magnificent accomplishment." The professor smiled, "I believe that I contributed a little over ten thousand dollars to your fund in 1994. This was the foremost reason you were selected to aid in this study."

Carol looked mildly embarrassed, "I believed in their cause. Their demands for women's rights and equal justice spoke to me." Looking Dr. Redding in the eye, Carol continued, "The Zapatistas were the only chance these people ever had at escaping the blatant greed of the Mexican government."

The aged professor of anthropology placed a well worn hat, made from palm, on his head, "You are going to work out wonderfully, Carol. In a month or so, I am going to introduce you to the leader of the local Zapatista army. He is very insightful and his people desperately need our help right now. It is also important that he understands you and your family are here as friends and supporters."

With that said, the professor climbed into the passenger's side of the Jeep, "I'll see you and your family in two weeks in San Cristobal. We'll meet for lunch at *Casa del Sol* next to the Maya Medicine Museum. They serve wonderful coffee there."

With a wave, Dr. Redding's Jeep pulled onto the dirt road and climbed the mountain toward the village of Ocosingo.

Jim and Taylor approached Carol as she stood watching the professor depart in a cloud of dust, "You look very troubled, *Senorita*," Jim offered lightly.

Carol smiled, "It's *senora*, Jim. If I were a *senorita*, we would have men at our door every night asking me to marry them."

Jim pulled Carol close and kissed her gently on the forehead, "Impossible," he chided, "We have no door!"

Nine

As the afternoon progressed in Tojolaba, the Iverson's worked steadily to prepare their new household for the approaching night. Taylor swept the dirt floor clear of chicken droppings while Jim cleaned the fire pit of old ash and collected enough firewood to last the evening. Carol stayed busy organizing the supplies brought by the professor and put together a quick meal for the famished family.

Sitting on a hundred pound bag of corn seed, Taylor chewed hungrily on a sandwich made from canned chicken spread, "Mom, why are the dogs here so skinny and afraid of us? I tried to get one to come to me so I could pet it, but it yelped and ran into the forest. Are they wild dogs?"

Carol thought for a second before replying, "The Mayans generally don't like canines. They particularly don't appreciate a dog's bathroom habits around their homes. Consequently, they are treated very poorly and kept out of the village."

Taylor wrinkled his forehead, "Then why do they even have them around?"

Carol quickly fell into her role as teacher, "Mayans believe that after they die, a dog will lead them through a series of gates and across a large body of water to the underworld." She winked at Taylor,

"You watch carefully during the day and you will see older women sneaking food to the dogs and whispering to them."

"What do they say?" asked Taylor playfully, "Please stop peeing on my house?"

Carol laughed then continued her instruction, "No silly, she is telling the dog to remember her after she dies and to help her across the river to the afterlife."

Jim finished his sandwich and cleared his throat, "I'm going to have to find out who did the original decorating in here. They obviously have an abundant stash of Corona beer hidden somewhere in these hills. I see a beautiful friendship on the horizon. *Comere otra cerveza por favor.*" Jim smiled at Carol, "That is the extent of my Spanish vocabulary."

Carol laughed, "Do you have a history in Mexican bars that I am unaware of?"

Jim stood and opened another bottled water, "I've never been to a Mexican bar my love." He held his water out in a mock salute, "Now, ask me about Columbia and I will share a colorful history with you."

Carol groaned and looked at Taylor, "I'm not sure that is a story Taylor and I want to hear." She finished stacking the canned goods on a small shelf mounted to the wall and turned toward the open door, "I think we have visitors."

Jim, Carol, and Taylor stepped outside of their new home and were greeted by several families gathering in a semicircle at their door. An elderly man stepped forward and spoke in an odd dialect of Spanish, broken with several pauses intermingled with an occasional clucking of the tongue. When finished, he handed a gift to Jim.

Carol translated for her family, "They are welcoming us. I will pick up the nuances of their language before long and we'll be able to communicate much better."

The Iverson's nodded and smiled at the elder and accepted his offering. It was a sharpened axe with a hand carved handle. Jim tested the blade with his finger then shook the man's hand.

Another family stepped forward with a heavy wool blanket and held it to the door to suggest the family hang it for a temporary covering.

Hand shakes were abundant and smiles were plentiful as Jim, Carol, and Taylor accepted gifts of chickens, pots and griddles made from fired clay, hallowed gourds filled with fresh tortillas, sacks of dried beans and corn, and baskets of squash and fresh flowers. The Iverson's graciously thanked family after family as they brought their generous offerings. Some brought colorfully spun wool thread while others brought armloads of chopped firewood. Every gift was placed in its appropriate place as the bearers walked in and out of the Iverson's hut.

One family of four, each carried a two foot pine bough into the home and hung them together on the far wall.

Carol whispered to Taylor, "The four pine boughs represent the four corners of the Mayan world. Every home here has them."

As the visitors said their final goodbyes and hands were shaken one last time, the Iverson's stood outside their now quiet home and were overwhelmed by the generosity they had just experienced, "These people have so little," Carol said with deep humility in her voice, "And they willingly shared it with us to make us feel welcome."

Taylor glanced inside the darkening hut, "Mom, someone planted a dead tree next to our fire pit."

Carol looked through the door and laughed out loud. She grabbed Taylor and hugged him tightly, "That's not a dead tree you silly goose. That is a pine rack to hang all of our new clay pots from."

Before sunrise the next morning, Carol rose to join the village women at the spring. She took two bright red plastic jugs that were given to her the night before and quietly slipped aside the heavy wool blanket acting as a door. Carol knew that Mayan women gathered at the spring each morning to collect water for their families. She also knew that these women would stand about while they filled their pots and jugs and gossip about who was pregnant and who was sick. Carol expected this to be a primary source of information for her study.

As Carol stepped through the door, she looked back to her husband and son, sleeping side by side on a bedroll brought by the professor. Jim seemed to be resting fitfully. Carol watched closely for a minute, hoping that he was not having another nightmare. She was frustrated that he refused to share with her what his nightmares were about and he absolutely refused to seek professional help. She frowned and shook her head as Jim moaned quietly in his sleep. Whatever was haunting him seemed to be growing in intensity as their son got older. Lately, she sometimes caught Jim staring at Taylor with a look of pure sorrow on his face. When confronted, Jim would shake out of it and make some excuse about how his job was getting to him. Carol knew better. This man, that she had devoted her heart to, was in pain and there was absolutely nothing she could do until he opened up to her and allowed her to help him. Jim moaned again and raised his hand to his face. Carol shook her head mournfully, let the wool blanket slip back to its intended place, and walked quietly through the early morning smoke and mist toward the bubbling spring.

January 16, 1991
Hwy 1, twelve miles North of Baghdad, Iraq

The small boy stood about four foot tall with coal black hair that blew in the desert wind. He wore loose fitting white cotton pants and a white pullover shirt. As he walked straight to where Jim was concealed, he whistled an unfamiliar tune. Jim peered at the boy as he approached and feverishly but silently willed the youngster to turn around and return to the bus. He kept coming.

As the young boy walked, he used a discarded piece of rebar, he had picked up at the tracks, to trace a line in the sand. Jim watched the point where the steel rod touched the desert sand, creating a shallow line which followed the boy's progress. Jim believed that if he looked at the youngster's face, the boy would instinctively look up and spot the camouflaged American hiding among the debris. The line grew closer—the whistling grew louder—the boy was not going to stop.

Jim focused intently on the approaching line in the sand until it was less than six feet away. Bare feet, covered in sand, froze in place, the whistling stopped, and the rusted metal rod dropped to the ground. Jim slowly brought his eyes up the folds of the young boy's pants, along the dirt stained shirt, and stopped at the boy's trembling lips and saucer sized eyes. The boy's eyes were as black as night and fear resonated through them as he stared at the deadly soldier before him.

"Lopez! Call for immediate evacuation!" the captain's hurried voice came over Jim's earpiece. Staff Sergeant Anthony Lopez was the team's communications specialist. He secured a direct link to the Tactical Operations Center in northern Saudi Arabia by satellite phone, "Tell them our cover is compromised and we are going hot!"

Jim looked into the frightened boy's eyes and held his finger to his lips, then motioned slowly for the boy to come to him. The trembling youth took one step back, opened his mouth and...

———※

"Dad, wake up!"

Jim opened his eyes quickly and focused on Taylor, sitting next to him, shaking his shoulder.

"Wake up, Dad! You're having another bad dream!"

Jim sat up and looked around the cramped quarters, unsure of where he was. Gazing around the room, he locked onto Taylor's eyes and was calmed by the radiant blue staring back at him. Now sweating in the humid air, Jim cleared his throat and asked, "Where's your mother, Tot?"

"She's gone. Don't call me Tot."

Jim looked around the shelter once more, "Is it morning?" he asked.

"Yes. What were you dreaming about, Dad?"

"Nothing, Tot—sorry! Taylor."

"You kept saying 'don't shoot, don't shoot!' Who was shooting, Dad?"

Jim stood and walked over to the door, pulled aside the heavy blanket and looked outside, "No one was shooting, Taylor. Please drop it!" Jim scolded, showing his frustration.

Taylor sat quietly for a moment, "Dad, you always tell me to talk to you about my nightmares. You say that it helps chase the monsters away and it really does!"

Taylor peered into his father's sad eyes, "Tell me about your bad dream, Dad, and I'll help you chase the monster away."

Jim shook his head solemnly, "The monsters in my dreams are too hideous for a ten year old, son. I'm sorry!" Jim tried to change the subject, "Let's get these bedrolls picked up and find something to eat, okay?"

Taylor sat on the thin mattress and didn't budge, "I don't want to eat. I want to help you have nice dreams, like the one I had last night."

Jim smiled and sat next to his persistent son, "What was your dream about?"

"I dreamt that I brought my whole class from school down here… well, not the girls… and we swam and played all day in that waterfall we were at yesterday. It was really cool!"

"That does sound like a nice dream. We'll go back to that waterfall soon and play in it all day, okay, tiger?" Jim ruffled Taylor's hair, "Now let's get things picked up and then you and I will put together a plan on how to turn this mud hut into a mud castle."

Taylor held onto his father's arm and wouldn't let him stand, "Was it about the war you were in?"

Jim sighed deeply and surrendered, "Yes, son. My nightmares are about the war I was in. A lot of terrible things happened. Some very good friends of mine were killed and a lot of innocent people died too. That's what I have nightmares about."

Taylor looked down at the dirt floor, "Mom told me that some of your friends died in Iraq. Did you see them get killed?"

Father and son sat quietly, side by side, for what seemed like an eternity. Jim was focused on his own hands while Taylor watched the sadness grow in his father's face.

"I can't talk about that right now, Taylor Paul," Jim said solemnly, "Maybe someday, but not right now, okay?"

Taylor rubbed his dad's back for several seconds then smiled, "We should build a door today, Dad. So those cannibals don't come in here and eat us."

Ten

Village of Perdido
Chiapas, Mexico

C ristobal Salinas rose before the sun that morning as was his custom. At the center of his home he blew on embers in the fire pit and brought them to life to chase the chill from the confined interior. His two children slept soundly as their mother brought water from the village well. Cristobal helped his young wife, Lucia prepare corn for the morning's meal of fresh tortillas and a small serving of scrambled eggs. Before using the tortilla press to fashion the flattened staple of the Mayan diet, Lucia quickly braided her ebony hair to keep it from interfering with the task before her.

The couple worked quietly at well rehearsed tasks to start their day before Cristobal had to leave for a long shift driving bus. Cristobal squatted and placed a pot of water on the small fire and added a generous helping of hand ground coffee beans. He watched in silence as his youthful wife kneaded the corn paste in preparation for the tortilla press. He loved to watch her work. Cristobal tried to think of a time when his wife of four years did not have a smile on her face. The image failed him. He loved her broad nose which symbolized Mayan royalty from a time long passed. He loved her brown eyes which revealed her innocence and playfulness. He loved her blazing white teeth that made a broad appearance every time she smiled.

The children began to stir at the smell of cooking food. First to the fire was Cristobal's oldest son Gabriel. The three year old yawned and wiped the sleep from his eyes as he dug his toes into the dirt floor. Luis, the youngest son by almost a year, sat at the edge of his small bed and began to cry. Luis had been ill for much of the past year. The shamans had tried several herbal concoctions, mixed with long prayers, to no avail. Finally, after a visit to the doctor in San Cristobal, it was discovered that Luis had problems with the development of his heart and was not expected to live past the age of five.

Cristobal stood and gently plucked the crying boy from his bed, "*Papa le ama mi hijo*," he said soothingly, "Your daddy loves you!"

Luis snuggled into his father's shoulder and cried mournfully while Cristobal slowly rocked him back to sleep, "*Shhhhhhhhh, mi pequeno muchacho, Shhhhhhhhh.*"

Cristobal laid the sleeping boy back in his bed and pulled the blanket over his frail shoulders then joined Lucia and Gabriel at a small table for a simple meal and sweetened coffee.

Eleven

T aylor held the long plank as Jim hammered another nail into a brace that would add strength to their new door. With tools borrowed from a village craftsman and lumber scavenged from behind their new home, Jim and Taylor were able to construct a sturdy door for their dwelling. It was Taylor's idea to use the durable hinges from one of the family's trunks to complete the new entry.

"Your mom may just decide to keep the two of us around," Jim said, admiring their handy work, "We need to be careful though," he continued, "She'll have us building her something new every day if she sees how much we enjoyed doing this."

Taylor smiled at his dad, unwilling to let the moment pass, he suggested, "We should make a window now so it's not so dark inside."

"That's a great idea, son," Jim said, "but in places where it gets really hot, people don't put windows in their homes. It keeps the heat out so the house stays cool inside."

Jim and Taylor put together a long list of projects that would keep them busy for several months. They planned to build an actual fireplace on the south facing wall of the hut to free up space and keep smoke from choking them out in the early mornings. They also planned to fashion several handmade clay bricks to install as a hardened floor to keep the dust down.

After getting the door hung and leveled and a homemade latch installed that locked from the inside, Jim and Taylor set out to explore the mountain that rose majestically to the west of their home. Unlike the mountains of Colorado, there was little undergrowth here and most fallen or dead trees had been cleared for firewood. Also, the predominant tree in this region was the young mahogany. Most of the old growth forest had long since been logged out by greedy timber companies.

Jim enjoyed taking time to instruct Taylor in direction finding methods and other survival skills.

"See, by marking the two points of this shadow after fifteen minutes and drawing a line through them, we know east and west." Jim stood after drawing a straight line with his stick, "Now, we can place our left foot on the first point we marked, and our right foot on the second point and bingo!" Jim said pointing directly in front of him, "We are facing north!"

"Cool!" Taylor replied, "But what if it's cloudy, or night?" Taylor smiled at his father, positive that he had stumped him.

"That's easy," Jim answered, "We can use the moon and stars at night to find north, or on a cloudy day we can use these tree stumps over here." Jim walked over to a recently cut tree stump and knelt down.

Taylor mimicked his father's movements and paid close attention to his instruction. Quality time with his dad was sometimes hard to come by back at home, so he relished the focused attention he was receiving now.

"Do you see how the growth rings on this tree are spaced farther apart on this side?" Jim used his stick to point out the widened rings.

"Yeah, I know that each ring stands for one year the tree has lived. This tree wasn't very old," Taylor observed sadly.

"You're right. I don't think any of these trees are very old. The wider rings always face toward the equator. So, which way is the equator?" Jim quizzed.

Taylor pointed in the proper direction.

"And which direction is the equator on the point of a compass?"

"South?" Taylor responded hesitantly.

"Outstanding!" Jim proudly hugged his son.

"But Dad, what good does it do me to know which direction north is if I'm lost? Even if I walked north, I would still be lost."

Jim sat in the dirt and pulled Taylor down next to him, "Young man, I know highly trained soldiers who never bothered to ask that question. You, Taylor Paul, are a thinker!" Jim looked around and thought about how to answer his son's foresighted question.

"Okay, say you are lost out here in these woods and don't know which direction you have gone or which direction our home is."

Taylor looked around the forest that surrounded him and shuddered a little at the thought.

Jim asked, "Do you remember the last village we traveled through before we got to Tojolaba?"

"Yes, it was Ocosingo, right?" Taylor beamed with pride.

"Exactly! Do you remember which direction we traveled to get from Ocosingo to Tojolaba?"

"I think it was east, because the sun was in front of us and it was morning."

"Brilliant! You're not only smart as a whip, you're also very observant." Jim ruffled Taylor's hair and looked at him proudly, "So if you're out here, lost in this forest with no idea how to get home, what could you do to save yourself?"

Taylor thought for a long minute. He didn't want to get this wrong and disappoint his father. He stood and brushed the dried leaves from his pants, looked at the tree stump, then at the sun. Using what he had learned, Taylor pointed directly west and proudly stated, "I would walk west until I came to Ocosingo."

Jim laughed out loud and grabbed Taylor's feet, tackling him to the ground. After a brief wrestling match, he pinned his laughing boy to the ground, "Son, I cannot begin to tell you how many young soldiers I had to go out and find in the backwoods of North Carolina because they could not grasp the very concept you just mastered."

Taylor sat up and smiled broadly. Pleasing his father had to be the greatest feeling in the world. Not wanting this moment to end, he pointed to a bright blue bird, preening its feathers while sitting in a tree not far from where they were now resting, "I think that's a Macaw, Dad. It belongs to the parrot family. Oh, and this is really cool! Did you know that Macaws have bones in their tongues?"

Jim glanced at his son with a surprised look on his face, "I thought teenagers were the only ones with bones in their tongues."

Taylor missed the joke and shook his head with a confused look on his face, "The bones help them break open nut shells and stuff."

Jim watched as Taylor stuck his tongue out and pushed it against the palm of his hand.

"Can you imagine if you broke that bone?" Jim joked, "You would have to wear a cast on your tongue for several weeks. It would be horrible. All your friends would want to sign it. Your tongue would itch and you wouldn't be able to scratch it. Oh, and the smell, can you imagine the horrible smell?"

Taylor and Jim laughed out loud and startled the beautiful bird into flight. As they watched it disappear through the deep green canopy of mahogany trees, Jim patted his son on the shoulder, "Let's get back to the village. Your mother is probably wondering what happened to us."

Taylor jumped up and excitedly announced, "I will lead us back home!"

Carol sat against a tree outside her home and admired the new door Jim and Taylor had obviously built that morning. It was a beautiful day with mild temperatures and low humidity for southern Mexico. The village women had welcomed Carol warmly that morning and took turns tutoring her language skills. The dialect of this village was unique in a sense that it used strategically placed pauses throughout a sentence to change or accentuate meaning. A pause wrongly placed in a sentence could modify the implication just enough to confuse the listener. Needless to say, there were lots of giggles shared among the Mayan women as they instructed Carol in the nuances of their village dialect.

Carol had been amazed by the strength and endurance of these women. She had followed three middle-aged wives into the forest to collect firewood. They walked for an hour, using machetes to cut branches from trees until they had fashioned large bundles which were carried on their backs. The weight of these large bundles of firewood was supported mainly by a strap that fit across the crown of the women's heads. Carol had a bundle less than half the size of the village women and had to stop several times to rest her neck and lower back.

The women of Tojolaba seemed to enjoy this work. They smiled often and gossiped freely as they carried out their morning chores. Carol had studied the Mayan culture for years and was always infatuated by the stories, traditions, and myths that dominated this people. She now realized that what she had learned from books and studies was insignificant compared to the education she was now receiving.

During one of the many unscheduled rest stops, Carol learned that almost all newly married couples from Tojolaba were choosing to live in the cities. This behavior used to be a rarity in Mayan culture but had become a trend in the past decade. Village life was difficult, as Carol was now learning. The men, women, and children worked steadily from sunrise until sunset just to survive. She was impressed that this was not viewed as a hardship by the villagers. This was just the way things were. Carol was also impressed that these women did not think less of her for her frequent stops. They explained that they had been doing this their entire lives and were used to it.

As she sat in the shade of the forest that surrounded her new home, Carol realized that her definition of *poverty* was changing. Yes, the Mayan people did not own nice homes and fancy automobiles. Electricity had still not found its way to this remote village, and communication was still accomplished by word of mouth. By western standards, the Mayan villagers of Tojolaba were poor. Carol stood and brushed the grass from her jeans. She looked around the busy rural community and watched as mothers trained their daughters in the art of weaving. Old men sat in groups and carved animal figures from hardwood while little boys watched in fascination. A village craftsman was concentrating on a new violin he was creating from raw materials. A shaman was returning from the jungle with a pouch overfilled with herbal remedies, harvested during his morning walk. Carol realized that these villagers were rich in tradition and family. They did not see themselves as poor. They were blessed with clean water from the Earth lord. They were blessed with resources from the Lacandon jungle to their east as well as the highland forest to their west. These villagers were rich in ways that Carol never imagined.

Twelve

Village of Perdido
Chiapas, Mexico

E very Mayan has a companion animal spirit to guide him
through life. Cristobal Salinas told Lucia, shortly after they
were married, a story of when he was a young boy and had wandered
into the jungle to find his animal spirit. Cristobal had roamed for
days without food and water. He began to worry that he would never
find his animal spirit and that his life would be meaningless. Finally,
on the verge of exhaustion, Cristobal collapsed near a small stream
and was prepared to die. He told Lucia how he woke to a beautiful
black leopard drinking from the stream next to where he lay. He
asked the leopard, "Are you my companion spirit, mighty jaguar?"

Cristobal shared with his wife how the great cat turned from
the stream and stepped over his chest, pausing long enough for him
to raise his small hand and stroke the leopard's velvet coat. The cat
then vanished into the jungle and Cristobal was reinvigorated. He
quickly found his way home and informed his father of his experience.
Cristobal's father sat for a long period without responding. He finally
told his young son that he had dreamt that Cristobal would be an
important man among the Mayans someday. He told Cristobal that

the jaguar was a spirit that would lead him to do bold things. He told Cristobal to always listen to his companion spirit and to never question the path it had laid out for him to follow.

By mid-morning, Lucia had finished with her chores and took some time to assemble her loom to finish a new shirt for her handsome husband. Her intricate brocade told the story of a heavy storm passing over the Mayan land. Water from the storm flooded the land and forced the people from their villages. In this story, the jaguar, who is lord of the animal spirits, stood on its hind legs and ordered the toads, which were musicians of the Earth lord, to be silent. The jaguar then used his mighty roar to chase the storm away. Lucia stopped to admire her work and watch her two sons play nearby.

Luis was so frail from his weakened heart and Gabriel was always aware of his brother's fragile condition. He would recognize when his younger brother grew tired and he would quickly change the game to something less strenuous. Lucia often found them sitting in the dirt drawing pictures of animals or great battle scenes.

The young mother turned her attention back to Cristobal's new shirt. She was proud to have mastered the difficult art of brocading at such an early stage in her life. Most women who brocaded were older, without the responsibilities of young children. Therefore, they had much more time to devote to this complicated task.

Lucia was startled when Luis crawled under her loom and poked his head up through the woolen fibers to surprise her. Lucia sat back and looked sorrowfully at her youngest son smiling at her through the webbing of white thread. This was a bad omen in Mayan culture. When a child was allowed to play under a working loom, this usually meant that the child would become very ill. If the child was unfortunate enough to stick his head through the wool fibers stretched out on the loom, this meant that the child would die sometime soon.

Lucia gazed at her delicate boy with bluish lips and could only reach out to rub his cool forehead. She had known that Luis's life would be cut short due to his failing heart, but this omen hinted that the end would come sooner rather than later.

With her attention solely on Luis, Lucia yelped in surprise as Gabriel poked his head through the loom next to his brother's and growled at his startled mother. Lucia scolded the two boys and told them to go to their beds until she was finished. The boys, who were rarely scolded for being playful, sulked off to their beds to figure out what they had done wrong.

Lucia was frantic. How could she be so careless to let her sons play around her loom? She could not share this revelation with Cristobal. He would be so angry at her recklessness. She would seek the shaman's help and stay extra vigilant to keep her sons from harm. Lucia would go to the church and ask God's forgiveness and she would beg the ancestors to watch over Gabriel and Luis and protect them from harm.

Lucia felt better with this plan firmly in mind. She would keep the boys away from the river and sleep next to them at night. With God's help and the ancestor's blessing, her precious boys would be safe.

Thirteen

Mexican Army Garrison
Oxchuc, Chiapas

S pread throughout an open field that once provided fertile land for much needed crops, the Mexican army camp watched over the impoverished community of Oxchuc, much like the Spanish lords in a past century. Soldiers languished outside small tents, waiting for their rotation to various roadblocks throughout southern Chiapas. Some played cards, a few cleaned their weapons while others slept, anticipating their often uneventful night shifts in the dark forests of this occupied state. Smoke floated from the mess tent where the camp's daily hot meal of beans and squash was being prepared.

Captain Eduardo Marquez stood behind his field desk inside the largest canvas tent. The sign on the door read *"Jefaturas."* A young lieutenant stood at parade rest on the opposite side of the four legged table and listened obediently to the ravings of his *comandante.*

"Senator Zentella from Chiapas, has personally requested that we send a message to the villagers that supporting the Zapatista *insurgentes* will not be tolerated. These rebels are like wild beasts who will steal food from the mouths of Mexican children. They live like dogs, they behave like dogs, and we will shoot them down like dogs."

The captain's voice got louder as he continued, "These *animales* in the villages provide for the rebels and then say to me, 'Oh no, *el Capitan*, there are no Zapatistas here. You have scared them all away. '*Gracias, gracias, gracias!*' I am sick of these peasant pigs."

The lieutenant shifted nervously. Captain Marquez was obviously waiting for a response, but the young officer intelligently decided to remain quiet.

The angry captain waited for a brief moment then snorted when his junior officer failed to reply, "You are from southern Mexico, Lieutenant Mateos, what would you suggest we do to get the villager's attention?"

Lieutenant Omario Mateos was born and raised in the Mexican state of Veracruz, just north of Chiapas. His family owned no land and had very little means to support themselves. When Omario turned sixteen, his father asked him to join the Mexican army to help support the family. Not having much stomach for the life of an ordinary soldier, Omario became a driver for the commander of his battalion in Monterrey, just north of the Mexican Capital. The commander, Colonel Fernando Garcia, was impressed by Omario's obedience and sense of duty. The Mexican army was under immense pressure from the *politicos* to diversify and reform its elitist officer corps, so Colonel Garcia sent his skilled driver to officer's training. Omario was proud and excited to be earning a higher wage. He could send money home to his family and still afford to keep some for himself. Two years later, having visions of renting an apartment in Mexico City, Lieutenant Mateos was stunned after he was transferred to an army garrison in Chiapas under the command of Captain Eduardo Marquez. At this moment, he would much prefer his former job as a lowly, enlisted driver.

The lieutenant offered reluctantly, "I recommend that we capture a rebel and publicly hang him in the courtyard of San Cristobal de Las Casas."

The young officer glanced at his commander for reassurance. Receiving none, he continued, "We could distribute flyers pledging the same treatment to any villager found supporting the Zapatistas."

Lieutenant Mateos swallowed hard. He did not want to hang any person, let alone a Zapatista rebel. When he was a teenager, growing up poor in Veracruz, Omario dreamt of running off to the mountains of Chiapas and joining the Zapatistas. He would never admit to that now, and Lieutenant Mateos felt it was much safer to adopt a hard line in front of this unpredictable commander.

The senior officer shuffled some papers on his desk while he contemplated the lieutenant's suggestion. Ready to pounce on the peasant officer for his incompetence and lack of aggression, Captain Marquez was surprised by the bold proposal.

"Very good, Lieutenant Mateos. I did not think you were capable of such intrepid vision. I'm beginning to see why Colonel Garcia was impressed by you." The captain walked around his desk to size up his subordinate officer, "Zapatista rebels have proven very difficult to capture and I do not have the resources to canvass the highlands of Chiapas to find their camps."

The captain paused and drilled his eyes into Omario looking for any trace of treasonous design. Deciding he could trust him, the captain continued, "With the Senator's approval, I have laid out a plan to assault a remote village close to here. There is information from America's CIA, that the villagers openly support the Zapatistas and are trafficking drugs to support them. By the time we finish killing a few of the rebellious peasants who live there, I promise you, a clear message will have been sent."

Lieutenant Mateos felt his commander's eyes burning into him. Omario's face became flush with anger as he contemplated the captain's plan.

"*El Jeffe*, do we have proof that the people of this village have become traitors to Mexico? Will the Senator from Chiapas really allow us to kill civilians based on information from the Americans?"

Captain Marques slammed his fist down on the table in front of him, collapsing one corner and scattering papers to the floor, "I do not need proof!" The captain screamed, spittle spraying from his lips, "The Senator does not need proof! These peasants exist only with our permission, and Mexico has decided to rid our nation of these pests."

Lieutenant Mateos looked at his commander and came to the position of attention. Visibly shaken by the captain's outburst, Omario immediately regretted challenging his commanding officer.

"These pigs laugh at us!" the captain continued loudly while waving his arms, "They should be afraid of us! They *will* be afraid of us! Do you understand me, Lieutenant Mateos?"

The junior officer straightened even more, "Yes, sir!" he replied smartly.

"Prepare your soldiers for battle, Lieutenant. All passes from this garrison are canceled effective immediately. Do I make myself clear?"

"Yes, sir," was all Omario could think to reply.

"Dismissed!"

Lieutenant Omario Mateos quickly exited the commander's tent and called for his soldiers to form up. Never in his life did the young peasant from Veracruz think he would be called upon to kill his own countrymen.

Fourteen

The Iverson's had survived two weeks in the village of Tojolaba and were starting to interact with the villagers on a regular basis. An artisan in the community led Jim and Taylor to his natural supply of clay for making pottery. He then showed them how to fashion blocks from the clay and fire them in a kiln they would build themselves.

After three days of non-stop labor, the father and son team had enough bricks made to cover the floor in their small quarters. They hauled sand from the streambed and dried it to use as a locking device between the individual tiles and were now prepared for the final step of laying the floor in place.

Carol spent several hours each day working with village women. She had learned how to make tortillas from boiled corn and was well on her way to weaving her first blanket made from home spun wool. Most importantly, Carol had gathered a wealth of information on the culture of Tojolaba. The anthropologist had learned that due to the heavy logging in this area, much of the land now owned by villagers was barren and infertile. In the past thirty years, Tojolaba had transformed from a farming community to a population who depended mostly on selling trinkets to tourists at several archeological sites in the area. As a result, young couples were moving away for better prospects in the city, leaving more work to the aging population. At this rate, Carol estimated the village of Tojolaba would cease to exist in the next ten to twenty years. With the accelerated pace of immigration and development in Chiapas due to the free trade agreements, Carol believed the end would come much sooner.

Another recent phenomenon was working rapidly to unravel the cultural glue that held this community together. The spread of evangelical Christianity throughout Chiapas was causing a rift between the young and the old. Stories that had been passed down through generations were now deemed irrelevant by the younger, *born again* Mayan families. The older Mexicans held strongly to their beliefs that their lives were guided by the Earth lord as well as their ancient ancestors. Evening gatherings, where stories were shared between young and old, were becoming a lost practice. The elderly were being left to share stories among themselves as the younger Mayans traveled several miles to hastily set up churches to worship Jesus Christ.

In Tojolaba, a rare blending of new and old ways was taking place. Elders combined stories of Jesus Christ with the stories of their ancestors to draw in the young. Legends of how a young Jesus farmed corn for his virgin mother who in return would make tortillas for him was a common unification of past and present in Tojolaba.

Carol had also completed the nuts and bolts of her cultural study of this rural community. The population of Tojolaba now stood at two hundred and eighty-one, ninety-seven of which were children under the age of fourteen. There were forty-two separate families living in the immediate area. Through various accounts shared by the local women, not one villager had lived to the age of sixty five in the past fifty years. Most died in their early sixties as a result of various illnesses, as well as malnutrition. Infant mortality appeared to be high due to a lack of trained medical professionals in the state.

Carol shook her head in disbelief as she studied the notes in her journal. On paper, these villagers were quickly descending toward disaster. When she raised her head from the cold figures and notations, Carol witnessed a vibrant community. Children were happy and for the most part healthy. Parents were working hard to provide for their families. She didn't see the violence and tragedy that predominated most poor neighborhoods in America. Carol would be sure to ask the professor for his interpretation at their meeting in San Cristobal, tomorrow morning.

Jim and Taylor began moving items from inside their temporary home. Among the belongings were two newly made frames for the bedrolls the professor had provided. Jim decided to pay a local craftsman to build the beds for the family. He had to admit, the frames were constructed much better than anything he could have put together. A lack of professional power tools was proving to be a serious handicap for Jim.

As father and son twisted and turned the last bed frame to fit it through the small door, the village shaman approached and stood quietly, watching Jim struggle to get his end out the opening.

"We got this dang thing into the house," Jim grunted, "There has to be a way to get it out."

Taylor set his end of the bed down and cleared his throat to get his father's attention.

"Are you giving up already, Taylor Paul?" Jim asked, "I haven't even cussed yet."

Taylor pointed to the colorfully dressed man standing behind a pile of luggage at the corner of the house.

Jim turned, "Oh! Excuse me," he said, setting his end of the bed down as well, "May I help you?" Jim asked uncomfortably, looking over his shoulder for Carol.

The older man spoke rapidly in the odd language and shook a cloth bag at Jim. Jim smiled back sheepishly and shrugged his shoulders at the smiling medicine man.

"Carol, honey," he called out loudly, "I think this man is casting a spell on me. Could you please come translate?"

Carol came from the shady side of the house and approached the shaman with a broad smile on her face, "*Senor Banuelos, de la bueno manana.*"

The shaman shook Carol's hand and said haltingly in English, "Good morning, Carol."

Carol laughed and turned to Jim, "I've been teaching *Senor* Banuelos a little English during our conversations together."

The shaman repeated what he had attempted to tell Jim and again shook his cloth bag.

Carol translated, "He says that he has something very important for the three of us and he would like to sit down to tell us about it."

Jim looked at Taylor trapped inside the hut by the wedged bed frame, "Hop on over here, tiger. The Union says it's break time."

Taylor climbed over the bed and the Iverson's, with their guest, sat in the shade under a nearby tree. The shaman launched into a long story. Carol followed along knowingly while Jim and Taylor tried to interpret the few words they had picked up while in Mexico.

Carol finally shook her head and held up her hand to the healer, "He says that he is worried about our health and safety in this village. He suspects that we do not have animal spirits to guide us while we are here."

Jim smiled playfully, "I know that I am in serious need of some spirits to guide me, but I don't believe we are talking about the same thing." Jim missed his nightly Michelob Light.

"Stop it!" Carol scolded, "This is serious."

Jim chuckled and elbowed Taylor, "Pay attention, son."

The village shaman continued his story. Carol fell into a groove and translated as *Senor* Banuelos continued uninterrupted.

"He says that he has watched us closely since we arrived and has consulted the ancient ones." Carol listened carefully, asked a brief question, and then continued translating.

"The ancestors are suspicious of our motives and predict a terrible outcome for us."

Carol glanced at Jim to catch his reaction to this revelation from the shaman. Jim was more serious now but shared no other response. *Senor* Banuelos continued.

"He says that the ancient ones have given him permission to show each of us our personal companion spirits." Carol held up her hand to the shaman once more. She wanted to explain the importance of this to her family.

"Usually, the Mayans are responsible for finding their own animal companions. Special arrangements are sometimes made for those who are too ill or otherwise unable to go out and discover which native animal will guide them through their lives."

Jim sat up straighter, "I guess we qualify as special cases."

Carol smiled and translated her husband's words for the Indian healer.

The Mayan nodded his head and continued in a grave tone.

"He believes that our lives are in danger because of visions the ancestors have shared with him. He has fasted for several days to gain access to the spirit world so he could interact with our guardian spirits."

Carol listened carefully, then smiled, "He says that our companion spirits are strong spirits and should keep us safe while we are here." She added after listening further, "We must listen to our spirits and do what they say or they will abandon us."

Taylor took advantage of a brief pause in the conversation, "What kind of animal protects me, Mom? I hope it's a mountain lion or a wolf."

Carol asked the question in Spanish. After listening to the shaman and watching him gesture to the sky, she reported, "He says that all of our spirits are birds. The bird is significant because it can easily escape one place and fly to another."

Taylor did not seem upset by this news. He loved all animals and enjoyed learning about birds in particular.

Jim watched Carol as she listened to the medicine man. Her acute attention to his unfamiliar language amazed him. Carol smiled and nodded politely as the Mayan continued without interruption. Jim still felt stunned at times, that this incredible woman was in love with him.

Carol turned and smiled at Jim, "He says that my companion spirit is an owl. Owls are wise and listen very well to all that is happening around them. He says that in the animal world, the owl brings balance and is rarely shaken by danger. He noticed that I constantly watch everything that is happening, much like an owl sitting in the trees."

Carol spoke briefly to the shaman, then listened as he continued.

"He was not surprised by your animal spirit, Jim. He says that you are guided by the Harpy Eagle. The Harpy Eagle is one of the most patient hunters in the forest. He says they are fast, agile and determined predators. The ancestors told him that you will hunt in the Mayan world much like this fierce bird and that your prey will not escape you."

Jim laughed uncomfortably and made eye contact with the Mayan medicine man. The man nodded at Jim as though he had journeyed through his soul. Jim felt a little embarrassed that he had allowed himself to get caught up in this superstition. He pulled Taylor close and tried to lighten the moment.

"I hope he says you're a woodpecker so you can peck that damn bed frame apart."

Taylor giggled then asked his mom, "What is my animal spirit, Mom?"

Carol scowled at Jim while she asked the shaman to continue.

"He says that he was most surprised by your spirit guide, Taylor. The White Hawk rarely offers itself as an animal guide. He says the spirit was intrigued by you because you stand out in this forest much like it does. He thinks the White Hawk will protect you from dangers that cannot be seen from the ground. He says that you must always listen to what this spirit tells you."

Taylor's eyes were wide with excitement, "Cool beans!" he exclaimed, "I'm going to go out right now and see if I can find a White Hawk in the forest."

"Not so fast, partner," Jim interrupted, "We have a big job to finish before sunset. We'll set aside tomorrow morning to go bird watching, okay?"

"But we're going to San Cristobal tomorrow," Taylor protested.

"We can squeeze in an hour or two right after the sun rises in the morning. That's when most birds are out anyway."

"Awesome!"

The medicine man spoke and held up his cloth bag. He pulled three small wood carvings from the bag and handed one to each of the Iverson's.

"Wow!" Carol exclaimed, "These are wonderful." Her carving was that of an intricately detailed owl. Jim's was an eagle, and Taylor's a hawk.

"It looks like he used white ash for Taylor's hawk," Jim noticed, "That tree doesn't grow south of Texas. I bet it was very difficult to find here."

The shaman gave instructions to Carol that she shared with her family, "He says that we must always keep these carvings with us. They will help keep us safe."

The Iverson's took turns thanking the gracious healer. He looked very proud that he had accomplished his mission. Carol left for a minute and returned with one of the extensive first aid kits she had packed for the trip. She handed it to the shaman and explained what it was in his native tongue. The healer beamed with pleasure and thanked the family for their generous gift.

As the shaman was leaving, he stopped and turned toward the road leading from Ocosingo. The sounds of approaching large trucks reached the Iverson's ears long before they could see who the vehicles belonged to. The medicine man seemed to instinctively understand the significance of the approaching trucks. Jim gathered his family close as the Mayan ran for his home on the far side of the village.

Fifteen

The Mexican army troop carriers bore down on the rural Mayan village. Civilians could be seen standing, holding children close, as they tried to determine the military's intention. Coming to a halt among the local's run down automobiles, soldiers unloaded off the trucks and quickly formed a perimeter around the immediate area.

Captain Eduardo Marquez stepped from his vehicle and gave orders for the soldiers to lock and load their weapons. Lieutenant Mateos circulated through his troops and quietly cautioned them not to point their weapons at the villagers. The soldiers, excited to break away from the humdrum of uneventful duties, were ready for a fight. The Lieutenant could see it in their eyes. Worse yet, he could see it in his commander's eyes.

"*Coloque abajo.*" The lieutenant whispered to his troops, "Settle down. These are our countrymen." The young officer could see that his words were having little effect on the men under his command.

A village elder reluctantly approached the heavily armed platoon of Mexican soldiers. The older man, stooped by age and endless labor, tried to smile as he limped toward the captain.

Captain Marquez was immediately angered by the man's obvious weakness, "Look at this old man," the commander spoke loudly, "he looks like an old dog that is about to be kicked by his master."

Several soldiers laughed quietly as their lieutenant stood heartbroken with knowledge of what was about to happen. The village elder looked much like Omario's grandfather before he passed away several years before.

The old man tried to hurry as he sensed the commander's impatience. Smiling, he raised his right hand, waving to the soldiers, "There are no Zapatistas here. We do not like the Zapatistas."

Before the village elder made it to the platoon's perimeter, Captain Marquez pulled his sidearm and shot him in the forehead. The noise was deafening, then absolute silence followed.

The lieutenant closed his eyes and prayed to God to stop this from happening, but God would not intervene this day.

From a fog, Lieutenant Omario Mateos heard his commander's order to clear the village. He watched the dust rise as soldiers opened fire on the stupefied civilian population. Brass casings from expended ammunition clinked to the ground as women and children were massacred where they stood. Soldiers broke rank and ran after the fleeing population. Screams could be heard from inside homes as women unsuccessfully tried to shield their children from hostile gunfire. Thatch roofs were set ablaze while the soldiers finished their murderous rampage.

No gunfire was returned on the armed troops now occupying the village. Very few local men were even present. They were elsewhere, trying to earn a meager living to support their families. No guns were found in the now burning huts. There was no sign of any drugs or Zapatistas.

Lieutenant Mateos walked among the carnage that his men had created. Tears streaked his face as he stared into the sightless eyes of a three year old boy who had fallen across the body of his younger brother. Screams from a nearby hut, announced the violation of these dead boys' mother. The smell of cordite mixed heavily with the odor of blood and opened bowels. Omario fell to his knees and vomited. A hand was placed on his shoulder and the young officer stood to meet the eyes of his commander.

"It is okay to feel sick after such an engagement," Captain Marquez instructed like a caring father, "I remember my first battle with drug runners on the northern border."

Lieutenant Mateos wiped his mouth then shoved the commander's hand from his shoulder, "This was not a battle, *el Capitan*. This was murder!"

The senior officer stood for several seconds before responding, "We are soldiers, Omario," the captain instructed calmly, "We are trained to murder. We are expected to murder to protect our nation. The lives of these villagers are nothing compared to the security of Mexico."

A gunshot erupted from the nearby hut and the mother's screams were silenced.

Lieutenant Mateos wiped a stream of snot from his face and refused to break eye contact with his captain, "I am not a murderer!" he said.

Marquez watched as two soldiers exited the hut, laughing as they buttoned their trousers, "There are over one hundred million Mexicans who are counting on you to do your job, lieutenant." The captain was now growing impatient, "This country is on the verge of prosperity. The only things that stand in our way are these villagers and their Zapatista friends. If we must kill to make Mexico a great nation, then we will kill." Looking back to his junior officer, Captain Marquez asked, "Do you understand me, lieutenant?"

"The people of Mexico will not stand for what happened here today," Omario yelled, "I will not stand for what happened here today. Do you understand me, *Captain*?"

Captain Marquez stepped back from the fuming officer. Shaking his head sadly, the commander pulled his sidearm and shot Lieutenant Mateos in the heart.

Walking back to his vehicle, the captain gave orders to recover the dead lieutenant's body, "He will be a hero!" Captain Marquez shouted to his troops, "The Zapatistas shot him as they fled into the forest. What a glorious day for Mexico!"

Sixteen

Village of Perdido
Chiapas, Mexico

C ristobal Salinas arrived home just as the sun was setting over the highlands to the west. Smoke was heavy in the valley where the village of Perdido sat, isolated from the rest of the world. At first, Cristobal thought another farmer was clearing land for crops. He soon realized that something very wrong had happened in the community where he and his family lived. Many of the Zapatistas from the rebel camp in the mountains were armed and walking throughout the village. Homes were burned. The carcasses of dead horses and goats were strewn about. Cristobal's chestnut gelding lay silent at the entrance to Perdido, riddled with bullet holes.

Cristobal panicked. He set off at a dead run for his home at the far end of the village. Rebels called to him as he ran through them to get to his family. He called out feverishly, "Lucia! Gabriel! *Venido al papa*! Luis! Come to Papa! Lucia!"

Blood stained the ground that Cristobal passed over. Before he could reach his home, Cristobal was stopped by his brother. Sergio had waited for him in anguish.

"Don't go there, brother. They are gone." Sergio held his brother tightly and whispered into his ear, *"Han cruzado el rio, mi hermano. They have crossed the river."*

Cristobal stared at his older brother with a wild look in his eyes, "You lie!" he screamed, "Why do you lie to me, Sergio? Where have they gone?"

Sergio spoke in a low tone, "They are dead, Cristobal. Your family has been killed. Many of the villagers have been killed." Tears streaked Sergio's face as the reality finally sank in.

Cristobal broke free from his brother's embrace and quickly covered the remaining distance to his home. Blankets covered still bodies in several locations. Cristobal saw the bare feet of Gabriel protruding from a stained blanket. *His dirty toes*! Gabriel always had dirty toes. Cristobal fell to the earth next to his murdered family. He openly sobbed as he pulled the blanket from their broken and blood spattered bodies. Cristobal Salinas lay next to his wife and pulled the lifeless bodies of his children close. A deep wale rose through the forest that night. All living creatures of the jungle stopped and listened to the cry which they understood all too well.

Seventeen

E arly the next morning, the Iverson's climbed into their Jeep for their first trip to San Cristobal. Dust was heavy in the air as trucks rumbled past the rural community. Jim had to wait several minutes for an opening onto the rutted two-lane road to Ocosingo. A new lumbering operation had begun close to Tojolaba the previous afternoon so large trucks, loaded with equipment going east and large mahogany trees going west, had clogged the dirt road continuously.

"Dad, where do the birds live after their trees are cut down?" Taylor asked from the backseat.

"They move on to other parts of the forest, I guess."

"But the White Hawk we saw this morning has a territory," Carol added, "When their territory is disrupted, they usually have to fight another hawk to take control of their hunting grounds. Either way, one of the hawks will probably die. It's tragic!"

Taylor prodded his mother for more information, "Is the White Hawk an endangered species?"

"I'm not sure, honey," Carol responded, "Maybe you and your father can find an internet café in San Cristobal and do some research."

"Can we, Dad?" Taylor asked excitedly.

"Absolutely, young man. I can send emails to everyone to let them know we're running around in loin cloths and fig leaves."

Carol turned to Taylor and rolled her eyes in a dramatic fashion as Jim pulled to the side of the road to let an oversized flat bed truck pass in the opposite direction.

"I wonder why the shaman reacted the way he did when he heard these trucks coming yesterday?" Jim asked.

Carol thought for a moment, "You wouldn't believe what the logging industry has done to the people down here. They come in and clear out every tree. Sometimes, they obliterate the entire forest surrounding these rural villages. They don't let anything get in their way, and the people really suffer for it."

Jim wrinkled his forehead as he pulled back onto the dirt road, "I thought the citizens of Tojolaba owned the forest around the village. How can the lumber companies get away with what they are doing?"

Carol fell into her teaching mode, "Land ownership in Chiapas is a shaky issue," she said, "It seems that the only people who recognize and honor private property down here are the villagers themselves."

Carol continued, "Thousands of displaced migrants move to Chiapas from other regions of Mexico and settle on private property with no repercussions from the government. It can get quite dangerous down here when that happens."

"I'll bet it does!" Jim offered, "It would get pretty dangerous back in Colorado if squatters moved onto my piece of the mountain."

Jim pulled over at the military check point half-way between Tojolaba and Ocosingo. A single soldier approached their vehicle and spoke in Spanish. Carol responded for a short time and the soldier waved them through.

"That was easy!" Jim remarked.

"I told him we were going to San Cristobal for a couple of days. I think this truck traffic has him irritated."

Taylor spoke up from the back seat, "Dad, what kind of weapon was that Mexican soldier carrying?"

"That was an old American made M-16A1 rifle. The United States gives Mexico a lot of its old weaponry after we upgrade to new systems. Why do you ask?"

"It just looked cool," Taylor responded.

"It's a piece of crap!" Jim stated, then turned his attention back to the road.

Arriving in San Cristobal, Jim, Carol, and Taylor were awestruck by the crowded farmer's market at the edge of town. Cabbages lay heaped on tarps and blankets. Carrots, onions, and tomatoes were displayed on boxes while blocks of salt, harvested from the salt mines of Salinas, were displayed in wooden barrels.

Locals wandered with bags filled with purchased vegetables and colorful fruits. Carts overflowed with brilliantly displayed carnations, gladiolus, and calla lilies as young girls sat nearby, ready to sell their harvest. Smoke rose from cooking fires and the heavy odor of open living hung in the air.

Jim maneuvered the jeep through pedestrians as he searched for a place to park near the Maya Medicine Museum. Carol was not scheduled to meet Professor Redding for another two hours at a nearby café, so the family took time to wander the streets of this historic city on foot. The classic white washed adobe architecture with red tiled roof captured the cultural significance of this commercial hub of the Chiapas highlands. Cathedrals rose to impressive heights while radiating the historic influence of Spanish Catholicism on southern Mexico.

As the family stood outside the *Templo y exconvento de Santo Domingo,* Carol explained that this cathedral was built around 1560, and is considered San Cristobal's most beautiful church.

Carol gladly accepted the role as tour guide and explained to Jim and Taylor, as they traversed the city plaza, "Spanish conquistadores built this city in 1524, after defeating the Mayans in the surrounding mountains. It was the capital of Chiapas when Guatemala controlled this area, but lost out to Tuxtla Gutierrez when Mexico took over in the late 1800's."

The sounds of traffic and blaring radios met their ears as the Iverson's crossed a busy street near the center of town. Carol raised her voice to compensate.

"All roads in Chiapas lead to San Cristobal. It's the principle trading town in this state, plus it's the most popular tourist destination."

"Looks like mostly Europeans come here," Jim noticed, "I don't see many other Americans."

"Most of the Americans here are researchers like us," Carol explained, "American tourists seem to prefer the beaches of Cancun, to the steamy jungles of Chiapas."

Time flew and Carol quickly found herself racing the family across town to meet the professor. He was sitting at a small table outside the café, *Casa del Sol,* reading a newspaper from Mexico City.

"I am so glad to see the three of you enjoying yourselves in this beautiful city," the professor shared as he stood from the table. He took Carol's hand and guided her to a seat, "I trust that you have been instructing Jim and Taylor on the colorful history of San Cristobal de la Casas?"

"Very little, I'm afraid," Carol laughed, "There is so much to experience here and too little time to do it."

Dr. Redding looked at Jim as he and Taylor found seats next to Carol, "I made arrangements for your family to stay the night at the hotel across the street." He looked to Carol, "It's very nice and the university is picking up the tab for one night. If you choose to stay longer, of course you will have to make arrangements."

Carol smiled, "Thank you so much, Dr. Redding. You have been very gracious to me and my family."

"Don't mention it." The professor leaned across the table and whispered, "It is just a shameful attempt to justify my continued importance down here."

Jim chuckled, "Taylor and I have some important research of our own to do," he stood and put his hand on his son's shoulder, "So we'll leave you two to your work."

The professor shook his head and looked very troubled, "Please stay for a bit, Mr. Iverson. I'm afraid that I have some very unsettling news for the three of you."

Jim looked at Carol, who shrugged and motioned for him to sit back down.

With Jim back in his seat, the anthropologist began, "This may be somewhat inappropriate for your son's young ears."

"Taylor, honey," Carol said, "Why don't you go over and throw some coins in the fountain." Carol pulled a handful of *pesos* from her purse and handed them to her son.

"Don't get out of our sight, okay, tiger?" Jim included.

Taylor agreed and ran to the fountain to play in the bubbling water.

Dr. Redding, receiving nods from both Carol and Jim, continued, "Yesterday, in a small village much like Tojolaba, forty-four villagers, mostly women and children I'm afraid, were killed during a Mexican army raid."

Carol gasped while Jim leaned forward in his chair and drilled his eyes into the professor, "Was this raid drug related?" he asked pointedly.

Dr. Redding was expecting this question, "No, no. There are no drugs in Perdido. It is a simple farming community with less than two hundred occupants. A very quiet community off the beaten path, close to Guatemala."

"What on earth was the Mexican army looking for?" Carol asked, already realizing the answer.

"The official word is that they were sweeping the village looking for insurgents. They say that they were fired upon by Zapatista rebels in the village and had to fight back. An army officer was apparently killed during the battle."

"If they were fighting rebels, then why the hell were so many women and children killed?" Jim asked, not believing a word of the official story.

The doctor looked around before continuing. He spoke in a much quieter voice this time, "My sources tell me that this was a massacre, plain and simple." He leaned closer to the table, "I've heard that the Mexican government has authorized a final push to eliminate all remaining rebellion from Chiapas. This raid was supposedly a message to everyone down here that the hydroelectric dams will be built." The professor leaned back and took a sip of his coffee before continuing, "The Central American Highway will run through the valley Perdido sits in, and Mexico cannot afford delays caused by rebel uprisings. So they say!"

Jim shook his head, "So they believe that killing a few women and children will quiet everybody down? When will governments ever learn that murdering innocents only makes people angry and more rebellious?"

"I can't believe the government sanctioned the murders," Dr. Redding offered, "I would wage a bet that this was the work of a certain Captain Eduardo Marquez." The professor looked over his shoulder, apparently shocked that he had spoken the captain's name out loud, "Please excuse my paranoia," he said, "Foreigners who become politically involved down here tend to find themselves deported to Guatemala rather quickly."

Carol put her hand on Jim's arm, "Captain Marquez was the officer you tangled with at the checkpoint when we first arrived here. You shouldn't have provoked him," she scolded.

The professor's eyes widened dramatically.

Jim spoke up, "That captain was ruthless. He was baiting us on the road that day. He knew I had him figured out and it really threw him off his game." Jim looked at Carol, "I've met men just like him who would smile and hold your hand while they cut your throat."

Professor Redding cleared his throat and jumped in, "I'm afraid your husband is right, Carol. There is also substantial rumor in Chiapas that children tend to disappear when the captain is near." The professor glanced at the water fountain, "I'm afraid a boy, like your son, would not stand much of a chance if he ever fell into the clutches of a man like Captain Marquez."

Both Jim and Carol quickly searched the fountain with their eyes to ensure Taylor was safe. He was sitting on the edge of the concrete structure handing the *pesos* to a group of children rather than tossing them into the water like his mother suggested.

"Oh my God!" Carol whispered, "Why does the Mexican government allow this man such autonomy down here?"

Dr. Redding sighed deeply, "Unfortunately, Chiapas is just land to be used for the advancement of Mexico's economy. The Mayan population here is basically irrelevant to the politicians in Mexico City." The professor removed his hat and rubbed a hand through his thinning white hair, "As long as the captain is making progress down here," he continued, "he will have free reign to do as he chooses."

"That's just disgusting!" Carol proclaimed.

"And unfortunately, a common practice in every country on this planet," Jim allowed, "including ours."

"Very true, Mr. Iverson. We are crossing our fingers that this will be an isolated incident, but we are not going to hold our breath. Once word of this spreads, I'm afraid another uprising will occur. The situation could get very bloody down here."

Jim looked at Carol with a stern expression, "We will make arrangements to leave Chiapas as soon as possible." He turned to Dr. Redding who was nodding, "Would you please contact the university and ask them to book us tickets out of here by the end of the week?"

Carol jumped from her seat, "Now wait just a minute, Jim!" she exclaimed, "I have waited my entire life for this opportunity. I will not abandon it on a whim without any discussion."

Jim got angry, "I will not have my family butchered in the middle of a damn war that doesn't concern us." His face red and his posture unrelenting, Jim continued, "Look at our son over there, Carol. Did you listen to anything the professor just said? These bastards are killing women and children without recourse."

Carol would not back down. As a highly educated woman in a man's world, she had learned early not to be intimidated, "I understand the situation, Jim. I am just informing you that *we* will make a decision after *we* have discussed it fully."

The professor stood and wiped the corners of his mouth with a cloth napkin, "Why don't we agree to meet here in the morning for breakfast? This will give the two of you time to come to an agreement." The professor pulled Carol's chair for her to stand, "The

University will understand fully if you decide to leave, and I will personally guarantee you a spot on my research team down here after things calm down."

Carol looked troubled but tried to smile, "Thank you, Dr. Redding. We'll meet you here in the morning then."

At the hotel that night, Carol and Jim quietly compromised on their next course of action. Jim agreed to stay in Tojolaba for the remainder of the month. Carol felt that she could collect enough data during that time to finish her dissertation and complete her PhD, while Jim felt he could ensure his family's safety by keeping them off the roads and close at hand.

Both parents agreed not to inform Taylor of the massacre in Perdido. He would have plenty of time in his life to discover mankind's atrocities committed against one another.

The next morning, after informing Dr. Redding of their mutual decision, the Iverson's bought supplies, then headed back to Tojolaba. The military checkpoints, although stressful, passed without incident and the family arrived safely.

The mood in the village had obviously changed from news of the killings at the small village, not twenty miles to the south as a crow flies. Children were kept closer to mothers. Fathers were finding reasons not to leave the village, and animals were not allowed to wander freely in the community as before. Tojolaba was once again adapting to a new world.

Eighteen

Zapatista Camp
Chiapas Highlands

After the bodies of the massacred villagers were laid to rest, Cristobal Salinas abandoned his job, his home, and most of his belongings. He then moved to the rebel camp in the mountains with his brother.

Sergio stood outside his makeshift headquarters and watched as his only brother sat and talked to three other men. He knew that Cristobal was angry and heartbroken and wanted vengeance for his murdered family.

Since the assault on Perdido, the Zapatista camp had swollen with volunteers. One of the men sitting with Cristobal, lost his pregnant wife during the raid. Sergio spit in the dirt. It was not a raid. It was calculated murder. Dropping the stick in his hand, Commander Salinas walked to where his brother was sitting. The conversation stopped abruptly.

"What are you planning to do, *hermano?*"

Cristobal glued his eyes to the ground and focused angrily on a map drawn in the dirt, "We have to do something, Sergio." Now staring defiantly into his brother's eyes, he continued, "They take our

85

land. They burn our crops. They steal our livestock. They murder our women and children. What do we do?" Cristobal stood and for the first time in his life, stepped face to face with his older brother, "The Zapatistas do nothing!" he yelled, "You, brother, sit there in your plywood castle and play with your balls!"

Sergio stepped back to slap his younger brother, then changed his mind. He could not imagine what Cristobal was going through. Never marrying and never having children, sheltered Sergio from ever having to face the loss that now permeated this camp. He bowed his head, "I want to help you, brother." Raising his eyes to meet Cristobal's painful expression, Sergio asked, "What are you planning? What do you want me to do?"

Cristobal looked at his brother for several seconds then looked at the three men still sitting. Emilio, the young man who lost his pregnant wife, nodded.

"We want to fight these fucking *Ladinas*." Searching his brother for reaction, Cristobal continued, "We want to kill as many Mexican soldiers as we can. We want to send them all straight to *Mitnal*, brother. Will the Zapatistas join us?"

Sergio frowned at his brother's question, "Of course we will join you, but we do not have enough weapons to fight the army. The only thing we would be able to do is throw rocks and die." The commander looked at the sitting men, "This is what they want us to do. Don't you see? They want to draw us out into the open and kill us once and for all." Sergio pleaded, "We have to plan carefully. We have to use our resources wisely. Killing Mexican soldiers will only bring more Mexican soldiers."

Cristobal grabbed his brother's shoulders and spun him around, "You have no plan!" he yelled, "The Zapatistas have no resources. We act like scared rabbits hiding in a bush, too afraid to come out. Pissing our pants every time we see a Mexican soldier."

Sergio bowed his head again. Everything his brother was saying was true. The mission had become more about hiding from the government than standing up to it, "Where will we get guns and ammunition?" the commander asked.

Seeing his brother capitulate, Cristobal spoke enthusiastically, "We are working on a plan to bring in a million dollars." He smiled for the first time in days, "It will take a few weeks to get the money, then we will be able to buy all the guns and ammunition we need. We will take Chiapas from the Mexicans for good this time."

Sergio was shocked. A million dollars was unheard of. He could not even imagine a plan that would bring in such money, "Where will we ever get a million dollars?" he asked.

Cristobal sat in the dirt and pulled his brother down close, "There is an American family in Tojolaba. I brought them from the airport in Villahermosa a couple of weeks ago. They are staying here for one year to study us like rats." Cristobal stopped to search his brother's face for a reaction. Not seeing any form of agreement, he continued more passionately, "There are three of them. The husband, the wife, and a young boy. If we take them, the university that they work for will pay us for their safe return."

Sergio shook his head, "You don't even know what university they work for. How can you demand a ransom?"

Cristobal got angry, "They are from Colorado. I heard them talking on the bus. Their bus tickets were paid for by Colorado University. I am not a stupid little boy, Sergio! I am a man whose family was butchered two days ago while I ate popcorn and drank a cola at Palenque." Tears rolled down his cheeks, "Are the Zapatistas with us, *hermano*? Or are we going to do this by ourselves?"

Sergio sat back, shocked by everything he had just been told, "You know that I do not have the authority to decide this kind of action. I will have to consult the elders. I will probably have to ask Commander Marcos himself. I do not think that any of them will agree." Sergio pleaded with his brother, "What you are proposing is madness! This will turn the world against us. We will be hunted like dogs and killed. Where will Chiapas be then? Please, brother, I know your heart aches and your blood boils, but this plan can only end in disaster. The ancient ones will not stand for it."

Cristobal stood and screamed at the top of his lungs, "Where were the ancient ones when Lucia was being raped by those bastards, Sergio?" Crying now, Cristobal grabbed his brother's shirt and stood him up, "Where were the ancient ones when my little Gabriel tried to shield his brother from those murderers? Did you see them, Sergio? Did you see their little bodies shredded by the bullets?"

Cristobal released his brother and began to walk away. Finally stopping, he turned and pointed threateningly at his brother, "Don't you ever talk to me about the ancient ones, Sergio. The ancient ones are dust in the ground."

Sergio stood quietly, shaken by his brother's outburst as the remaining three Zapatistas rose and followed after their new leader.

Nineteen

Jim and Taylor walked slowly through the short grass of the hillside forest. Eyes glued to the ground, father and son searched intently, kicking over rocks and scraping at piles of dirt with their feet.

"Wow! Look at this, Dad." Taylor used his net to capture a butterfly from the climbing vine of a colorful pokeweed.

Jim walked over to his excited son to inspect the latest addition to their growing insect collection, "That is a terrific looking butterfly."

As Jim placed the flying insect into a mason jar, lined with dried clay and a little bit of Carol's fingernail polish remover, Taylor quickly opened his *Guide to Central American Insects* to discover what he had found, "I think it's a Zebra Longwing, Dad." He read on enthusiastically, "Heliconius Charitonus. Brown body, black wings with yellow stripes. This is definitely a Zebra Longwing," Taylor said as he examined the fluttering insect inside the jar.

"Well, somebody named this one properly," Jim mused, "It sure looks like a zebra."

"I can't wait to find an assassin bug. My friends back at school are going to think it's so cool." Taylor turned the page in his book to find a photo of the insect he was referring to, "What did *Senor* Banuelos call this bug, Dad?"

Jim stood and stretched his back muscles, "I think its pronounced *conenoses*. Your mom said that it means bedbug." He continued, "When we catch one, we have to treat it with that bleach solution she made for us this morning. I guess they carry some pretty bad diseases."

"I know, that's why they are so cool," Taylor explained, shaking the jar to see if the butterfly was still alive, "They crawl on your face in the middle of the night and give you a kiss. That's really gross, but I think I would rather be kissed by a bug than a girl."

Jim took the jar from his son and unscrewed the lid. He helped Taylor use a pin to attach the Zebra Longwing to a small foam board.

"This bug hunting kit your mother brought was a great idea. I think you and I should do something nice for her to show her our appreciation. What do you think?"

Taylor's face brightened, "I know! We could make her a fancy dinner tonight and eat outside at the picnic table we built yesterday."

Jim smiled, "That, young man, is a wonderful idea." He thought for a moment, "Seeing how we do not possess a microwave oven or the electricity to run it, we should probably head back and get started pretty soon."

Taylor packed away the newest member of his collection. Taking his father's hand and leading the way back to the village, he proclaimed, "I want to live down here forever!"

Carol sat next to two village women who were patiently weaving colorful threads into a grid work of fine woolen fiber. One used a deer bone pick to separate cream colored strands while the other, kneeling on a mat made from palm, tightened the tension of her loom to better observe the pattern she was creating.

The women had been subdued for the past few days as they struggled with the news of the massacre. They spoke quietly of families they had known from the shattered village and shared stories of weaving contests that were consistently won by the women of Perdido.

Carol recognized a nervous tension in the villagers as they raised their eyes to every approaching vehicle, expecting the same fate as their sister community to the south. For the very first time since she arrived in Tojolaba, Carol heard mention of the Zapatista rebels.

"The Zapatistas used to help the Mayan people," she heard an older woman explain, "They taught us better ways to grow our crops, and they encouraged us to return to our roots and learn the art of weaving again. Now, we can be killed just for saying the word Zapatista."

Carol learned of at least four young families who were making arrangements to leave the village permanently. Fed up with the difficult farming lifestyle, the added danger of a rural campaign by the Mexican army was too much to bear. These families would rather take their chances in the cities among others who had fled the countryside.

As children played quietly near their mothers, the anthropologist struggled with the changes she was seeing in the day-to-day lives of the people who surrounded her. An almost sad surrender to a fate that was not in their control. She had never really studied the effects of war on indigenous peoples. Her focus of study had always been the impact of economic change on civilizations.

Carol had read books on the Montagnard people who lived in the mountains of Viet Nam, but was always more interested in the cultural metamorphosis that took place after the war. An economic explosion in Southeast Asia had fundamentally changed that society forever. She made a mental note to ask Jim for any insight he might have regarding this matter.

The smell of delicious food greeted Carol as she stepped through the door of her earthen home. Jim was pulling something from the glowing embers of the recently constructed fireplace, while Taylor was gathering supplies to carry outside to the pine table.

"What on earth smells so scrumptious?" she asked, giving her husband a peck on the cheek.

"Taylor and I thought it would be nice to show you how much we appreciate you," Jim said.

Placing the sizzling dish, wrapped in aluminum foil on a small table, Jim hugged his wife tightly and returned the kiss.

"Gross!" Taylor exclaimed, walking through the door, "Didn't you know you can get diseases from doing that?"

Carol looked at Jim for an explanation.

Turning back to the chicken, Jim filled her in, "We've been looking all day for a Kissing Beetle. He thinks it's cool that they spread mayhem through an action he considers disgusting."

"Trust me, son, your father's kisses are worth the risk." Carol laughed while Taylor wrinkled his nose and walked outside with more supplies. "What are we having for dinner, and to what do I owe this extravagant treatment?"

Jim folded down the edges of the foil to reveal a roasted chicken with carrots and potatoes sizzling in the bird's juices, "I killed our only chicken," he said, "She refused to lay eggs so her days were numbered."

Carol frowned then breathed in the succulent aroma of the delicious fowl, "Well," she said, "She gave her life for a good cause. Now tell me what I did to deserve all this."

"We just love you, Mom," Taylor offered, coming back through the door, "*Senor* Banuelos let me pick the vegetables from his garden. I gave him my binoculars in exchange. He really liked them."

The family walked out to the picnic table under the trees at the south end of their home. "I have candied squash cooking for desert," Jim shared while dishing up steaming slices of breast meat.

Jim sat across from Carol as she spooned some vegetables onto Taylor's plate. He watched as his hungry son licked his lips and picked up a fork, waiting to dig in.

Carol said, "So this is the secret to getting you to eat more vegetables. We should just require you to grow your own."

"Dad and I are going to plant a vegetable garden when we get home next week," Taylor shared excitedly with his mother, "I wish we could stay longer, but I really miss my friends and video games."

Jim laughed while watching his son devour the food on his plate.

Turning and catching Carol with a solemn look on her face, he asked, "You look a little down in the dumps, honey. Are you upset that we're leaving next week?"

"No, not really," Carol responded, picking at her food, "This family's safety is more important than my work right now. I fully accept the reality that we need to return home." Carol paused and thought for awhile, "I have grown very close to some of the people in this village and I am really worried about what might happen after we leave."

Jim looked at Taylor as the eager boy added more vegetables to his plate, "Maybe you should devote the rest of the year to getting this story out. Write a book or blow the whistle to any news channel that will listen."

"I've thought about that, Jim. I haven't made a decision yet. If I go public, I will never be allowed to work down here again. I have to weigh the possible good I can achieve through exposing these atrocities, with the possible good I can do down here at a future time."

Jim watched Taylor pick at a pin feather on a drumstick he pulled from the platter of meat. Choosing his words carefully, he explained, "Atrocities happen in war, Carol. These people need you now. Their lives depend on you going home and telling their stories. If word of this doesn't get out today, they will not need you in the future."

Carol took a bite of potato and chewed slowly, "Jim, I don't understand. What kind of butcher would shoot innocent women and children?" she asked, "I mean, what kind of man could point a gun at a defenseless child and pull the trigger?"

Jim sat in stunned silence. Always teetering on the edge of horrific memories, it was as if Carol had glimpsed into his secreted past and was now demanding an explanation.

Carol watched in shock as her husband stood from the table and walked into the forest, "Jim?" she called after him, "Honey, are you okay?"

Jim wandered through the trees trying to make sense of his reaction to Carol's question. What happened in the desert of Iraq was in no way comparable to what happened in the village of Perdido. Jim was a soldier in a foreign country during a time of war. 'Atrocities happen in war, Carol'. Why did he say that? There was no war in Chiapas. Just innocent people trying to live out their lives. Just like the civilians on that bus in Iraq, over a decade ago.

Looking to the setting sun, Jim sighed deeply then walked back to the village. He dreaded the questions he knew he would have to avoid when he returned and the nightmares he would have to face when he finally slept.

Twenty

Jim returned home just after sunset. The food and dishes had been cleared away from the picnic table and his family had gone inside for the evening. He could hear bleating goats and nestling chickens across the village, fussing as they settled in for the night. The moon would not rise for a few hours, leaving the stars to dance in its absence.

As he sat on the table to clear his head, Jim could hear the mournful sobbing of a child in a nearby hut. An owl hooted in the distant woods as it watched the jungle prepare for darkness. Some settled in to rest, while others were organizing to hunt.

Jim opened the door to the hut and stepped inside. The north wall was bathed in candlelight as Carol snuggled with Taylor and read a story about wizards from a time only imagined. He stood and watched in silence as shadows danced in golden light, across the faces of his wife and son. The scene before him was overwhelming and Jim stood transfixed by its beauty.

"Are you okay, Daddy?" came the sweet voice of his only child.

Carol looked over the top of the cloth bound novel and smiled at her husband with nothing but understanding of his struggle against the demons that haunted him.

"I…" Jim hesitated, searching for the right words, "I love you two more than either of you will ever know." He stood, unable to move, "And I promise that I will get help as soon as we return home."

Carol pulled aside the blanket that covered her and Taylor and patted the bed for Jim to join them.

January 16, 1991
Hwy 1, twelve miles North of Baghdad, Iraq

The small boy, expecting to find discarded treasures in the debris below the abandoned water tower, was surprised to find a camouflaged soldier staring at him instead. Danger flooded his senses like the instinctual warning received from a rattlesnake ready to strike. He wanted to run but froze instead. The only thing he could do now was yell.

"Soldiers!" the boy screamed in Arabic while pointing at Jim, "There are enemy soldiers hiding in the garbage."

Jim broke eye contact with the boy and watched as two of the Republican Guard soldiers raised their weapons and started toward them.

Sergeant Wesley Burns, the other weapon's specialist on the team, opened fire and immediately brought down one of the approaching Iraqis.

As the action began to spiral at untold speed, Jim's mind slowed events and filtered unnecessary information, which transformed him into a highly focused killer. Three rounds from his Colt Commando brought down the other soldier.

"Stingray, Stingray, this is Bravo Team. We are engaged with enemy and are requesting immediate extraction, over." Jim could only hear one side of the call for evacuation.

Civilians scattered in all directions. The six remaining Iraqi soldiers returned fire and ran for cover. Jim could not get a clear shot without killing innocent civilians. The boy stood perfectly still and covered his ears.

"Heavy machine gun on the truck!" came an excited yell over the team's radio.

Jim watched as the barrel of a Russian made "Kord" heavy machinegun swung toward the team's location. Outgoing fire increased and was directed onto the truck, equipped with armor plating.

Civilians screamed and fell to the earth as stray rounds and ricochets claimed their lives.

The heavy machine gun opened up with a loud burp as 12.7 millimeter rounds were directed onto the team at 650 rounds per minute. Metal flew as empty drums shattered behind the awesome force of the copper jacketed rounds.

First to fall was Staff Sergeant Lopez. Caught in the open on his perch on the water tower, the communications specialist fell twenty feet to the ground in a tangle of blood, equipment and torn body parts. The call for help had just been silenced.

Small arms fire came from the ditch at the side of the road. Civilians, frightened by the loud firefight jumped to their feet to escape. Mistaking them as soldiers, the team dropped them before they could fully stand. A mother, running for her boy who now stood in front of Jim, was cut down before she could reach the railroad tracks.

The "Kord" was working a steel culvert that concealed Sergeant Burns. Finally punching through, the Kevlar helmet that protected Wesley's head was not enough to stop the hunger of the Russian weapon. Sergeant Burns died in a vapor of bone, blood and brain matter.

"Somebody take out that God damned machine gun!" This was Captain Miller trying to direct the fight from behind a pile of concrete.

Jim launched to his feet and ran the short distance to the small boy who still stood, hands clasped on top of his head, facing his dying mother on the far side of the tracks. Before Jim could reach for the frozen child, small arms fire from the ditch found him. A ricochet off his Kevlar helmet forced him to the ground. He returned fire while rolling for cover behind a discarded railroad timber.

A short squeak escaped the boy's lips as a round struck him just under the right shoulder blade. He fell to the ground and fixed his eyes on Jim's face. Not more than twelve inches away, Jim watched as life drained from the ten year old. Pink foam bubbled from his nose and mouth as he tried to cry.

Fire from the Iraqis swung toward the captain and Corporal Carpenter as they tried to lay down covering fire for Jim. Jim grabbed the boy's hair and dragged him to relative safety behind the abandoned pickup.

"Medic!" he screamed over the radio.

Corporal Brian Rhodes was the team's medic. Highly trained, a Special Forces medic is as good as any doctor on the battlefield.

As the heavy machine gun reloaded, the corporal made his way to where Jim held the Iraqi boy.

"Are you wounded, sergeant?"

Jim yelled as the "Kord" opened up again, "The boy! The boy has been shot!"

Corporal Rhodes took one look at the child and said, "He's dead, sergeant. There's nothing I can do for him."

Sergeant Iverson released the boy's body and let him slide slowly to the ground. His lifeless stare drilled into Jim's soul.

The heavy machine gun was now working the concrete pile that concealed Captain Miller and Corporal Carpenter. Jim rose above the pickup and took careful aim at the Iraqi machine gunner. Firing a short burst, he missed the enemy soldier completely. Armor deflected any rounds that might find their way into the fortified position.

The machine gun turned back toward Jim and ended Corporal Rhodes' life in a blink of the eye. Jim hugged the ground as blood from his fallen friend pooled at his feet.

"Medic's down, Rhodes is down!" Jim reported over his radio to the two remaining team members. In less than five minutes, the elite army unit had been cut in half. With open desert to their rear, there was no avenue left open for escape. The Russian "Kord" would find them among the dunes and kill them all. The only thing left for the team to do was hunker down and pray for support.

Captain Miller had never been one for "hunkering down." Timing his movement to the reloading of the "Kord", the officer made his way to Burns' body and recovered his M-203 grenade launcher.

His timing impeccable, Captain Miller stood as the machine gun stopped, and fired one round at the armored truck. Small arms fire found the captain easily in his compromised position and the ten year veteran of

Special Forces fell before he could see the truck erupt in flames. The heavy machine gun had been silenced.

Sergeant James Iverson and Corporal Nathan Carpenter exchanged fire with the five remaining Iraqi soldiers. Two were killed easily while changing positions and the other three reduced their rate of fire to conserve ammunition. Eventually, all gunfire stopped.

Jim looked across the battlefield and saw the red stained cotton of dead civilians blowing in the breeze. The military truck burned and belched out thick black smoke. The bus sat motionless among shattered glass and unmoving bodies.

An odd sound broke the silence that had befallen the killing field. A rhythmic clicking grew louder and louder as Jim looked for the source of the clatter. Click, click. Click, click.

Jim sat up in bed as the odd sound woke him from another nightmare. The room was dark and Carol lay at his side, softly snoring. Click, click. Click, click. The sound hadn't come from Jim's nightmare at all. The noise was emanating from the latch on the door to their small home. Someone was trying to open the door.

Twenty-one

Jim moved the blanket aside and stood in the absolute darkness of the confined quarters. The door rattled again, almost imperceptibly, as someone outside worked the latch to release it. He moved closer to the door, careful not to make a noise. His heart pounded, partly from the fading nightmare, and partly from the unexplained event now taking place outside the door to his dwelling.

Jim weighed his options carefully. There were no guns in the hut to protect his family and his hunting knife was packed in a knapsack in the back of the Jeep. If the person or persons outside intended to do harm, Jim was left with his bare hands to defend his family. No problem, as long as the intruder did not have a weapon. Chances were, he did.

The handmade latch relented with a slight scraping noise and the door slowly swung open. Jim could see nothing but felt the pressure change as cool air rushed through the opening. He could hear whispers from outside, meaning there was more than one intruder. What did they want?

In a flash, Jim's mind raced through several possibilities. Were the men outside bandits, looking only for money and possible treasure? Or was it Captain Marquez, seeking revenge for his humiliation on the road that day, three weeks before? Was it a village peasant, hoping to steal a few scraps of food for his family? Or was it lonely workers from the lumber company, planning to do harm to his wife? This last thought scared the hell out of Jim and he quickly settled on a course of action. The person or persons coming through that door would pay for this mistake with their lives.

"Honey, is everything okay?" It was Carol, calling from the bed.

Momentarily distracted by his wife's call, Jim was late responding to the first intruder through the door. A light came on and bathed the interior in bright white luminescence from a large flashlight held by someone still outside. Jim was blinded but threw a devastating punch to the head of the first man to step inside. The intruder fell into a small table and twisted to the ground in a heap.

Wearing brown ski masks that covered their faces, two more intruders came through the door and tackled Jim. Tripping over a folding chair, he went to the ground hard. A loud gasp came from Carol as she realized what was happening.

Grabbing one of the masked men who had tumbled to the ground with him, Jim tried to put his attacker in a sleeper hold to take him out of commission. It didn't work. The young man slipped from Jim's grasp and went for Carol and Taylor, now standing on the bed.

Carol woke in the middle of the night to find Jim out of bed. She could see his outline as he stood motionless by the door to the hut.

"Honey, is everything okay?" she asked, assuming he was struggling with another nightmare.

Jim never answered. Instead, a bright light illuminated the inside of their hut and Carol squinted as she watched her husband being driven to the ground by two masked men.

Carol reacted quickly, grabbing the still sleeping Taylor and shielding him against the wall with her body. She screamed as the house swarmed in a flurry of action. Jim was fighting furiously on the floor as two masked intruders approached the bed. One was holding cloth bags in his hand while the other held a flashlight. They tried to coax the mother and her trembling son from the bed.

Carol yelled, "Taylor! Run!" She watched as her son, consumed with fear, ran for the door. The hooded bandit holding the flashlight dropped his burden and reached for the escaping boy.

Darkness enveloped Carol when a bag was placed over her head. A bolt of lightning flashed through her mind as she was struck in the face by one of her attackers. Sounds of the assault faded as she quickly slipped into unconsciousness.

Jim was in a struggle for his life. Now standing, he was locked in a death grip with a strong opponent. In the struggle to stand, the mask had been pulled from the head of his attacker. Jim was shocked when he recognized the long hair and face of the bus driver whose life he had saved at the military checkpoint. Finding an opening, Jim locked his grip onto the windpipe of his assailant with a *ranger choke hold*. The bus driver's eyes went wide as his air supply was cut off entirely. Jim knew it would be a short time before this madman lost consciousness.

Cristobal was stunned by the fierceness of the man he was fighting. The American's punches felt like bricks were being pounded into his face. Losing the battle on the ground, Cristobal broke free and stood to give himself more maneuvering room. As the man reached for him, Cristobal's mask was torn from his head. He could see recognition in the man's face just before he grabbed the Zapatista's throat with his right hand.

Cristobal was shocked by absolute pain as his airway was crushed in the American's steel grip. Sensing death, he grabbed for the hunting knife sheathed on his belt. As consciousness was dimming and death approaching, Cristobal plunged the knife into the American's stomach. The grip on his throat never abated and Cristobal collapsed to the floor with his opponent. Blood warmed his hand that held the knife deep inside the man who was killing him. Cristobal finally relaxed his grip on the knife and crossed the river to the underworld.

Jim was losing blood at an alarming rate. Sliding the body of his attacker to the side, he tried to sit up and take note of the situation. Carol and Taylor were gone. He prayed that they had escaped. The intruder who had been knocked out by Jim's first blow was now standing and struggling to get out the door. The failing husband and father tried to stand. Struggling to his knees, his head swam in an ocean of urgency and approaching death. Jim fell to the clay floor of his small home in Chiapas, Mexico, and succumbed to the darkness that stalked him.

Twenty-two

Taylor slipped by the hands of the intruder and was out the door in a rush. For a brief second, he hesitated on whether to run to another house in the village or to head for the shadows of the forest. Sounds of his mother screaming inside the hut and the sight of one of the attackers coming through the door, determined a course of action for him. Taylor ducked around the corner of the house and ran for the dark woods.

Hearing footsteps in pursuit, Taylor picked up his speed and changed course several times. This always seemed to work when he was being stalked by one creature or another in his video games, so he prayed that it would work in real life. Amazingly, it paid off. The footsteps grew fainter and fainter which allowed Taylor to slow down and trade speed for stealth.

Finally stopping, he tried to calm his breath and slow his heart so he could listen for the man who was trying to follow him. There! He saw his pursuer's outline pass far below on the hillside.

Taylor remembered a shallow cave further up the mountain that he and his father had discovered on one of their hikes. The cave gave Taylor the creeps because it was overgrown with vines and the entrance was blocked by several ornately carved wooden crosses. He thought it might be some sort of burial ground but his mother had informed him later that evening that the cave was a place where the village shaman went to pray to the Earth lord for rain each spring. Taylor didn't think the Earth lord would mind if he used the cave as a hideout until daylight. Plus, he would have a pretty good view of the village and his home from up there.

After quietly snaking his way up the mountain, Taylor was surprised when he easily found the cave's entrance in the dark. His dad had always required him to memorize landmarks wherever they went. Taylor thought it was silly and sometimes got mad when his dad would quiz him on what markers he could remember from their hikes.

"Thanks, Dad!" he whispered under his breath as he reached the spooky altar.

Taylor sat perfectly still in the darkness for several minutes, listening to the sounds of the forest. His father had taught him how to pick out noises that were distinctly man made. The slight clink made by metal. A whispered cussword. A trip over a stone or log. Sniffles. Lots of things that would identify the noise maker as human. He heard none of these noises now. In fact, the forest was eerily quiet.

Feeling a little safer now, Taylor stood and moved to a clearing just ten feet away and peered down into the village. He could see light inside his home, sneaking through cracks in the mud walls. He could also make out four shadowed individuals standing outside the house. One had a white sack covering her head. Taylor was stunned when he realized that this hooded figure was his mother. Tears flooded from his eyes. He desperately wanted to cry out for the men to leave his mom alone.

Taylor stood silently and watched one of the men return to the house. A moment later, he returned with the flashlight and gestured wildly to his two companions. The three seemed to be arguing about what to do next. Finally, they led his mother, hands tied behind her, to the edge of the forest on the opposite end of the village. After several minutes, Taylor distinctly heard horses as the attackers rode south into the Lacandon jungle.

An hour later, the sun began to rise over the foggy highlands of Chiapas. Taylor had decided not to return to the village after the men rode away with his mother. He remembered seeing four intruders in the house as he ran out the door and realized that only three had left with his mom. That left one intruder plus his father unaccounted for. He knew without a doubt that if his father were okay, he would have gone after the kidnappers like a wild man. If his father was not okay, and the other intruder was still alive, Taylor would probably be captured if he went back to the hut.

Instead, the frustrated boy was high-tailing it to the village of Ocosingo, just like his dad told him to do. He had been moving through the forest in the dark for the last hour, keeping the Big Dipper and the North Star to his right. After leading his father home each day following their adventures in the forest, Taylor was confident in his land navigating abilities. Now that the sun was coming up, it was even easier. He just kept the shadows in front of him as he walked quickly through the young trees.

Coming across no water, Taylor was parched and worn out. Ocosingo was still hours away by foot, so the ten year old stopped to rest at the edge of a clearing. Once his mind was allowed to rest from the tiresome task of navigating, the events of the night before came flooding back and Taylor fell to his knees and began sobbing uncontrollably. His mother was gone, his father was probably dead and he was alone in a thick forest in an alien world. He couldn't stop crying and finally quit wiping at the tears and snot that ran down his face. Giving in to the exhaustion that overwhelmed him, Taylor curled up next to a log and fell asleep.

His eyes stinging from sweat that rolled down his face, Taylor woke to a screeching sound from a nearby tree. Using his shirt to wipe the grime from his eyes, Taylor stood and squinted into the forest to see what had awakened him. The sun was directly overhead now and most branches of the young mahogany trees were illuminated by its rays. A stark white hawk sat on a limb a few feet above the youth's head. Another screech escaped from the beautiful bird and it spread its angelic wings to change positions in the tree where it sat.

"If you're planning on eating me you dumb bird, I'm not dead yet."

Another screech was the hawk's only response.

Taylor looked for the shadows he had been following earlier that morning, but they had all but disappeared with the cresting sun. He walked to the edge of the clearing and found a stump from a tree that had been cut in the past. He knelt and observed the rings closely.

"They all look the same to me, Dad!" Taylor spoke into the sky, "They all looked the same that day you showed me in the woods, too. I was just too embarrassed to tell you."

Taylor watched the sky and half expected his father to answer but only heard another screech from the White Hawk sitting in the tree.

"You're supposed to be my guide, you dumb bird. Why do you just sit there?"

Taylor kicked a dead branch off a fallen tree and stuck it into the ground. He marked the end of the small shadow with a rock and walked over to the tree where the bird sat unfazed by his presence. Taylor sat in the shade of the tree and stared up at the beautiful hawk, now pruning its feathers.

"Okay, companion spirit. Tell me if my mom and dad are going to be okay." Tears welled up in his eyes again.

Louder this time, "Tell me if I am going to be able to save them!"

Finally shouting, "Tell me which way it is to Ocosingo you stupid bird!" Taylor picked up a rock and threw it with all his might at the fretting bird. With another screech, the White Hawk sprung from its branch and glided through the trees and out of sight.

Taylor yelled after it, "I can see why you're not a companion spirit for many people. You're not very good at it!" He stood and listened to the hawk screech some more as it circled above.

Walking back to his shadow stick, Taylor quickly determined which way was north and set out again in a westerly direction toward the village of Ocosingo. Before he had made it through the clearing, the White Hawk dove from the western sky and frightened him when it came within inches of his head. Taylor ducked and yelped in surprise.

"Knock it off!" Taylor picked up a stick to fend off another attack by the aggressive bird, "I'm sorry I threw a rock at you, okay? Now leave me alone!"

A loud rumbling in front of Taylor caught his attention and he froze in place. Finally recognizing the sound as that of a large truck, he quickly forgot about the angry animal guide and hurried across the clearing toward the sound of the truck. Before he reached the road, the hawk took one final swoop at his head, missing by a short distance. Taylor ducked again and took a swipe at the passing bird with his stick, missing completely but sending a strong message that he wasn't to be trifled with. The screeching hawk circled once, then flew away to the north.

Taylor reached the edge of the road and knelt behind a fallen tree to watch the activity in front of him. He was happy to see that he had made it all the way to the road block just outside the village he was trying to reach. A Mexican soldier stood on the step of a truck, loaded with cut timber, and spoke to the driver. He finally laughed and waved the truck through.

As the dust settled, Taylor watched three soldiers, dressed in olive drab, sit and play cards in the shade of a White Pine. One soldier spoke into a radio then quickly jumped up and stowed the deck of cards away in one of his cargo pockets. The other soldiers also jumped up and grabbed their weapons.

"Did they see me?" Taylor wondered.

His concerns were lost when he heard another vehicle approaching from the direction of the village. The soldiers stood at attention when a military truck approached with more militia in the back. Taylor slid down a little further, still not sure of his next course of action. Three Mexican militia jumped from the back of the truck and snatched their M-16's from a rack.

"Pieces of crap!" Taylor said under his breath, remembering his father's description of the U.S. made weapon.

Taylor watched an older man step from the front of the truck and yell at all the soldiers. He recognized the man immediately as the captain who had spoken to his mom and dad at this roadblock, the day his family came to Chiapas. He remembered that his father didn't seem to like the man very much, but he also remembered that the captain spoke English. That was a big plus! Taylor turned his face to the sky as he heard another screech from the circling White Hawk.

"See, you stupid bird? I did it without your help!"

With that said, Taylor Paul Iverson stood and walked onto the road toward Captain Eduardo Marquez of the Mexican army.

Twenty-three

Carol lay on a dirt floor with her hands tightly secured behind her back and a hood draped over her head. She estimated that she had been alone now for at least twelve hours. Her fingers had lost all sensation and now her arms were beginning to tingle.

Dressed in one of Jim's T-shirts and a pair of cut-off sweat pants, Carol began to shake uncontrollably as a chill crawled across her skin like a thousand dancing beetles. Her lips were dry and cracked from a lack of water. Her nose was swollen and still bleeding from the punch she had received during the first minutes of the kidnapping.

Carol prayed that her family was safe. She strained to hear any noises that might reveal the fate of her son and husband. She had heard nothing and there were no answers to her cries for assistance.

"Dear God. I know that you and I don't talk as often as we should. Please keep my little Taylor safe. Please make sure that he is in his father's arms and not worried about me. He is such a sensitive boy, Lord." Carol cried huge tears that mixed with the dirt on her face. She shook her head one more time and tried to remove the suffocating bag that blinded her.

Carol strained to fight off an overwhelming urge to urinate. Unable to hold out any longer, her bladder released and added one more act of humiliation to this tragedy that threatened to consume her.

"Jim!" she called out to the empty space that surrounded her, "Don't worry about me. Just keep our little boy safe. You really are a great father. Your son cherishes you, so you have to be okay. Please be okay, Jim." Carol cried again and finally surrendered to the fatigue that enveloped her.

Through the bag that covered her head, Carol heard the door open to the shelter she was being kept in. She had slept more than ten hours. By now, her tongue had swollen inside her mouth from dehydration and her eyes were no longer producing tears. She felt cold and her breathing was strained from lying on her belly for so long.

A gentle set of hands brought her to a sitting position and untied the rope that bound her wrists. Another set of hands untied her hood and removed it as the first person began to massage her aching arms and fingers.

The light, although faint, blinded Carol when her prison was finally revealed to her. She was in a small building, made of plywood and corrugated metal. Morning light from outside filtered in through gaping holes along the roof. A Mayan woman knelt next to Carol and continued to rub her limbs. Her hands began to ache horribly as blood resumed its intended path through her arms and fingers.

An Indian man dropped to one knee and held a gourd full of water to Carol's lips. Water dribbled from her chin as she greedily tried to gulp down the cool liquid. He pulled the gourd away before she was finished, "Easy now," he cautioned with a whisper, "Just a little at a time."

The man had a kind face. He smiled at Carol as she wobbled, trying to remain in a sitting position.

Carol's world swam with thirst, confusion, and disgrace. Her tongue began to loosen with the welcomed fluid that flowed once again from the gourd, and she found her voice, "Where's my son? Where is my husband? What have you done with them?"

The kind man hushed Carol with a gentle, "Shhhhhhhhh." He used a wet cloth to softly clean her bruised face, "Let's get you feeling better, then you and I will talk."

"When?" Carol asked angrily.

"Soon, *mi mujer pobre*. Soon!"

Sergio Salinas stood and spoke to the woman who was now rubbing Carol's legs, "Feed her some boiled squash and chicken broth. I'll have the food sent over. Do not leave her! Do not let anyone else in here, do you understand, Maria?"

"*Si*," was her only response.

Sergio left the shanty and Maria unfolded a dark green wrap for Carol to put on in place of her soiled sweats.

"*Gracias*," Carol offered as she took the soft fabric and tied it around her hips. She then slipped out of the wet and mud stained cut-offs and tossed them into a corner, "Have you seen my husband or son, Maria?"

After no response from the Mayan woman, Carol asked again in Spanish.

"*Ha visto a mi marido o hijo, Maria?*"

Maria looked sad and only shook her head.

"Where am I?" Carol continued in Spanish.

Still no response, just more head shaking.

"What have they done to my family, Maria? Why did you do this to us?"

Maria stood and walked to the door, avoiding the persistent woman's eyes. She peeked through a crack in the door, then opened it and received two bowls from an unseen visitor. The slightly plump woman brought the bowls to Carol and sat in front of her. Dipping a rolled tortilla into the steamy chicken broth, she offered it to Carol.

Slapping the tortilla away from her mouth, Carol lost her temper and knocked the bowls of food from Maria's hands. Knowing how precious food was in Chiapas, and how generous Maria was for offering it to her, Carol felt a pang of guilt through her chest. Tears welled again and she looked pleadingly into the brown eyes of the sorrowful Mayan woman.

"Maria, please? You have to tell me if my baby is okay. Please, Maria!"

Maria frowned deeply and bowed her cheerless face. She stood and walked out the door of the shanty.

"Maria!" Carol yelled after her, "What have you done to my baby? What have you bastards done to my family?"

Several hours passed before Sergio returned to speak with Carol. Cleaned and somewhat re-hydrated, the American was ready to do battle with her kidnappers. Looking into the Mayan's kind eyes, she quickly decided to appeal to the man's heart rather than try to overpower him physically.

"Why are you doing this to us?" she asked pointedly.

Sergio turned an empty five gallon bucket over and sat in front of the beautiful woman. He looked deeply into her eyes. A painful expression washed over the Zapatista's face as he struggled with the news he was about to share.

"I am very sorry that this has happened to you and your family."

Carol shuttered and asked through gritted teeth, "What have you done with my husband and son?"

"Please *senora*, let me tell you what brought you and I to this camp in the highlands of Chiapas. When I am finished, you will know everything that I know."

Carol nodded, then waited patiently as the rebel commander told his story.

"My younger brother, Cristobal, lost his family in the village of Perdido only ten days ago."

Carol recognized the name of the village. She nodded at Sergio to continue.

"Lucia was very young and very beautiful. She gave my brother two handsome sons. Gabriel who was three years old and Luis who was two years old. They were all killed when the Mexican army stormed the village." Sergio stopped and searched the woman's eyes for compassion. He was going to need it for what he was about to tell her.

Carol offered, "I understand the army was looking for Zapatistas in the village."

The Mayan shook his head, "There were no Zapatistas in the village. The Zapatistas were in Guatemala getting food and supplies. No, the people of Perdido were killed because their village sets in the path of a highway that is going to be built through Central America. The Zapatistas were threatening a new uprising if the village was moved. The native people of Chiapas are tired of being relocated each time the Mexican government finds a new use for the land we live on."

Carol nodded, "What does this have to do with my family?"

"Please, be patient. I must be allowed to tell the whole story," Sergio pleaded, "My brother was devastated at the loss of his family. He wanted to fight the army today! The ancient ones advised against this. Cristobal wanted to kidnap you and your family and ask for money from the university you work for. He never wanted to hurt you. He never intended for this to turn out the way it has."

Carol panicked at the turn this story had taken, "What have you done to my family?" she asked angrily, "What do you mean, your brother didn't intend for things to turn out this way? Where is your brother? You tell him that I want to see him, now!"

Sergio bowed his head, "My brother is dead. Your husband killed him as they fought in your house." The saddened man raised his head and looked into Carol's eyes, "I am sorry to tell you that your husband is dead as well."

Carol's mouth opened wide as she struggled to catch her breath.

"When I went to Tojolaba to claim my brother's body, they had already taken your husband away."

"Then he's not dead!" Carol struggled with the news, "Why would they take him if he was dead? Where is my son, Taylor?"

"I went into your hut to get Cristobal's body. There was a lot of blood on the floor. None of it was my brother's." Sergio paused before continuing, "The villagers said that your husband was covered when they removed him from the house and loaded him into an American helicopter. They said that it was obvious that your husband was dead. This was corroborated by the other men who were with Cristobal that night."

Carol began to cry, "What about my son? Where's my little boy?"

Sergio shook his head sorrowfully, "No one knows what happened to your son. He never returned to the village. I am afraid he is lost in the jungles of Chiapas. He will not last long in the forest. There are animals and other bad things that will claim his life as their own."

Carol was now shaking uncontrollably and crying.

"I have sent out many Zapatistas on horseback to look for your boy. They have searched day and night for him in all directions. They have found nothing. They believe he may have been taken by a jaguar. They are very active this time of year."

Carol could not accept what she was hearing. She looked for any discrepancy in this sad man's story that would allow her to cling to the belief that her baby boy was still alive, "How could you send Zapatistas to look for my son? Why would they do what you ask?"

Sergio was confused by the question, "I am the commander of the Zapatistas in this part of Chiapas. They do what I ask them to."

Carol sat back, staggered by this revelation. When it finally clicked in her mind, she exploded with anger, "You son of a bitch!" she yelled, "How could the Zapatistas do this to my family?"

Carol was off the floor now, towering over the still seated commander, "I have devoted my life to helping the Zapatistas! I believed in you! I believed in your cause!" She bent and slapped Sergio across the face with surprising force, "I brought my family down here to help you. I was going to bring your plight back to the attention of the world, and you butcher my husband and kill my son for it?" She slapped Sergio again, knocking him from the bucket he was sitting on.

Stunned, the Zapatista commander remained on the floor, "This was not done with the Zapatista's blessing," he offered, "I told Cristobal that only bad things would come from his actions. The ancient ones were angry at him for straying from the path, and took his life as a consequence. I am sorry that my brother did this to you, but he did not do it as a Zapatista."

Finally standing, Sergio reached out and touched Carol's arm, "He did it because of the same rage you now feel in your heart. It is a terrible thing to lose your family."

Carol softened as she connected with the man who invaded her home and destroyed her family. She sat again and sobbed uncontrollably, "What about me? What do you plan to do with me?" she asked with a heavy breath.

"I need time to get you out of Chiapas. I cannot turn you over to the army; you would not be safe there. I will smuggle you to Mexico City where you can contact the Americans directly, but I need time."

Carol looked up, "I will not return to America without my son. Either you find him, or let me go so I can. Taylor is a very smart boy. He is a survivor like his father was. I will not go home until I know for sure what happened to him."

Sergio walked to the door and opened it, "We will look harder for your son. You may even come with us if you like; you are no longer a prisoner here. I will treat you like a friend, and together we will discover what happened to your boy."

Carol sighed with relief. As long as she had hope in her heart, Taylor would remain alive.

Twenty-four

January 16, 1991
Hwy 1, twelve miles North of Baghdad, Iraq

*C*lick, click. Click, click. Jim finally recognized the rhythmic metal on metal vibration as a train rolled across the jointed tracks.

"Corporal Carpenter," Jim called over his radio, "As soon as the train's engine passes, double-time it to the DPV's. Two minutes and I'll be hot on your tail."

"Affirmative," was the soldier's only reply.

As the train lumbered between the two opposing forces, headed toward Baghdad, Jim watched as Carpenter ran for cover behind a barren hill, one hundred meters to the west. Two Desert Patrol Vehicles were hidden there under camouflaged netting.

Using the last drops of precious water from his canteen, Jim took a minute to wash the blood from the dead boy's face. A heaviness washed over him as he sat stroking the child's matted hair.

Losing fellow soldiers was always tough. Sergeant Iverson looked around at the bodies of his fallen comrades, his friends. The carnage was brutal, but always expected. This was a treacherous job, so a soldier trained hard and accepted the fact, long before going into battle, that he or his fellow soldiers might not return.

Looking into the face of the dead child once more, Jim swallowed hard and forced his emotion into a deep, dark place in his soul. He laid the boy flat and tried to close the child's eyes. As Jim stood to make his way to the vehicles, the boy's eyelids slid open and fixed their lifeless gaze upon the retreating American.

The DPV's made their way west at a high rate of speed. The extraction point was twenty kilometers into the province of Al Anbar. Hopefully, if the request for evacuation was received before Sergeant Lopez was killed; the MH-53J Pave Low helicopter would be there to pick them up. If not, Sergeant Iverson was prepared to go to ground and wait. The fifty caliber machine gun and forty millimeter grenade launcher mounted to the formidable vehicle would keep an enemy at bay until help arrived.

Coming to a halt five kilometers short of their objective, Sergeant Iverson and Corporal Carpenter dismounted the vehicles to scout ahead on foot. There was always a possibility that their extraction point had been compromised and an enemy lay in wait. The timbered area, next to a dry streambed appeared to be quiet. No enemy, no helicopter. Jim and Nathan waited patiently for thirty minutes, watching closely, before returning to their heavily armed dune buggies. They drove slowly and silently to the rally point and waited for the chopper.

Shortly after midnight, a vibration in the air caught Jim's attention. He could feel the approaching Pave Low before he could hear it. Setting out the infrared strobe lights, the two soldiers watched the perimeter as the Air Force Special Operations team arrived to take them to safety.

The noise from the helicopter was deafening. Jim opened his eyes and had trouble focusing on the soldiers who knelt around him. Someone was poking his arm with a large needle that led to an I.V. bag. Another person was pumping a blood pressure cuff tight around his other arm. Jim was confused and tried to search the soldier's faces for Corporal Carpenter.

"Was I wounded?" he asked around a tongue made of cotton, "Where's Corporal Carpenter?"

Two men in olive green jumpsuits looked at each other, "Is this guy military?" one of them asked, "What the hell was he doing in a knife fight in rural Mexico?"

Sergeant Iverson, still over the Iraqi desert, said, "We have to recover the bodies. We can't just leave the captain and the others there for those bastards to parade in front of a T.V. camera."

Marty Oaks of the United States Drug Enforcement Agency leaned forward and got the copilot's attention, "Get the State Department on the horn and have them meet us at the Angeles Hospital in Villahermosa. This guy might be military. It sounds like his whole team may have gotten wasted back there."

The sounds of the hospital finally brought Jim back to present day. Waking up slowly, his senses picked up the distinct odor of alcohol and iodine. A voice, in Spanish, was summoning someone over an intercom, and the conspicuous sound of a heart monitor wrestled its way into his consciousness.

Finally opening his eyes, Jim tried to remember the events that brought him to this odd place. Looking around the room for Carol and Taylor, he spotted two American men sitting at a small table playing checkers.

Clearing his throat, he asked with a gravely voice, "Where is my wife and son?"

The two men stood and approached the bed with serious looks on their faces.

"James Patrick Iverson?" one asked, pulling a small notebook from his pocket.

"Yes," Jim responded, "Where is my wife, Carol and my son, Taylor?"

"That's what we are here to ask you," said the taller of the two. Turning on a miniature voice recorder, he continued, "This conversation is being recorded, Mr. Iverson. Do you understand me?"

Jim nodded his head.

"You have to say it sir, so I can record it. Do I have your permission to record this conversation, Mr. Iverson?"

"Yes," Jim responded, looking around his bed for something to drink. There was nothing.

"Mr. Iverson, my name is Rick Stephens. I am a consular agent with the American Embassy in Mexico City. This is Marty Oaks with the Drug Enforcement Agency. It was Marty's helicopter that pulled you out of Tojolaba and brought you to this hospital."

Hearing the name of the small village brought Jim to full alert. He tried to sit up in bed but was flattened by a burst of pain through his abdomen.

"Oh my God!" he said, "My wife and son, are they okay? Did you find them?" Not getting any response from the two Americans, he finally yelled, "Where the hell are they? How long have I been in here?"

Rick Stephens cleared his throat, "Mr. Iverson, you need to calm down. Mr. Oaks and I are here to take your statement about what happened in Tojolaba."

Jim, ignoring the overwhelming pain, pulled himself up in bed, "We were attacked in our hut by four men in masks. I think I killed one of them, but not before he stuck a knife in me. Please tell me my wife and son are safe."

The DEA agent finally spoke, "Mr. Iverson, you are very lucky to be alive. We were running drug intervention on the Guatemalan border when we overheard radio traffic about a dead American. Thinking it might be one of our agents, we landed near the village to check it out. You were lying in a hut, just about bled out. The Mexican army told us you were dead, but when my medic checked you, you still had a pulse. We loaded you up, against the objections of a Mexican captain, and brought you here. He was going to let you die on that floor. You're very lucky we came along!"

"Where are my wife and son?" Jim asked angrily, his face turning dark red.

"That's just it, Mr. Iverson. There were no other Americans in the village. Just you!"

Jim started to swing his feet out of the small hospital bed, pulling leads from his chest, sending the monitors into blaring alarms.

Rick Stephens put his hand out and spoke in a forceful tone, "Mr. Iverson, it is my duty to inform you that you are under arrest for the murder of a Mexican citizen. When the state police, along with the Mexican army, complete their investigations, further charges for the murders of your wife and son are highly probable."

Jim collapsed back onto his pillow, partly from exhaustion, mostly from the words spoken by the agent. He watched as a nurse came in to turn off the alarms.

After she left, he asked, "What the hell are you talking about? Are Carol and Taylor dead?" Jim felt his head spin with disbelief and unbearable pain.

Stephens relaxed a little, "We're not sure what the status of your wife and son are. Now, if you will just settle down, I will tell you everything the Mexican army and state police have told us."

Jim ground his teeth together and relented with a brief nod.

"After interviewing the villagers that you and your family were living with, a Captain Eduardo Marquez filed a statement of events that led to the murder of one," Stephens looked at his notebook, "Cristobal Salinas."

Agent Stephens pulled up a chair and sat next to the bed, "According to some members of the village, your wife was having an affair with the Mexican citizen you assaulted and killed."

"Horse shit!" Jim spouted.

The agent continued, uninterrupted, "Villagers who lived close to you reported hearing a loud argument between you and your wife, two nights before. They reported seeing you later that night, dragging heavy items into the jungle. They say that your wife and son were not seen in the village after that night."

"What the hell kind of scam are you pulling here, Agent Stephens?" Jim wanted to strangle the arrogant official, "You know damn well that none of this is true!"

"Please, Mr. Iverson, let me finish. I will take your full statement after I have informed you of the charges against you." Never raising his eyes, Stephens continued, "According to witnesses, your wife's lover entered the village after dark to meet with her and you ambushed him in your home, strangling him to death."

Jim ground his teeth together, "My wife was not having an affair. She would never do that. What you are saying is absolutely ridiculous. We were attacked in the middle of the night by four masked men. While I was fighting with this 'Cristobal Salinas' the others must have taken Carol and Taylor."

Jim locked eyes with the DEA agent, "And while you bastards are sitting here playing checkers, God only knows what is happening to my family!"

The drug agent looked away and remained silent.

Rick Stephens scoffed, "Are you telling us that your wife and child were kidnapped by masked men, Mr. Iverson?"

"That's exactly what I am telling you, Agent Stephens. Now get off your ass and put together a search party to find them!"

Stephens looked at his notepad again, "It's been three days since you were brought to this hospital, Mr. Iverson. To the best of my knowledge, there have been no demands for ransom for the release of your family. Were you aware that Mr. Salinas, the man you murdered, was a member of the rebel movement in southern Mexico known as the EZLN?"

"I know that Mr. Salinas, the man I killed while trying to protect my family, was the bus driver who brought us to Tojolaba four weeks ago."

Agent Stephens peaked his eyebrows and wrote in his notebook, "Are you aware that your wife was very active supporting the Zapatistas during their uprising in the early nineties?"

Jim was growing tired, "I know that she attended some demonstrations in college. I honestly doubt that even you could consider that as giving aid and comfort to the enemy."

Stephens smirked and sat back in his chair, "Your wife, Mr. Iverson, personally collected and sent a quarter million dollars to the Zapatista rebels in March of 1994."

"You're lying!" Jim said vehemently.

"We have the paperwork to prove it! Do you realize that your wife is on the United States Terrorist Watch List?"

Jim laughed, "Along with over thirty thousand other American citizens you jackass. You government types today, remind me of the Keystone Cops."

"Did she tell you that homeland security interviewed her at the airport before you flew out of Denver? Did she inform you that they searched her belongings and made copies of all her travel documents?"

Jim remained silent, remembering Carol's short disappearance at Denver International Airport.

Agent Stephens leaned forward, "It seems that there is an awful lot of information your wife fails to tell you, Mr. Iverson. Don't you think she would accidentally forget to tell you about her torrid love affair with a rugged Zapatista rebel?"

Jim sprung forward and grabbed the smiling American official by the shirt collar, "You son of a bitch!" he yelled, spraying the man's face with spittle, "I would know if my wife was fucking around. She wasn't! Now get off your ass and go find my family or so help me God, I will! And I'll start with that piece of shit Mexican captain who made up this bullshit story."

Agent Oaks circled the bed and pried Jim's hands from Stephens' shirt. Standing and stepping away from the bed, Agent Stephens straightened his collar and tie.

"Unfortunately, you will not be going anywhere, Mr. Iverson. As soon as you are ready to travel, you will be transferred to Cereso prison here in Villahermosa, to await trial for murder. I understand that it can take several years before a court will hear a complicated case like this one. Enjoy your stay in Mexico, Mr. Iverson."

The two Americans left the room and walked down the narrow hall of the hospital.

"I've interviewed my share of bad *hombres* who lied through their teeth to me." Marty Oaks offered, "This man is not lying to you about what happened in that village."

Agent Stephens stopped and stared at the DEA officer, "It doesn't matter. We have other plans for Mr. Iverson, Agent Oaks. Besides, his wife is a traitor to our country. The United States government could care less what happens to her and her family."

Marty Oaks stood and watched the Consular agent walk down the hall to the double doors that led outside.

"Asshole!" he said under his breath before following after.

Twenty-five

The line of eighteen horses snaked its way down a narrow path on the rocky hillside, while dark limbs from Black Brush reached in to pull the riders from their steeds.

Carol rode second in line on a white Appaloosa, marbled with browns and blacks. The young horse was not as sure footed on the steep trail as she would have liked. Sergio, who led the long procession from the highlands to the village of Tojolaba below, seemed unfazed by the treacherous trail. Years of riding through the heat and harsh environment of southern Mexico had filled the man with quiet confidence.

The plan was to interview the villagers of Tojolaba to determine the events of the last five days. Was Jim really dead? Had anyone heard from Taylor?

Carol felt in her soul that her son was alive. She could see his face and hear his calls to her. He was in trouble, but he was not dead. A mother knows these things.

Crossing a tributary of the Lacandon river, the column of riders climbed one last ridge before dropping into the village. Carol felt a dark apprehension seeing the thatch rooftops below. A place that, only days before held so much joy and wonderment, now painted her heart with sorrow. A dull ache reached into Carol's womb and radiated down her thighs as she anticipated what she might learn from the villagers about her missing son.

Entering Tojolaba from the south, Carol led her horse to the center of the village and dropped effortlessly to the ground. Sergio, wearing a ski mask to conceal his identity as a rebel, dismounted as well and stood next to her. Most of the guerrilla riders remained outside the community. It was a hot day, and they did not want to pull the traditional disguise of the Zapatistas over their faces.

Women and children began to gather around the American woman and rebel commander. Some of the women who knew Carol were shocked by her return and immediately started crying and rubbing her back and arms.

"Thank you!" Carol offered, tears welling up in her eyes, "Please, has anyone here seen or heard from my son, Taylor?"

An older woman named Perla was the first to speak, "We have heard nothing *Senora* Iverson. We only know that something very terrible has happened to your family. We are very sorry!"

Carol wrapped her arm around the smaller woman and walked to a set of benches outside the town hall. The small crowd of women chased the children away and followed. Sitting, arm still around Perla's shoulders, Carol asked, "Please tell me everything you know that happened. It's very important that I find out what became of my husband and son."

Perla nodded somberly, "*Si Senora*. We know very little. The Mexican army came to our village in the afternoon, five days ago. We thought they were coming to kill us, so many of us hid. They made *Senor* Banuelos show them where your family lived. The soldiers would not let us get close to your house. The American man who was with them said that everyone was dead inside. Our hearts were broken, *Senora*. We like your family very much."

Carol asked, "There was an American here? Do you know who he was?"

Perla looked at the other women. No one responded, "We do not know who he was. He had dark hair and wore glasses *cuadrados*."

Carol cleared her throat. She had no idea who the American with square glasses might be, "Thank you, Perla. You have been very helpful. Did you see Taylor at all that morning?"

Perla shook her head sadly, "I am sorry *Senora* Iverson, we did not. We saw your husband as they carried him to the helicopter. He was very pale and limp. I think his spirit had left him. After the army left our village, we looked inside your house and saw the dead bus driver and lots of blood. We thought your family had all been killed. Rita's husband knew the bus driver and sent word to his brother."

Carol glanced at the masked Zapatista commander. Something about Perla's story didn't seem right. Carol could not quite get a grip on it as it tickled the back of her mind. She looked to the crowd of women and asked, "Does anyone know if my son has been seen in any other village? Maybe Ocosingo? Have any of the lumber trucks stopped and mentioned anything about him?"

The women shook their heads and mumbled, "No."

Sergio placed his hand on Carol's shoulder, "When your son ran from the hut, which way would he have gone? Did he have a favorite hiding place?"

Carol put her head in her palms and sighed loudly, "I don't know. He and my husband caught bugs in the jungle. They cut wood together up the mountain behind our hut. They went north to watch the lumber crews. They were all over this place and I rarely went with them."

The Zapatista commander mounted his horse, "We will search the mountain to the west. We cannot go too far or we will stumble on the army check point outside Ocosingo. It will take three hours; will you be okay until then?"

Carol nodded and Sergio rode back to his soldiers to begin the search.

As Carol watched, her mind recounted Perla's story. Something was setting off alarms in her head, but she could not figure it out. Shaking it off as stress, the troubled woman stood and thanked the villagers for their kind words. She walked slowly through the community and tied her horse outside the hut that had been her family's home for the past month.

Stepping through the door, Carol was overcome by the stench of fear and sweat and death. The pool of blood had soaked into the floor and left a black stain. Jim's blood.

Carol gasped for air as the realization of what had taken place here, wrapped around her like a suffocating blanket. She sat in a folding chair and tried to cry, but the tears stopped coming and anger flooded her heart.

"Why did you let this happen to us, God?" she yelled at the sky, "What did we ever do to deserve this fate?"

Carol slid to the floor and curled up next to the dark stain, "He was such a good man," she cried, "Do you hear me?" she yelled.

An hour passed as Carol traced the cracks in the stain with her fingers. Light from the door played with dust in the air above her head. She thought about the time they brought their baby boy home from the hospital the day after he was born. Jim was a mess. He was videotaping and talking on the phone to his father at the same time. He tripped over Carol's luggage and fell into a glass coffee table, shattering it. It was all caught on tape. It became tradition to play the scene back every year on Taylor's birthday. They would sit and laugh for what seemed like hours.

Carol caught sight of Taylor's and Jim's journals beside the bed. She slid over and sat with her back against the wall. Opening her son's diary first, Carol read quietly to herself.

"Today, Dad and I found a Red Eyed Tree Frog, east of the village in the jungle. It was so cool. I wanted to capture it and bring it home but Dad wouldn't let me. He said that if every little American boy down here captured a frog and took it home, pretty soon there wouldn't be any left in the jungle. He tries to act serious, but I know he's joking with me because I think I'm the only American boy down here." Carol laughed and wiped her nose with her sleeve.

Turning the page, she continued reading, "Today, Dad showed me how to find my way if I am ever lost in the forest. He taught me lots of cool ways to find out which direction is north so I could walk to Ocosingo to find people. I don't think I will ever get lost, though. My mom and dad never let me out of their sight."

Carol closed the journal and thought for a brief moment. She decided to look for Taylor in the village to the west. She could find a phone there and contact Professor Redding. She would ask him to use his contacts in Chiapas to learn what happened to Jim. She would also ask for his help in finding Taylor. If no one in Ocosingo had seen her son, then she would walk east, through the forest, to Tojolaba. She felt fairly confident that her son would stick to what his father had taught him. At least the Zapatistas were looking in the right direction. When they returned, she would inform them of her plan. Until then, she decided to read Jim's journal.

"Absolutely amazing!" Carol read to herself, "I still can't believe that she chose me out of all the men she must have known in her lifetime. I watched her today as she listened to the stories being told by the elders of the village. Her face lit up as she translated a language that I cannot make heads or tails of. Less than one week and she has already mastered this dialect. I look at Taylor and see his mother. They are both at home among these people. How did I ever get so lucky?"

Carol closed the journal and sat quietly. She was finding it hard to concentrate as her mind kept replaying the story Perla had shared.

"What took the army so long to get here?" she asked herself, "Why didn't *Senor* Banuelos use the first aid kit I had given him, to help Jim?"

Carol stood and walked to the door, "Perla said they didn't know anything was wrong. The shaman couldn't help Jim if he was not aware that Jim was in trouble."

She opened the door to the hut and looked out at the village, "If they didn't know, who told the army?"

Stepping from the earthen home, Carol studied the women as they stood and talked where she had left them, "How did the army find out, if no one here knew anything about what had happened?"

A brief flash of excitement sparked across Carol's heart, "Taylor told them! He was headed for Ocosingo, like his father taught him, and found the check point instead."

Running back to the group of women, she found Perla, "Who told the army that there had been an attack on my family?"

Perla looked at the crowd of women. Each woman was shaking her head, "We do not know who told the army, *Senora*. We did not even know that your family was in trouble until after the army told us."

Carol grabbed Perla by the shoulders. With a smile, she said, "Taylor told them, don't you see? My little boy brought the army here to help us. He's alive, Perla!"

She turned to the village women, "Did any of you see Taylor with the soldiers? Was he in one of their trucks?"

The women shrugged and shook their heads. Perla looked worried, "*Senora*, Captain Marquez would never allow us to look in the army's trucks. He is a very bad man."

Carol stopped dead at the mention of Captain Eduardo Marquez. She immediately remembered Professor Redding's warning.

"I'm afraid a boy, like your son, would not stand much of a chance if he ever fell into the clutches of a man like Captain Marquez."

Carol panicked, "Oh my God!"

Running across the village to her horse, Carol repeatedly called out, "Oh my God! Oh my God!"

The Appaloosa sprinted up the mountainside at a breakneck pace. What the young horse lacked in confidence, it more than made up for in sheer power. Carol held the reigns tightly as she urged the mount to go faster. Her mind was flooding with conflicting images.

"That bastard has had my son for five days now." Carol ducked under a low hanging branch that passed overhead at lightning speed.

"No, no, maybe not," her rational side was telling her, "Taylor is probably on his way to Jim's parent's home in Phoenix, this very moment. He's safe Carol! Please God, let him be safe."

Catching a glimpse of several riders on horseback, Carol slowed her winded Appaloosa and finally stopped in front of Sergio.

"He's got him, Sergio! That son of a bitch stole my son, I know it!" Carol gasped for air behind great sobs.

The Zapatista slid from his horse and took the reigns from Carol's hands and helped her to the ground. Rubbing the horse's lathered neck, he calmly asked, "Who has him, *Senora*? Who do you think took your boy?"

Her mind in a whirlwind, Carol could not recall his name, "That fucking army captain!"

Sergio froze, "Marquez? Do you mean Captain Marquez? Why do you think the captain took your son? What did you learn?"

"No one from the village knew about the attack on my family. I asked them! They learned about it after the army arrived later that afternoon."

Sergio stared at the frantic woman and waited for her to continue.

Carol opened her eyes wide and shook her head, "Don't you see? If the villagers didn't know, then how did the army find out? Taylor went to the checkpoint and tried to get help for us."

The commander reflected on this new information for a moment. A worried expression crossed his face, "We must contact someone who can find out if your son is safe. This could be very good news." Sergio did not smile.

"I know about the rumors, Sergio. Dr. Redding told us that children disappear whenever that bastard is around. We must go now! Let's ask the soldiers at the checkpoint if they saw my son."

Sergio shook his head, "*Senora*, we are rebels. We are outlaws in Chiapas. The soldiers will shoot us on sight before we even ask them about your son. We must ask the professor to inquire for us."

Carol yanked the reigns to her horse from Sergio's grip, "I don't have time!" she yelled, "That monster may have Taylor in his hands right now! I have to help him."

Sergio grabbed Carol's arm and held tightly, "You will do your son no good if you are dead," he said sternly, "If Marquez has your boy, then he will kill you as well as Taylor." He released Carol's arm and placed his hand on her shoulder.

"We must be very careful if you want to see your son alive. The professor can inquire whether he has been turned over to the Americans or not. If he has, then we will get you home quickly."

Carol clenched her fists, "And if he hasn't, I am going to kill that bastard!"

Twenty-six

Cereso Prison
Villahermosa, Tabasco
Mexico

Jim shuffled through the double doors on the second floor of the federal prison in Villahermosa. Hands cuffed in front, legs shackled together, the chains rattled harshly as he tried to keep up with the Mexican guards who were leading him to his cell. Jim was dressed in a stained brown jumpsuit with no shoes on his feet. The guards had offered to sell him a pair of sandals as he was processing into the prison, but the American had no money and nothing of value to trade.

The puncture to Jim's stomach had not yet begun to heal. The ride from the hospital, on the floor of a police van, had jostled the wounded prisoner enough to tear stitches and start the blood flowing again. Jim tried to hold pressure over his wound, but the guards kept jerking his arms away from his stomach as they raced him down the darkened hallway.

This Mexican prison bore no resemblance to any facility Jim had ever visited. Water dripped from the ceiling, causing a slippery film to form on the hall floor. The doors to each cell were made of solid steel, with a small barred opening at the top.

A pungent odor of human waste, mixed with cigarette smoke caught in Jim's throat as he stood before a rusted metal door, waiting for keys to turn the lock and open the gate to his new reality. More keys rattled as restraints were removed from his wrists and ankles.

Jim set aside the pain that raked through his midsection and stood tall to confront whatever lurked behind this grinding steel menace. The cell was dark. A low wattage bulb hung high from the ceiling and offered little illumination to the shadowed figures inside. Whispering rose and fell as the tall, blue eyed American stood ready for whatever awaited him. A half empty can of beans materialized from the shadows and bounced off the door to Jim's left, striking one of the Mexican guards in the shoulder. A shove from behind propelled the stoic prisoner into the cell, and the door slammed shut behind him. Laughter rose from the shadows as Jim's new cell mates praised the one with good aim.

Jim stood quietly and allowed his eyes to adjust to the darkened interior. The cell measured twelve foot by twenty foot with three sets of bunk beds along the far wall. He counted twenty men, sitting and standing around a room obviously intended for no more than six. Spots of red flared in the darkness as inmates puffed their cigarettes while staring at the new arrival.

"*Que estas mirando, estupido?*" someone hollered from one of the beds.

Jim stood perfectly still, panning the crowd of men for any hostile movement toward him.

"He asked what you are staring at, stupid?" came an English translation with a heavy Mexican accent, "You better stop looking so tough *muchacho*, or you are going to have to fight every bad ass in here."

Relenting, Jim backed against the wall and slid to a crouching position. Head tilted toward the floor, the attentive American never removed his gaze from the group of prisoners.

The English speaking Mexican moved closer and sat next to Jim, "Are you an American?" he asked quietly.

"Who wants to know?" Jim asked in a low tone.

"Me, you dumb ass!" The prisoner snickered, "I went to high school in Roma, Texas. Have you ever been there?"

Jim shook his head, never taking his eyes off the crowd.

"It's on the border. My parents worked cotton fields near there and made me go to school. They thought an education would straighten me out."

Jim glanced at the thin Mexican, "I take it, their plan didn't work."

The young man laughed, "No, I got busted bringing drugs into Mexico from Guatemala. I sell them to *coyotes* who sell them in America."

Leaning closer and whispering, "My name is Lucas. Why are you here, *gringo?*"

Jim thought carefully. The last thing he wanted to do was make friends with some scumbag drug dealer. Having someone close, who could translate, might come in handy though.

"My family was kidnapped in Chiapas. I killed one of the bastards, so they threw me in here."

Lucas whistled under his breath, "Must have been a *federale*, huh? Did the man you killed work for the government?"

Jim watched as a prisoner walked past to take a leak in the filthy commode, ten feet away.

"He was a tour bus driver. I don't know who he worked for."

Emerging from the shadows, a middle aged man, wearing pointed boots and a western shirt, stepped in front of Jim and stared down at him.

"Me debes el dinero, americano."

Lucas stood and backed away, leaving Jim alone, "He says that you need to pay him money for staying in his cell."

Jim stood and looked at the well kept prisoner, "I don't have any money."

A group of men gathered behind the man, arms crossed, showing loyalty to their leader.

Lucas translated, then listened to the response, "This is Armando. He runs this cell and he says that you pay in money or you pay in blood."

Staring Armando directly in the eye, Jim asked, "His blood or theirs?"

Lucas looked alarmed, "If I translate that, he will kill you."

"Tell him that I do not have any money and that I do not wish to fight him."

Lucas spoke in Spanish for an extended period. The men gathered around Armando laughed and patted their leader on the back. Armando spoke to one of his cronies then nodded to the translator.

"Armando says that if you cannot pay, then you have to fight one of his men. If you win, you can stay here for free. If you lose, then you have to keep fighting the others until you finally win...or die."

Jim brought his left arm in close to cover the stab wound he had received in Tojolaba. One blow to this area and he would be finished.

"Let's get started then," he said, bringing his right fist up.

A well built Mexican, about Jim's height, stepped out of the crowd and stood to Jim's right side.

"Watch his feet, *gringo*," Lucas advised, "This jackass fights dirty."

The Mexican prisoner stepped in and jabbed at Jim's face. Easily dodging the blow, Jim drove his fist into the man's nose, breaking it with a loud smack. The prisoner stepped back and wiped blood from his swelling beak. He smiled at Jim and came back in a flash of fury.

One handed, it was impossible to fend off the angry attack the Mexican was unleashing. Jim took a solid blow to the chin and another to his right kidney. Stunned, Jim stepped back to catch his breath.

"This guy is not going to go down easy," he told himself.

With the crowd cheering, the Mexican stepped in again and kicked at the American's right knee. Raising his bare foot just in time, Jim deflected the boot and set the prisoner up for a devastating punch to the ribs. He felt the bone and tissue give way under his crushing blow. The Mexican gasped for air and turned away to protect his broken ribs. Spotting the perfect opening, Jim drove his left fist straight into the man's lower sternum, breaking the bone that anchored his diaphragm to his rib cage.

Out of breath, and unable to take another, the Mexican collapsed to the floor and struggled to fill his lungs with oxygen. Jim stood and waited for another attacker. None came.

The crowd was eerily quiet. Armando watched as his prized fighter slipped into unconsciousness. Smiling, the leader of the cell turned and walked back to his bunk. No one bent to offer help to the injured fighter.

"He needs medical attention or he will die very soon," Jim told Lucas.

"Let him die," Lucas said. "He rapes women and kills them."

Jim walked to the steel door and banged loudly with his right fist.

"A man is dying in here!" he yelled, "Help!"

Keys jingled in the lock from outside the door. The steel gate swung open and several guards rushed through the opening, clubs in hand. Jim was pushed against the wall and immediately cracked in the forehead with a wooden baton. Sliding to the floor, he watched in waning consciousness as he was drug from the cell behind his dying opponent.

James Iverson woke to absolute darkness. The absence of any light or sound sent flashes of panic through his system. His forehead throbbed and his stomach ached from torn stitches deep in the muscle. He would have thought he was dead if it wasn't for the pain and extreme thirst that plagued his body.

Jim could sense that he was not alone in this dark place.

"*Eres despierto, amigo?*" came a whisper from the darkness.

Jim sat still and stopped breathing. The voice had echoed in this hollow chamber, making it impossible for Jim to discern which direction it had come from.

"*Estas lastimado?*"

There! It was coming from directly in front, not four feet away. Jim remained silent.

The voice came in broken English now, "I saw you when they opened the door to throw you in here. Are you American?"

"Yes," was all Jim would say.

"My name is Thomas Cortez. I was named after the ancient god Chac. He is the ruler of rain and thunder."

"I don't get it." Jim replied, "Is your name Thomas or Chac?"

The voice in the darkness chuckled, "It is Thomas, *amigo*. Chac is the name of a Mayan God. After the Spanish came in the 1500s, they changed it to Saint Thomas. The elders would never permit my parents to name me Chac, so they called me Thomas instead."

Jim peered into the darkness and could barely distinguish the outline of his new cellmate, "Well, Thomas, I'm afraid my name is pretty boring. It's Jim. James actually. I was named after James Coburn, the movie actor. My dad's favorite movie was, *Hell is for Heroes*."

"Ah, yes! *Snow Dogs*. *Senor* Coburn was a fine actor."

Jim chuckled, "My father is more the war movie type. I doubt he would ever watch, *Snow Dogs*, even with Coburn in it."

Sitting up, trying to take pressure off his aching stomach, Jim asked, "So, Thomas, where are we?"

"We are in *aislamiento, Senor* Jim."

"Is that Spanish for Hell, Thomas?"

The Mayan laughed, "Yes, Jim. In here, *aislamiento* is Spanish for Hell. Why are you in Cereso prison?"

Jim massaged a stiff jaw with his right hand. Thank God, the Mexican who fought him earlier didn't get in more punches. He hit very hard.

"I killed a man, Thomas."

Silence greeted Jim's statement.

"He was trying to kidnap my family in Chiapas, so I killed him."

"I am from Chiapas, *amigo*. Is your family safe?"

Jim chewed at the inside of his cheek, replaying the scene of that night in Tojolaba.

"I don't know, Thomas. I was stabbed and woke up in a hospital. The American Consulate says they have not heard from my wife or son. They are claiming that I may have killed them."

"Did you, Jim?"

Jim got angry and doubled his fists. Before lashing out at the man in the dark, he remembered where he was. Suddenly, the question didn't sound so ridiculous.

"That bastard, Cristobal Salinas, brought at least three other men with him. I think they may have taken Carol and Taylor."

Thomas slid over, face to face with Jim. A yellow flame flickered from his upheld hand, illuminating the tiny cell. The disposable butane lighter provided enough light that the two men could now see each other clearly. Jim could see two large scars, disfiguring the man's face. One above the left eye, replaced his brow with heavy scar tissue. The other, extended from the right side of the man's mouth and did not stop before reaching his ear. The deep wound gave the appearance of a permanent half smile. Thomas looked like a man who rarely smiled.

"I know Cristobal Salinas, *senor*. You say that you killed him?"

Jim tensed, ready for retribution from Thomas.

"He broke into my home in Tojolaba. He attacked me and my family in the middle of the night. You damn right I killed him." Jim leaned forward, coming nose to nose with Thomas, "And I would have killed his friends too, if the little prick hadn't stabbed me."

"Let me see your stab wound, *amigo*."

Jim gritted his teeth, "Back off, Thomas. I'm a very dangerous man right now."

Thomas hesitated, "Before I talk to you any more, I must see the wound you say Cristobal gave you. I must be sure you are telling me the truth."

Jim looked into Thomas's eyes and saw no malice. Unbuttoning the front of his jumpsuit, he revealed a blood soaked bandage to his cell mate.

"Remove the bandage. I must be sure you are not lying to me. I must know that you are not setting me up."

Jim was confused, but saw no harm showing the man his wound. Peeling the saturated bandage to the side, he revealed an open gash, three inches long. The edges were swollen and ragged from the torn stitches.

Jim looked up, "When I was a boy, I used to charge my friends a nickel to look at my wounds."

Thomas smiled and sat back. Letting the flame extinguish on his lighter, the Mayan prisoner sighed loudly.

"I am in prison because I am a Zapatista rebel, *amigo*. I lived in a camp in the highlands of Chiapas with Cristobal's older brother, Sergio. He was our commander." After a long pause, Thomas continued, "Jim, I think I might know where your wife and son are being held."

Twenty-seven

Cereso Prison
Villahermosa, Tabasco
Mexico

The warden's office was large and immaculately decorated. Three men sat around an oversized desk made from highly polished red maple. Several windows illuminated the air conditioned office with brilliant sunlight.

Colonel Benevito Carballes of the Mexican army spoke first to the prison warden, "Have you broken the Zapatista prisoners yet?"

The well dressed warden leaned forward in his chair and crossed his hands over the spotless desk, "We are still working on the rebels. One of them died last week after a session with Doctor Chavez." The warden smiled, "His heart did not appreciate the electrical shocks the doctor was administering."

Colonel Carballes frowned deeply, "You must understand the importance of the information we are trying to obtain. Mexico is on the verge of an economic explosion. Unfortunately, we are also on the brink of another revolution. The Zapatistas must be located and terminated before construction begins on the Central American

Highway this year. The President has assigned this the highest priority for national security."

The warden smiled and looked at the American, sitting quietly in the corner, "I understand the importance of the information you have requested, Colonel. Maybe Mr. Hatch can have his CIA interrogators work on the remaining insurgents for awhile. I understand they are well practiced at retrieving information from unwilling detainees."

The Central Intelligence officer removed his square Nautica eyeglasses and cleaned them with a cloth, "Did you put the American prisoner in a cell with the Zapatista like I requested?"

The warden stopped smiling, "Mr. Iverson has been placed in isolation with Thomas Cortez. It is very cozy in there. I suspect they will be good friends in a short time."

"Very good," replied Mr. Hatch, returning his glasses carefully back to the bridge of his nose, "We have to take full advantage of this fortunate set of circumstances. Jim Iverson has a distinguished record in the Special Forces. He was highly decorated during the first Gulf War. He will find out where that Zapatista camp is and then he will be determined to go there to get his family. We just need to arrange for him to escape unharmed so he can lead us there."

The warden sat back in his chair, "We have sewn tracking devices into the rebel's clothing as you requested, Mr. Hatch. I assume that Colonel Carballes has the proper equipment to keep the escaped prisoners under surveillance?"

The Colonel looked at the CIA officer. Mr. Hatch stood and crossed the room to the door, "The Mexican government has requested American assistance for this operation. We will be tracking the escaped prisoners from the air." Mr. Hatch had requested and received an MH-X stealth helicopter for this operation. "All the Colonel needs to do is have his army ready when we give the word. Give me forty-eight hours to put my assets in place, then make sure the prisoners get loose."

Richard Hatch opened the door to leave, "Gentlemen, your little insurgent problem will be purged by the end of the week."

Twenty-eight

Las Margaritas, Chiapas
Mexico

C arol and Sergio sat with Dr. Marcus Redding inside a small restaurant in the center of this historical town. Las Margaritas was known for its turbulent past and was visited often by Mexican military and paramilitary units. The professor would normally have chosen a smaller and much quieter location to meet, but this community of about nine thousand was on his normal rounds for collecting data from his researchers. Dr. Redding was shocked when Carol filled him in on the details of the past week.

"Carol, I am so sorry to hear about this tragedy. The University never informed me that you had not returned to Colorado. I was making plans to go back to Tojolaba next week to retrieve the Jeep and to hand out whatever supplies your family had not used. Have you contacted the American Consulate in Mexico City?"

"Thank you, Professor Redding. Sergio advised me against contacting the American Consulate right away. He thought we would have a better chance acting locally to find Taylor. He thinks the government might demand my return to the United States while they wade through official channels, and I completely agree."

The professor looked at the Zapatista commander and shook his head slowly, "I cannot believe that Cristobal would go against your wishes and try to kidnap Carol's family. This whole incident may turn popular opinion against the Zapatistas. Look at the Palestinian people. Israel bulldozes their homes, and fires rockets into their cities on a daily basis and the world turns a blind eye because the Palestinians condone this type of behavior. Nothing good ever comes from violence. It only breeds more violence."

Sergio sat quietly; his face burning from the anthropologist's scolding, "A man can be driven to do heinous things when his family has been butchered, Marcus. Cristobal's wife was raped and murdered. His two sons were shot at close range by Mexican soldiers. He was a desperate man and he paid for his mistake with his life."

Dr. Redding bowed his head for several seconds, "You are right, of course. I did not mean to speak ill of your brother, and I am very sorry for what happened to his family. Please accept my apologies, old friend."

Sergio nodded and turned to Carol, "If you would like to contact your family in America, now would be a good time to do that. We will need to leave shortly."

Carol stood and looked toward a payphone across the open air market. Dr. Redding pulled a plastic card from his shirt pocket and handed it to the departing woman.

"This calling card will make things much easier for you. Make all the calls you need, but please be very conservative with the information you relay to your family. It could be very dangerous for us to get them actively involved in this misfortune."

Carol agreed and walked quickly out the open door of the cafe.

"I am very concerned for the welfare of her little boy," Dr. Redding offered after Carol had left, "If that madman, Marquez, really has him, I'm afraid that we may already be too late to save him."

Sergio raised his elbows to the table and leaned in close to the professor, "If her child is dead, and her husband did not survive the attack by my brother, you must see to it that she returns safely to America. I will make certain that justice is delivered to the captain and his army for what they have done."

Dr. Redding's eyes pleaded with the Zapatista commander as he slowly shook his head.

Sergio interrupted before the professor could speak, "I understand that violence can only breed more violence, Marcus. But sometimes, that is all we are left with. Sometimes, only bloodshed can replenish the garden's soil."

"Hello Linda," Linda was Jim's mother, "It's Carol." A loud squeal came through the receiver of the telephone, "Yes, yes, we're still in Mexico. I just had a minute and wanted to touch base with you. Have you heard from Jim or anyone else?"

Carol listened for a moment, a deep frown crossing her face, "No, Linda, everything is okay. I just thought Jim or Taylor would have tried to contact you by now. They're always going to town for one reason or another."

Wiping tears from her eyes, Carol tried to remain calm, "Oh, they've been very busy. You know how they can get when they are discovering new things. I'll make sure they call you real soon, okay? Please give Richard my love. Okay, bye-bye."

Carol hung the phone back onto its cradle. She had envisioned a conversation with her mother-in-law that would wash away this nightmare, "Sure, Taylor and Jim are here and safe. We're all waiting for you to come home."

Carol picked up the phone again, prepared to call someone, anyone for help. A hopeless feeling washed over her and she banged the handset against the wall several times before sinking to the ground in a flood of desperation and tears.

Several minutes passed before Carol returned to the restaurant to sit with Professor Redding and the Zapatista commander.

Dr. Redding had gathered his things and was preparing to leave, "Were you able to discover anything from back home, dear?"

Carol sat and shook her head sadly, "No one has heard from Jim or Taylor, and no one has received any news about them either."

The professor stood and dropped some *pesos* on the table to pay for his coffee, "I will contact the American Consulate in Cancun and Mexico City. I have some friends there who will help me. If your husband was picked up by an American helicopter, as the villagers claimed, then someone at the embassy will know about it."

Carol reached out to stop the professor from leaving, "The women of Tojolaba mentioned a dark haired American with square glasses. Does this sound like someone you know?"

Redding thought for a moment then shook his head, "Not that I can think of right now, but I'll ask about him as well. I also have some contacts locally who can tell me if an American boy has been seen with Captain Marquez or not. Let's meet back here in two days to discuss what I have found out. In the mean time, Carol, you should return to Tojolaba and gather all your belongings. You will be safer in the mountains with Sergio and his guerrillas. Let's all pray for good news."

Dr. Marcus Redding climbed into his jeep and drove away toward San Cristobal while the Zapatista commander and American woman walked toward their horses being kept in a farmer's pen outside the village.

Twenty-nine

Cereso Prison
Villahermosa, Tabasco
Mexico

Jim and Thomas were finally released from isolation. Forty-eight hours in the cramped room had taken its toll on the American. His open wound had finally stopped bleeding, but Jim found himself weak from the loss of blood. Sitting in the dark, worrying about Carol and Taylor, had stretched his nerves to their limits and he was ready to do anything to get out of this hell hole.

The Mexican prison guard, who was leading the pair to a new cell on the first floor, was talking rapidly to the Zapatista prisoner. He kept looking back at the trailing American and smiling. Jim figured that he either had a new best friend, or the lanky guard was making fun of him. He doubted the latter. Word of the deadly fight during Jim's first hours at the facility had spread like wildfire through the dilapidated prison. Apparently, the prisoner Jim tangled with had died shortly after being removed from the cell. A lack of proper medical care and sheer indifference on the part of the prison staff sealed the man's fate.

The door to a cell was pulled open with a loud screech. Jim waited patiently as the guard removed his chains and cuffs. This time, there was no shove from behind to get him into the grimy room. Thomas and Jim entered the cell together and were surprised to find that they were the only two in the cell. Evidence of recent habitation was obvious, but now the cell was empty except for the two new arrivals. The guard spoke to Thomas again, nodded to Jim, then closed the door slowly.

"Why the special treatment?" Jim asked.

"The guard says that he will help us escape for two hundred dollars American."

"Are you serious? Two hundred dollars? Is this a joke?"

Thomas walked to a bunk, wiped some trash and filth to the floor, and sat, "He seemed very serious, *amigo*. He says that he will provide us with guard uniforms and we can walk out with him after his shift is over at midnight tonight."

"Is this some sort of trap, Thomas? Are they setting us up to kill us for trying to escape?" Jim felt excitement growing in his chest. For the past two days, he had been mulling over how long it would be before he found an opportunity to escape. How many more men would he have to kill? If Thomas was telling the truth, Jim stood an even chance of finding his wife and son still in good health.

"I do not think it is a trap, *senor*. This sort of thing happens all the time in Mexican prisons. Justice and freedom are for sale in Mexico, but it does not matter because my family has no money to pay the guard."

Jim was thinking and talking rapidly now, "If I pay the guard, will you take me to the Zapatista camp?"

Thomas sat for several seconds without responding, "I have been in this prison for two years now, *amigo*." The rebel pointed to the scars on his face, "They have tortured me. They have threatened to kill my family. They have promised to let me rot in here unless I show them where the Zapatistas make their camp in the highlands of Chiapas. I have never sold my brothers out. I will take that secret to my grave."

Jim crossed the room in a flash and grabbed Thomas by the collar of his jumpsuit, "You son of a bitch! You told me that my wife and son are probably being held at that camp, so you are going to show me where it is or so help me God, I'll kill you myself."

Thomas was limp in Jim's grasp. He looked into the American's flaming eyes and spoke slowly, "How do I know you are not working for the *federales*? This might be your plan to get me to lead you to the camp so the army can wipe out the Zapatistas once and for all."

Jim released his grip and let Thomas fall back to the bed. Kneeling down and looking his cell mate straight in the eye, Jim stated, "There is no plan, Thomas. My wife and son are missing and I am scared to death that someone is going to hurt them. From one soldier to another, I give you my word that I am not setting you up. Thomas, I need your help."

The tortured guerrilla fighter had to look away for a moment. It had been a long time since he felt camaraderie with another soldier. He wanted to help this man find his family and he desperately wanted out of this prison, "Okay, *amigo*. How do we get the two hundred dollars to pay off this guard?"

Jim explained how he would give the guard a debit card from his wallet that had been confiscated at the prison. All the guard would have to do is retrieve the wallet from wherever it was being stored.

"I'll give him the PIN number so he can go to any teller machine and pull the money out himself. I have over a thousand dollars in there now and he's welcome to all of it if he agrees."

Thomas smiled, "If this works, we could be at the camp by morning. The guard said that he will return in one hour to ask our decision."

Jim sat on the bed next to his new friend and smiled. For the first time in days, he had hope.

The prison warden sat behind his desk and listened carefully to the conversation between the American prisoner and the Zapatista. The cell they were in had been emptied of other prisoners and bugged just moments before they were released from confinement. The warden smiled broadly at the mention of Jim's debit card. He looked at the guard who was standing at attention near the door.

"Take them their uniforms. Tell them they must wear their jumpsuits underneath and give you the uniforms back once they are outside. We cannot risk them changing from the clothes we have provided for them."

The guard smiled and turned to leave.

"Juan," the warden stopped him before he could step out the door, "Take the thousand dollars out of the American's bank account. You can keep the two hundred, but you must bring me the rest. Do you understand?"

Juan nodded his head and closed the door behind him. He was not upset by the warden's demands. Two hundred dollars was almost as much as the prison guard made in a whole month, working twelve hours a day, six days a week. Maybe he could get his 1973 Ford Torino repaired now.

Thirty

Las Margaritas, Chiapas
Mexico

Carol and Sergio stood outside the small café waiting for Professor Redding to arrive. She held copies of the research she had completed during her short time in Tojolaba, hoping the University would find some use for the abbreviated study.

The day before, Carol had returned to the rural village to retrieve her family's belongings as Dr. Redding had suggested. Jim's visa and passport were missing, obviously confiscated by the Mexican army, but everything else was in its place. Carol expected to find the hut ransacked by poor villagers looking for items of use, but they had respected her and Jim's and Taylor's property by leaving it alone. She had asked *Senor* Banuelos while hugging him goodbye, to distribute the food and items she could not take with her.

"This is not a good sign, Sergio," Carol reported, "I doubt the professor has ever been late a day in his life."

"Do not worry, *senora*. The professor is probably living in old time." Sergio was referring to a local problem where some people refused to adhere to daylight savings time, at times making meetings and other scheduled events a real mess. Those who showed up an hour late were often referred to as "living in old time."

Carol paced back and forth in front of the aromatic coffee shop. Her stomach moaned loudly in protest. Carol had eaten little since the attack a week ago. She felt pangs of guilt every time she even considered meeting some need for herself. Her husband was probably dead and who knew what nightmare her little boy was facing.

"Taylor is okay, Carol," she told herself quietly, "The professor is going to arrive with a big smile on his face and tell me that Taylor is safe and sound at the American Embassy in Mexico City, and Jim is recovering in a hospital nearby."

Carol watched as a group of children played noisily in the middle of the street. They were enjoying a game of soccer, using an empty tin can as their ball. In her mind, she could feel Taylor standing next to her smiling as a goal was made, too shy to join in himself. She could hear Jim make some smartass remark like, "In my day, we only had large rocks to use as soccer balls and we never had shoes like some of these lucky kids!"

Carol laughed out loud then turned toward the sound of an approaching vehicle. It was Dr. Redding's Jeep, but he was not driving. Instead, a young man named Keith, the professor's assistant, was behind the wheel. He was alone.

Carol sighed, somewhat relieved and stepped to the Jeep as the driver skidded to a halt. A harried look consumed the young man's face.

"Dr. Iverson?" he asked as he set the brake.

"Carol Iverson, yes!" she corrected.

"Oh my God, Mrs. Iverson. I am so glad I found you." Keith took a deep breath to calm his obvious anxiety, "Dr. Redding asked me to bring this note to you. He told me it was most important that I find you and tell you to stay hidden. He wanted me to—"

Carol interrupted, "Keith, settle down. Now, what note? Where's Professor Redding?"

The assistant frantically checked his pockets then searched the floor of the Jeep, "Damn it!" he swore, "Dr. Redding said that it was very important that I get that note to you."

Slapping his forehead, Keith opened the glove box and extracted a folded piece of paper, handing it over to Carol, "I'm sorry, ma'am. Things have been very hectic this morning."

"Keith?" Carol asked calmly, "What is going on? What happened?"

The young man looked at Carol with wide eyes, "Professor Redding has been deported to Guatemala, ma'am. The state police came and got him this morning. It was horrible! They beat him to a pulp, then drug him out the door. He called from Santa Cruz this afternoon and told us that he was okay. That's when he instructed me to find you here and deliver this message to you." Keith pointed to the note in Carol's hand, "He told me to tell you that you should not go to the officials here. He said that you are to stay hidden."

Carol's face had gone white. She gasped for air once her lungs demanded that she start breathing again. The vision she had hoped for of a smiling professor with good news to report, vanished.

Carol unfolded the piece of paper and read the anthropologist's scribbled notes.

- *No word from American Consulate on any injured or killed American in Chiapas.*
- *No confirmation of any American helicopter in region.*
- *Mr. Iverson was not treated in any medical facility in Chiapas. Tabasco??? Will check tomorrow.*
- *University has heard nothing regarding Iverson's. No claims filed through Mr. Iverson's medical insurance.*

Carol dropped her research papers to the ground and held a trembling hand to her mouth. She sobbed loudly as she read the next line.

- *Captain Eduardo Marquez seen with light haired American boy in San Cristobal the day after the kidnapping in Tojolaba. Boy has not been seen since.*

Thirty-one
Cereso Prison
Villahermosa, Tabasco
Mexico

At ten minutes 'til midnight, Jim and Thomas stood in the deep shadows, on opposite sides of the prison cell as keys rattled to unlock the steel door. The guard uniform Jim was wearing stretched tightly across his broad frame and was made even more uncomfortable by the baggy brown jumpsuit underneath. The guard had insisted the uniforms be returned to him after they successfully exited the prison grounds. Jim would have been happy to surrender the stained jumpsuit as well, but the thought of streaking through the Mexican forest at midnight had no appeal for him.

Juan Berrazas stepped through the half open door and was puzzled for a brief moment by the lack of movement from within the cell. Jim waited as Thomas stepped from the shadows and spoke rapidly in Spanish to the guard. Thomas translated the guard's response.

"He says that we must hurry. The guards at the gate will become suspicious if we don't walk out with the rest of the staff at midnight."

Juan smiled as Jim stepped from the shadows as well. He threw a thick wallet in the American's direction and spoke to Thomas.

"He says that you can give him the card and the PIN number once we are outside."

Jim opened the wallet to ensure it was really his, then stuffed the leather mass into the front pocket of his khaki pants. Nodding to the guard, he walked through the open door.

The line of about fifteen staff members slowly snaked its way out the main gate of Cereso prison. Jim walked in front of Juan as Thomas followed, looking down and away to conceal the scars on his face. The two guards watching the gate seemed uninterested in those filing out and watched a recorded soccer match on a thirteen inch TV inside their post. Jim could not believe how easy this was going to be. Three more people and he would be through the gate. If he made it outside, he swore that they would never return him to this prison alive. The guards never raised their eyes as the two men walked to freedom.

Once outside the gate, Juan motioned for the escaped prisoners to follow him into an alley. Resembling a teenager who just accomplished his first illegal purchase of alcohol, the young guard laughed and dramatically hurried the two men to strip out of the borrowed uniforms.

Pulling the wallet out as he dropped the khaki pants to the ground, Jim retrieved his debit card and handed it to the smiling guard. Pulling a pen from the man's shirt pocket, Jim wrote a four digit number in the palm of Juan's hand.

"Tell him that there is a little over one thousand dollars in there and he may have it all, but he can pull no more than five hundred a day out of the machine. Bank's rules."

Thomas translated for Jim as he pulled the borrowed shoes from his feet.

"No," Jim said, "For a thousand dollars, we keep the shoes."

Thomas hesitated, then spoke to the waiting guard. Juan shrugged, picked up the pile of clothes and walked back out onto the street.

Walking south out of Villahermosa, Jim and Thomas moved quickly through rural farmland toward the village of Pueblo Nuevo. Thomas had assured Jim that they could steal a vehicle from one of the large ranches in the area. From there, it was about four hours of travel on the back roads of Chiapas to a point where they would abandon the vehicle and walk another ten kilometers to the Zapatista camp.

"I hope the Zapatistas have not moved their camp, *amigo*," Thomas whispered while puffing for air. The rainy season had begun in southern Mexico and the ground was slick from mud and puddled water.

"If they have, Thomas, do you have contacts to help us find the new location?"

Blisters were beginning to form on Jim's feet from the rough leather of his new shoes. He considered leaving them in the mud several times, but good sense forced him to reconsider each time.

"*Sí.* I have many contacts. I will get you to the camp," Thomas stopped and turned to his new partner, "but you must promise not to hurt anyone when we get there."

Jim stopped before colliding with the Zapatista. Backing up a step he replied softly, "If someone there has harmed my family, then I would have to break that promise." Placing his hand firmly on Thomas's shoulder, Jim pleaded, "Don't ask me to make a pledge I cannot possibly keep."

Thomas stared into Jim's eyes for several seconds. A battle raged in his mind as he weighed the loyalties he felt toward the Zapatista movement, and his new friend's search for his missing wife and son.

Thomas relented and nodded, "I cannot believe the Zapatistas would ever harm your family." He began walking again, toward the light of a distant farmhouse, "The Mexican government is our enemy, not innocent women and children."

Jim stood still and watched as Thomas walked ahead. Alone with his thoughts, despair enveloped his spirit as he contemplated the road ahead. Suddenly, a flutter of hope jolted through his body. Jim looked toward the silent sky with an overwhelming sensation that help was arriving. A faint vibration tickled his heart as he searched the sky for the coming cavalry. The sky remained silent.

Three thousand feet over Jim's head and a mile to the north, the CIA's MH-X stealth helicopter hovered and watched the escaped prisoners on an infrared radar scope. The two prisoners' bodies glowed brightly on the sensitive equipment.

"They're moving again, sir," the copilot reported to his passenger in the rear.

In the left seat, the pilot searched the air and ground, using night vision head gear to ensure no other air traffic was approaching, before moving again. From Mr. Hatch's vantage point, the pilot looked professional and scary as hell. These crews were selected from the best the military had to offer. Expertly trained, highly intuitive, and proud beyond measure, the CIA officer had no doubt that these men would accomplish their assigned mission. His confidence in their abilities freed the intelligence officer from micro-management and allowed him to concentrate on other pressing matters.

On a secure channel on his headset, Richard Hatch spoke to Colonel Carballes, who was waiting with a sizable force outside San Cristobal, "They're moving on a ranch house outside Villahermosa, Colonel. They will probably steal a vehicle and head your direction. Have you pulled the roadblocks like I requested?"

After listening for a moment, he continued, "Good, good. I will give you a heads up if they leave Highway 195, out."

Jim watched the dark house as Thomas worked under the dashboard of an old Ford F-100 pickup. The starter caught and the pickup roared to life. Several dogs sprang from a small shed and ran for the truck, snarling and baring their teeth. Thomas sat up behind the wheel and revved the engine as Jim climbed in beside him. The two men sped down the rutted dirt drive and turned south on

Highway 195 toward Chiapas, leaving the barking dogs in a spray of mist from the wet pavement.

"What about road blocks?" Jim asked after assuring no one was following.

"The army has a checkpoint at the village of Tapilula. We will abandon the pickup there and go around on foot, then steal another when we are safe."

"It sounds like you have this all planned out, Thomas."

"I have had two very long years to make this plan, *senor.* It is a good plan."

An hour later, the Zapatista coasted the old truck to a stop at the side of the road, "The road block should be just a little further," he said. "We will walk from here."

Jim climbed from the worn seat of the stolen truck and quietly closed the door. The night was hushed and dimly lit by a cloud covered moon.

The two men made their way into the trees that lined the road and walked south toward the village of Tapilula.

Thomas stopped and peered toward the road. Jim knelt beside the Mayan man and listened intently for any sound. The American looked toward the sky again, not quite sure why his attention had been drawn that way.

As the two men sat in absolute silence, Jim flashed, for a brief moment, back to the darkened desert of Iraq. He and Corporal Carpenter sat waiting for a helicopter to take them away from a failed mission.

Jim searched the sky again, but heard no sounds. Shaking his head, he leaned close to Thomas's ear, "What do you see, partner?"

Thomas waited a brief moment before answering, "The road block has been abandoned, Jim. There are no soldiers there."

"Are you sure?" Jim asked while peering at the road, "Are they just sleeping or something?"

"I do not think so, *amigo.* I think they are all gone."

The two men edged closer to the checkpoint on the road. Sandbags were still in place, but the arms of the crossing barriers were locked in upright positions. There was no evidence that soldiers still manned this post.

"Get the truck and drive up here slowly," Jim directed, "I'm going to have a closer look. I'll meet you before you reach the checkpoint and let you know if everything is okay."

Thomas didn't have time to respond before Jim slipped away into the deep shadows of the forest.

As the Zapatista edged the pickup slowly toward the checkpoint, Jim stepped from the side of the road and jumped into the seat beside Thomas.

"All clear. Let's keep moving."

The escaped prisoners drove down the deserted highway, unsure what to make of their continuing good fortune.

Three hours later, as the sun began to rise above the eastern horizon, Jim and Thomas made their way into the highland forest, outside the village of Las Margaritas, leaving the stolen truck for some lucky farmer to find.

Thirty-two

Zapatista Camp
Chiapas Highlands

Before sunrise, Sergio Salinas sat at his roughly constructed desk under the glow of a kerosene lantern. The night before, he and Carol had spoken at length about what steps to take to find her missing son. She was angry and wanted to confront the army captain face to face and demand that he return her boy. Sergio had warned Carol of the danger of this approach. If her son were still alive, which the Zapatista commander seriously doubted, then challenging the captain could lead to the young boy's immediate death.

Sergio shuddered as he contemplated the rumors he had heard of Captain Marquez and his affection toward little boys. In the four years since Marquez had taken command of the Chiapas garrison, over twenty local boys had gone missing while in close proximity to the army commander. Protests had been filed with local governments to no avail. Each year, the rumors grew more fantastic, with the latest being that Captain Eduardo Marquez was a servant of the Devil and he consumed the flesh of young boys to extend his immortality on this earth.

Sergio shook his head. He suspected a much more common and even more disgusting fate for the missing children. If given the chance, Sergio would take pleasure in ending the captain's life.

The Mayan rebel's thoughts quickly returned to the American woman who was now under his care. What a beautiful and powerful woman. If his thoughts were allowed to wander, Sergio could see himself offering a point of strength for this *mujer hermosa* who came to Chiapas with everything, just to have it all torn from her grasp and scattered like waste to the wind. So many people had suffered the same fate in this wonderful but dangerous nation. In Mexico, life and family and culture had become trivial to the corporate greed that now controlled his motherland. Sergio could see the same thing happening in America and the rest of the world. The Mayan bowed his head and looked at the palms of his calloused hands. God will never allow this to continue. He has to be looking down on the tragedy that permeates this earth. His heart has to ache terribly every time his children are brutalized by the predators that seem to control everything.

As his eyes blurred with moisture, the Zapatista commander stood and searched for his web belt with the old Colt .45 set in a canvas holster. It was time to fight. He would ask the American woman to return to the United States to rebuild her life. If she refused, then he would gladly accept her as a fellow soldier and someday ask her to be his wife. It was very odd to have a heart so full of sorrow, and yet tingling with excitement at what could be.

A commotion outside Sergio's door caught his attention. Someone was talking loudly and joyfully calling for the commander to come outside.

Carol sat in the darkness and damp chill of her shanty. It had rained most of the night which forced her heart into unknown depths of despair. She had lain awake all night, wondering if Taylor was cold and miserable. In his ten years of life, he had never been away from her or Jim for very long. What is he thinking?

Enduring the ache that seemed to radiate through her womb, Carol held her knees close to her stomach and rocked back and forth on the cold and soggy floor. Does he believe that his father and I have abandoned him? Does he know that I will find him no matter where he is, no matter what he has been through? Does he feel my heartache, my sense of loss, my determination to save him?

Carol sobbed as she remembered holding Taylor's tiny hands while he learned to walk across the hardwood floor to his smiling father. Her chest ached as she thought of cuddling her small child to her breast as he suckled milk from her. Anger flared as she thought of the bastard who took her son. Carol didn't know how, but she vowed to God and herself that today, she would find out what happened to her little boy, and she swore an oath that she would murder the man who was responsible.

Thirty-three

As the sun peeked above the eastern horizon, wisps of fog clung to the floor of the lush mountainous countryside. Humidity hung in the air from a night of rain and life was brought anew to the highland forests of Chiapas.

Jim and Thomas huddled on a rocky knoll, overlooking the quiet Zapatista camp below. Wet from rain and exhausted from a long night of travel, the escaped prisoners watched for signs of movement in the rebel camp. There was little activity below and Jim was growing impatient as he searched for signs of his wife and son.

"I'm going down," Jim said suddenly. "If Carol and Taylor are down there, I want to find them and get the hell out of here."

Thomas reached a hand out to his new friend, "Wait, Jim. If you walk into that camp and start searching through huts, someone will shoot you."

"I'm tired of waiting, Thomas. I'm tired of all this bullshit. My wife and son are probably being held captive down there, so I am going after them." After a brief pause, Jim added, "And the men who took them."

Thomas stood and faced the towering American, "Jim, *amigo*, let me go first. I know the people in this camp. They are my brothers."

161

Jim listened to the Zapatista's plan and calmed as his proposal took shape.

"I will find out if your wife and son are there. If they are, I will bring them to you or come back and tell you where they are. This will make a rescue more successful, *si?*"

Jim relented and nodded to Thomas, "I'll wait here. Please don't be long."

With that, Jim sat back among the rocks and watched his rebel friend navigate down the steep slope to the camp below.

As Thomas made his way into camp, Jim was impressed by the man's ability to move fluidly through the harsh terrain. No stones were heard tumbling behind the descending insurgent. No twigs were heard snapping under foot. The former Special Forces soldier was reminded of Contra rebels he had helped train in Central America, who moved as swiftly and quietly as Thomas. A new respect for this Mayan soldier washed over Jim while he observed the man's careful search through the encampment.

Jim watched as Thomas silently made his way around one of the largest shanties in the camp. Reaching for the door to the hut, Thomas appeared to freeze before turning toward a shouting man. Jim sprang to his feet, ready to aid his friend if needed.

As the rebel guard approached Thomas, Jim could see a broad smile of recognition cross his face. He yelled again and embraced the escaped prisoner in a bear-like hug. Jim could see his friend smiling as he returned the embrace and patted the man on the back. A loud and lively conversation seemed to be taking place between the two men as the door to the shanty they were standing next to opened and a man, wearing a sidearm, stepped from the hut.

Jim watched as the new arrival and Thomas exchanged handshakes and smiles. They spoke for a moment, then walked toward the center of camp. Jim thought that the rebel Thomas was talking to must be in command of the camp. He gave orders to other rebels as they approached the pair and sent them back to their posts.

After several minutes of conversation, the rebel leader stepped back from Thomas with a look of surprise on his face. He reached out to the escaped prisoner, then turned and looked to where Jim was now hiding. The American leaned back into the shadows, not sure if the rebel leader had spotted him or not.

The man turned and surveyed the mountainside for a long time as Thomas spoke excitedly to him. Finally, bowing his head, he turned back to Thomas and spoke. Pointing toward a small hut near the edge of camp, the commander began walking in that direction. Jim could have sworn that Thomas turned toward him and smiled.

Excitement raced through his heart as he watched the two men approach the door to a shanty and knock, "Yes! " A shout escaped Jim's lips as Carol opened the door to the hut and stepped out.

A thousand thoughts crossed Jim's mind as he raced down the slippery mountainside. Carol looked tired and beaten. Where was Taylor? There were no guards outside the hut, so his wife and son were obviously not being held against their will.

A vibration through Jim's chest stopped him dead in his tracks. He looked toward the sky as an olive Huey helicopter blasted over a ridge to the north and flew directly over the camp. Banking hard over the shanties, a machine gunner opened fire on the rebels standing with Carol. Horses, tied to saplings, broke free and scattered when automatic weapons opened up from the tree lines surrounding the camp. Explosions erupted from grenade launchers and Jim watched Mexican soldiers enter the camp from the east. Smoke began to rise while screams of death and murder reached Jim's ears.

Thirty-four

T he knock on the shanty door came as Carol was gathering her things to leave the Zapatista camp for good. She had decided to actively search for Taylor in San Cristobal, the last location he was spotted in the company of Captain Eduardo Marquez. If she made no headway by the end of the day, then she would contact her uncle Harry back in Colorado. It was a family rumor that Uncle Harry had many connections in the U.S. government and was possibly an agent with the Central Intelligence Agency. Even if that rumor proved to be false, Carol knew that she could count on her mother's brother to fly to Chiapas and help her in a search for her missing son. It felt good to finally have a solid plan under her belt.

Carol opened the door and stepped out into the muggy morning air. Sergio stood with another man who smiled big when he saw her. The scars on his face could not hide the man's gentle nature.

"*Buenos dias, Senor Salinas. Quien es tu amigo?*" Carol asked.

Before Sergio could answer, a loud roar from an army helicopter interrupted his response. An army helicopter banked hard as it passed overhead bringing a mounted machinegun to bear on the camp's inhabitants. Before anyone could dive for cover, death reached out from the door of the chopper and shredded the brown jumpsuit of Sergio's companion. As the scarred man fell to the earth, the

Zapatista commander ran for a group of rebels standing near the center of the camp.

"*Abajo, abajo, abajo!*" he yelled.

Carol dove for cover inside the metal sided hut. Hearing gunfire and explosions from outside, she quickly grabbed a box of important documents and ran from the shanty toward the closest hillside. She could feel the unmistakable zip of bullets as they passed close to her head. Ducking lower, she ran into the forest and began to climb the slippery mountainside. Sounds of a ferocious battle loomed behind her as Carol found a hiding place among a thick patch of wild gooseberry bushes. Dropping to the ground and scarcely daring to breathe, Carol visibly shook as she thought of the smiling man who died while she watched helplessly.

A noise from behind frightened Carol to utter stillness. She heard the faint sound of a hard soled shoe scraping across rock. Carol found a large stick within her grasp and silently waited for the noise to come closer. This close to going after her son, she would not be stopped by whoever approached.

Jim watched in horror as the door gunner on the helicopter unleashed his fury on Carol, Thomas and the Zapatista commander. There was no doubt in Jim's mind that Thomas had been instantly killed under the direct fire of the heavy machinegun. The commander sprang into action, directing his men into battle while Carol ducked back into the shanty. More than likely, she was getting Taylor to make a run for it.

Still high on the mountainside, Jim was surprised when Carol left the shanty without their son. She carried only a small box and ran full speed for the mountain he was now descending. Slipping in the mud in his haste, Jim fell hard to the earth and lost sight of his fleeing wife. Standing again, she was gone. *Must have gone to ground,* he thought.

Not wanting to alert the Mexican soldiers below, Jim refrained from calling out. He moved quietly toward a thicket of bushes and searched among their branches for his hiding wife. A wave of relief washed over Jim as Carol rose from the brush. Before getting a word out, his beautiful wife turned, with rage in her eyes, and struck him in the face, full force with a large stick. Daylight turned to darkness and Jim folded to the soggy ground.

Sounds of gunfire trespassed into Jim's thoughts as he slowly regained consciousness. Fireworks exploded in his head when someone shook him and rubbed his face.

"Jim, honey! Oh my God, I am so sorry. I thought you were dead." Carol frantically wiped blood from Jim's eyes and kissed his face repeatedly.

"They told me you were dead. Oh thank you, God! Thank you, thank you, thank you!"

Jim opened his eyes and peered through a film of red. Carol's expression quickly changed from horror to excitement as she pressed a torn shred of cloth to the side of his head.

"I am so sorry, Jim. I thought you were dead," Carol repeated.

"I should be, after a wallop like that. It's good to see you too, sweetheart" Jim smiled and held his frantic wife close.

"I didn't know it was you. You were the last person I expected to see. Oh my God, I am so thankful you are still alive."

Jim stood and reached out to his wife for support. A little wobbly still on his feet, he held Carol's arm and started up the mountain, "We have to put some distance between us and this camp. Where's Taylor?"

Jim turned and looked at his wife as she hesitated. 'Where's Taylor, Carol?" he demanded.

Tears streamed down Carol's face, "Let's get away from here. I'll tell you everything once we are safe."

Thirty-five

C aptain Eduardo Marquez stood next to his brand new Humvee at the top of a rolling hill, north of the Zapatista camp. He watched through binoculars as the attack against the rebel encampment progressed. Chuckling to himself each time he witnessed another insurgent's demise, the captain could not help but think of a promotion to colonel that was surely in his future.

The radio crackled to life in his ear as Colonel Carballes directed the battle from a Huey helicopter circling above. He was now reporting that a group of Zapatistas were escaping to the south toward Guatemala. Captain Marquez chuckled again. He had two teams of elite Mexican Special Forces waiting at the border to intercept and kill the fleeing rebels. It was understood that no prisoners were to be taken.

Lowering the field glasses, the army officer breathed deeply. Once his promotion came through, he would miss the highlands of Chiapas. In all of Mexico, this was his favorite place to be. The temperatures and humidity were mild, compared to the border region with America. The people were mostly passive and easy to control, and he enjoyed a certain sense of freedom down here, away from the prying eyes of the *politicos* in Mexico City. No one seemed to care what happened in Chiapas. As long as development and foreign investment continued unimpeded, the army pretty much allowed Captain Marquez to do anything he wanted.

He was paid handsomely by drug lords for looking the other way when shipments made their way through his area of operations. Politicians slipped money his way to ensure that elections were easily won. Lost ballot boxes were common and a village under siege on Election Day found it very difficult to vote for a politician's opponent.

The captain smiled to himself. A tidy little nest egg was also building from a lucrative business he stumbled across his first year in Chiapas. Trafficking children to various parties paid dearly whenever the opportunity arose. What happened to the young boys he sold was no concern of the captain's. Mayan children were like rats to him. They were dirty and poor and would probably die from one filthy disease or another before they reached adulthood.

Noting edginess and impatience in the eyes of the small group of soldiers left to guard the commander, Captain Marquez called to his new lieutenant.

"Lieutenant Rojas, take these men down into the camp and set fire to every building." The soldiers seemed to come alive with excitement, "Make sure that no wounded rebels crawl off into the forest. Do you understand?"

The young officer snapped to attention, "*Si, sir!*" he responded obediently.

The group of men moved down the hillside at a fast pace, leaving the captain to watch the carnage below as he contemplated his brightening future.

Sergio was out of ammunition for his sidearm. The thirty two rounds he had fired from his four magazines had not connected with one target. It was very difficult to hit a distant object with a .45. A lack of sufficient ammunition made practicing impossible, so Sergio was not a very good shot.

Separated from the remaining guerrillas, the Zapatista commander skirted the northern edge of his camp, looking for a path to escape. A Mexican officer and a small group of soldiers had nearly stumbled across his hiding place as they rapidly moved toward the buildings down below. Sergio decided to move north and put a ridgeline between him and the attacking force.

Moving quietly toward the top of the hill, the Mayan rebel was stopped in his tracks by the sounds of a crackling radio. Peering through the trees, he could see three army vehicles parked at the crest of the hill. A lone soldier stood with binoculars raised to his eyes. Sergio smiled. It would be very easy to sneak up on a distracted soldier and kill him.

Circling the army vehicles, the rebel commander was flabbergasted to find that the lone soldier was none other than the infamous Captain Marquez. Unguarded. Unarmed, except for a holstered sidearm. The ancient ones were smiling on Sergio Salinas right now. They had offered him this precious gift in exchange for his rebel command. He would take it, and relish this moment for the rest of his life.

Walking quietly around the first vehicle, Sergio approached the mumbling officer as he continued to watch the declining battle below. With the force of a Brahma bull, the rebel commander plowed into Marquez, driving him to the ground. Sitting atop the stunned and breathless captain, Sergio pinned his arms to the ground using his knees and pulled the Mexican officer's sidearm from its holster.

Smiling big, Sergio climbed from the captain's heaving chest and pointed the gun at his face.

"It looks like you will be vacationing in Hell today, *el capitan*."

Captain Marquez stood and backed against the Humvee, "Please do not shoot me, *senor*," he pleaded, "I have lots of money. I will pay you whatever you want if you let me live."

Sergio spit on the trembling man, "I do not want your filthy money, captain, I want your life."

A stain appeared in the crotch of Marquez's battle dress uniform as his bladder released.

Sergio pulled the hammer back on the captain's sidearm and pulled the trigger. The shot echoed loudly through the highland forest.

Thirty-six

J im and Carol had been walking southwest for over an hour. Finding a secluded clearing near a seasonal streambed, Jim pulled his wife close and held her for several minutes. Just breathing one another's scent calmed the pair and allowed them to finally relax.

"I was so worried about you and Taylor, honey. I thought for sure that I would never see you again." Jim held Carol at arms length, "Where's Taylor? Everything is okay, right? You sent him to Phoenix to stay with Mom and Dad, right?"

Carol could no longer hold her emotions. Grabbing her husband by the wrists, she shook his arms, "Taylor is gone, Jim! He's missing."

Jim pried loose from his wife's strong grip, "What the fuck do you mean, he's missing?" Jim yelled, "How is he missing? What the hell is going on, Carol?"

Carol began crying again, "He's been gone since the kidnapping. I told him to run and hide, and I haven't seen him since." Sobbing uncontrollably, she stepped close to her husband and let him wrap his arms around her.

Jim's mind raced as he pondered the possibilities, "He went to Ocosingo. I told him that if he became lost, to head west for

Ocosingo. That's what he would have done. Have you checked there or back in Tojolaba?"

"I checked, Jim," Carol said. "The Zapatistas searched the forest between the two villages and he wasn't there. I think he was kidnapped by that army captain who stopped us on the road when we came to Chiapas."

"What the hell would he want with our—?" Jim stopped short as he remembered the warning from Professor Redding, "Okay, honey. Back up a little bit and tell me everything you know. Don't leave out a single detail."

Carol spent several minutes explaining how she and the Zapatistas had searched for Taylor. She shared the news that led her to believe Jim had died in the attack as well as the conversation with his mother on the phone. Carol detailed how step by step, she discovered that their son had somehow contacted the army for help. She shared Dr. Redding's fate and pulled the professor's note from her box of papers and let Jim read it in silence.

"Jesus Christ, that son of a bitch took our son," Jim said under his breath.

Looking back in the direction they had come from, Jim tried to sort out these new revelations.

"The captain is probably back at that camp right now," he said. "I'm going to go kill him!"

Carol grabbed his arm and held fast, "Jim, you're angry right now. I want nothing more than to kill that piece of trash, but that is not going to give our son back to us. Let's go to where he lives and search his home, or go to his camp and ask questions." Carol paused and gasped for breath, "Let's find our son, Jim! He's alive, I know it! I can feel him calling for us, Jim. If you storm off and get yourself killed, then our whole family is finished. We're all dead if you do that." Carol was surprised at the words coming from her mouth. Just two hours ago, she was contemplating the exact action her husband was considering now.

Jim grabbed Carol by the shoulders and pushed her to the ground in a thicket of underbrush. Diving on top of her, he brought his face next to hers and put his finger to her lips, "Shhhhhhhh!" he cautioned.

A sound finally came to Carol's ears as she struggled with the confusion of her husband's forceful actions. It was a horse approaching slowly from the direction of the camp. Peering over Jim's shoulder, Carol could make out a rider on the bare back of a smoky gelding. As the horse stepped closer, she looked at her husband with wide eyes.

"It's Sergio!" she said, while struggling to stand in the thick brush.

Walking out into the clearing and placing her hand on the horse's neck, Carol asked, "How did you find us, Sergio?"

The Zapatista commander smiled and watched Jim carefully as he stepped next to his wife, "I've been following you for close to half an hour, *senora*. I knew you would stop eventually."

Carol patted the horse's nose and introduced her husband, "Sergio, this is my husband Jim. Jim, this is the leader of the Zapatistas, Sergio Salinas. He's been helping me search for Taylor."

Jim brought up his guard immediately after the introduction, "Salinas? Are you related to Cristobal Salinas?" he asked.

Sergio bowed his head and spoke solemnly, "Yes, *senor*. Cristobal was my younger brother. I am very sorry that his actions have brought so much grief to your *familia*."

Carol explained, "Cristobal's wife and two sons were murdered in the village of Perdido, Jim. Remember the army raid there?"

Jim looked at his wife as he processed the information she was telling him. His heart had been filled with hatred for the man he had killed. Now he felt sorrow for all the man had lost. Looking up at the Zapatista, Jim nodded his acceptance of the heartfelt apology.

"I have a gift for you and your husband." Sergio smiled at Carol and turned his horse so the couple could see the man tied across the rear of the beautiful animal. Sergio cut the ropes that held the man in place and Captain Eduardo Marquez fell to the ground in a heap.

"Please don't hurt me. Please don't hurt me," was all that escaped the beaten man's lips.

Sergio laughed, "I tried to kill him, *senor*, but it turns out that I am a very bad shot. Maybe you would like to help me."

Thirty-seven

The procession made its way slowly up the barren hillside. Carol, riding bareback on the smoky colored gelding, led the mumbling captain around stumps of large mahogany trees in a clear cut forest. Captain Marquez stumbled along, tripping over exposed roots and cursing the rope that bound his wrists to the horse. Jim and Sergio followed closely behind, discussing the battle that destroyed the Zapatista camp.

"I think Thomas and I were set up to lead the army to your camp," Jim offered. "Everything went too easily, I should have suspected but I didn't. I guess I was focused only on finding my wife and son."

"It is not your fault, Jim. I should have moved our camp months ago. It is easy to become," Sergio searched for the word, "lazy."

Captain Marquez yelled loudly and cursed in Spanish. Carol looked over her shoulder at the army officer, then smiled at Jim.

Sergio interpreted for the American, "He says his crotch is chafing from pissing himself. He wants to stop and rest."

Just then, the horse raised its tail and emptied its bowels onto the captain's feet. After a loud protest from the bound officer, Jim laughed.

"You train your horses well, Sergio. I couldn't have come up with a better response to the captain's complaint."

After walking in silence for several minutes, Jim turned to the Zapatista commander, "I'm going to need a secluded place to get some information from our friend here."

Sergio nodded, "I suspected that, *senor*. There used to be a village over this next ridge. It was abandoned after lumber companies came through and cut all these trees. On the hill above the village is a vacant church that was built by the Spanish in the 1600's. It is the only building still standing. Will that meet your needs?"

"That sounds perfect," Jim said. "When we get there, I will need your knife and something to heat up for cauterizing wounds. Can you manage that for me?"

Sergio stopped and stared at Jim, "I carry two knives, *hermano*. Do you mind if I ask what you plan to do?"

Jim turned to the Mayan man, "I plan to find out where my son is, Sergio. Is this going to be a problem for you?"

Sergio shook his head slowly, "I have no objections to torturing this *demonio*, Jim. I just wonder, is this something that you will allow your wife to witness?"

Jim looked up at Carol who was straining to listen to the conversation.

Quietly now, he asked Sergio, "I would appreciate it if you would take her out of earshot. I will need about two hours."

Sergio nodded and ran ahead to lead Carol and the captain around the abandoned village and up to the waiting church.

The church stood majestically on a hilltop, overlooking a ragged and unkempt graveyard. Crosses leaned in disarray and were all but covered by wild ryegrass. An eerie quiet surrounded the hallowed ground. No trees stood to harbor nesting birds and buzzing locusts. The land was barren and all life had forsaken it.

Built from mud and yellowed stucco, the place of worship had weathered the years with vigor. Doors still swung on their rusted hinges and windows remained intact. The pews and alter had been removed years before, possibly taken to a new church built for the displaced villagers.

Jim untied the rope that secured the captain to the mount and led him into the empty interior. Stopping at the back of the church, he kicked the army officer's legs out from under him and sat him down forcefully. Eduardo Marquez covered his head with his tied hands and begged for mercy.

Sergio approached the American and offered his two hunting knives with a sad look on his face, "What else will you need, Jim?" the sorrowful man asked.

"Will you bring me that wooden box in the corner and also start me a small fire right there?" Jim pointed to a large stone bowl once used for holding holy water.

Sergio looked into Jim's eyes and held his gaze, "Let me do this, *mi hermano*. I have no soul left anyway."

Jim stared back coldly as he remembered his last day with Taylor, "I've done this before," he admitted, "After you start the fire, please take my wife away."

Carol walked through the open door, "Take your wife away where?" she asked, her voice echoing in the empty chamber.

"I need you to go with Sergio. If the captain is stubborn, this could get very ugly."

"I'm not going anywhere, Jim." Carol pointed at the now crying captain, "This son of a bitch stole our son. I'm staying."

Jim shook his head, "Then you will have to wait outside. I will not do this with you watching."

Sergio set the wooden box Jim had requested in front of the sobbing army officer. A small fire crackled in the stone font with the blade of a hunting knife piercing the yellow flames. Sergio turned and led Carol from the church, closing the doors behind them.

Thirty-eight

Captain Eduardo Marquez stood naked on the unstable wooden box in the middle of the church floor. A rope, tied around his neck, led to a giant rafter that ran the length of the vaulted ceiling. The captain wept and pleaded for mercy as Jim checked the glowing blade of the hunting knife resting in the fire.

Jim turned to the naked man and heaved a great sigh, "I remember that you speak English very well, so let's dispense with feigned confusion about why you are now in the predicament you're in."

Jim pulled a small piece of wood he had fashioned, with a short loop of rope tied to its center, from the pocket of his jumpsuit.

"The fact is," Jim continued, "you took my son and now you are about to tell me where he is and what you did with him."

Slipping the loop of rope over the middle finger on the captain's right hand, Jim twisted the rope tight, cutting circulation from the appendage.

"Now, I know that you are going to try to feed me full of wild stories about how you have not seen my son, and how you would love to help us find him if I let you go right now."

Captain Marquez winced as Jim gave one more twist to the noose around his finger.

"So let me give you an example of what will happen each time I do not get a truthful answer from you."

Jim yanked down hard on the stick that was now tied to the officer's finger, dislocating it at the third knuckle. The captain groaned in pain as he tried unsuccessfully to turn away from his tormentor.

Raising the unheated knife to the separated knuckle, Jim removed the man's middle finger in one swipe.

Captain Eduardo Marquez screamed and tried to kick at Jim with his bare feet. The box wobbled viciously causing Marquez to dance to steady the crate. Growling like a wounded animal, the Mexican officer held his hand close to his body as blood poured down his bare leg.

Jim picked up the heated knife and pulled the crying man's hands away from his stomach. Holding his wrists securely, Jim burned the wound closed with the glowing red steel.

Captain Marquez screamed as slobber spilled from his mouth and snot ran from his nose. Losing his balance, he fell from the wooden crate and the noose tightened ferociously around his neck. The captain swung in mid-air while his legs flailed, looking for the missing platform.

Jim watched as Captain Marquez's face turned blue and his eyes began to bulge from their sockets. He walked to the commander's twisting body and wrapped his arms around the man's legs, lifting him from the strain of the tightened rope. Using his foot to retrieve the missing box, Jim stood the officer back up and steadied him on the creaky stand.

Captain Marquez was shaking uncontrollably and gasping for air. His feet held desperately to the wooden box.

"Now that you know that I am not here to play games, let's start with you telling me how you got your filthy hands on my little boy."

The trembling man looked at Jim pleadingly and began to shake his head. Without missing a beat, Jim repeated the process and removed the captain's index finger. After finishing the grisly task once again, the sweet stench of burning flesh permeated the once holy building.

———

Carol sat with Sergio on the steps of the abandoned church. The Zapatista seemed to be in another world. Carol assumed that this was a coping mechanism for a man who had experienced much tragedy in his life.

Screams from inside the church continued unabated. Carol found herself wrestling with the reality of what was happening on the other side of the double wooden doors. Her husband was torturing another man. She always knew that the man she had married had depths to him that she never wanted to see. There were times when he would slip and casually mention a horrific episode that occurred in the jungles of Columbia or a city in Libya. She never inquired further about his experiences while serving his country. She didn't want to know.

Another scream pierced the air and chills climbed Carol's spine and made her stomach ache with empathy.

Carol sat horrified that she had allowed herself to feel any sympathy for Marquez. God only knew what horrific things that beast had done to her son. He had ripped her entire life away. He had taken her little boy like he was a pair of shoes to be used, then discarded at his whim. Carol's face burned as she fixed a picture of Taylor in her mind. He smiled at her and whispered, "I love you, Mommy."

Overcome with emotion, Carol broke down and cried uncontrollably. She cried for several minutes until the screaming inside the church ended. With the sorrow washed away in a river of tears, the only thing that remained in her heart was anger.

Standing and opening the doors to the church, Carol was assaulted by the horrific odors of torture; seared flesh mixed with the metallic scent of blood. As she walked deeper into the smoke-filled chamber, the overpowering smell of urine and bowel assailed her senses.

Jim was standing next to a window, his back turned to her, as he gazed upon the battered grave yard.

Carol turned to the naked man, sagging against the straining rope. All ten fingers had been removed and thrown in a pile at the base of the stone font. The fire had burned itself out after its task was accomplished. Tracing the sallow lines up the man's quavering torso, Carol was shocked to see that Marquez was smiling at her.

"*Senora*," he said in a weak voice, "Please help me."

Carol was overcome by repulsion and pure anger. In a blinding rage, she kicked the box from under his feet.

He did not fight the strangling rope. He had no more strength to reach for the shattered platform. With tears flooding his straining eyes, Captain Eduardo Marquez simply died.

"He's alive." Carol heard Jim say from across the room. She looked at the swinging man and noted his dark blue face. Not saying a word, she turned to her husband with a confused look and shook her head.

"Our son is alive!" he said again, "That son of a bitch sold him to marijuana farmers not a hundred miles from here."

Carol struggled for breath as she listened to her husband's words.

Jim continued, "Taylor Paul is being used for slave labor to harvest the marijuana crop."

Seeing her husband covered in another man's blood, Carol fought to maintain her composure.

"I'm going after him," he said, "Are you coming with me?"

Thirty-nine

J im, Carol, and Sergio sat at the small café in Las Margaritas where Carol had met with Dr. Redding only a few days earlier. They sipped coffee and waited patiently for a produce truck to unload its supplies before heading back to the southern village of San Jose Montenegro. The marijuana farm where Taylor was being kept was hidden in the remote Sierra Madre mountains near the tiny village of Santa Apolonia. Sergio had made arrangements with the driver of the old one ton truck to smuggle the Iverson's past the army check points that dotted state highway 190 toward the border with Guatemala.

Carol had purchased new clothes for her husband and medical supplies to clean his wound. Red streaks surrounded the puffy and foul smelling lesion. Jim had begun to run a temperature and was becoming increasingly lethargic. In addition to the gauze and alcohol, Carol obtained some over the counter antibiotics to help fight the infection her husband was now battling.

The farm truck, now unloaded, pulled out of town and backed onto an overgrown lumber road. Sergio walked to the truck first, then motioned for the Iverson's to hurry and climb aboard. As the young driver helped Carol into the back and began covering her with empty crates, Sergio held Jim back and whispered into his ear.

"I wish you good luck, *Senor* Iverson. Please be very careful. The drug cartels in Chiapas are brutal men. They will not hesitate to kill you and your pretty wife."

Jim nodded to the rebel and shook his hand hard, "Thank you for taking care of my wife and searching for my son. I hold no ill will toward you or the Zapatistas and I wish you the best of luck in your coming fight."

Sergio smiled slyly at the American man, "There will be a fight, *hermano*. The Mayans will rise up again, as we always have."

Pulling Captain Marquez's sidearm from his pack, the Zapatista commander handed it to Jim, "There are twelve rounds left in the magazine, choose your targets wisely, *amigo*."

As Jim stuck the nine millimeter in the waist of his pants, Sergio also handed him the captain's binoculars, "These may come in handy."

"Thank you, brother. I'm not sure where we would be without your help." Jim climbed into the back of the truck and reached back to shake Sergio's hand once more. When the Zapatista released his grip, he left an item in Jim's palm. The American opened his hand to reveal a small figurine of a jaguar warrior carved from jade.

"The jaguar warrior is a symbol of might," Sergio said, "It will give you strength in battle and wisdom in peace."

Jim rubbed the small carving with his thumb and forefinger. It was highly polished from hours of massaging by previous owners.

"I think you might need this more than I in the coming years, friend." Jim said with humility in his voice.

The rebel commander bowed his head and seemed to drift back in time, "I have the souls of many dead Mayans to guide me in the coming battles. They will give me strength when I need it most."

Jim rubbed the figurine one more time before placing it in his pocket, "Good luck!" he said one last time before joining his wife among the vacant crates.

Jim and Carol rode quietly in the back of the farmer's truck for the first fifteen minutes. Jim, with his head rolling lazily to the movement of the vehicle, finally said, "Did you know that you are a terrorist, honey?"

Carol looked over to her husband. Thinking he might be delusional from the infection in his stomach, she decided to play along, "Well, you've finally figured me out, sweetheart. My real name is Hayaam Mawiya. I'm Usama bin Laden's fifth wife. What tipped you off?"

Jim looked over at her with a good-humored look on his face, "No really! The American consulate informed me that you are on the terrorist watch list. He said that in college, you raised a quarter of a million dollars for the Zapatistas. If you are that good at raising money, why in the hell did you ever take a thirty-thousand dollar a year job as a teacher?"

Carol looked away from her husband for a moment and tried to catch up with the turn of the conversation.

"I did raise money for the EZLN my senior year in college, but I had a lot of help. I have always loved these people down here and you have witnessed for yourself what they are going through." Carol rubbed her husband's arm, "Am I really on the terrorist watch list?"

"Yup!" Jim said, "You are a threat to America's way of life. You don't support the troops!"

Carol laughed out loud, then covered her mouth in embarrassment, "Well, you're a troop and I support you." She leaned over and kissed Jim on the forehead. Noting his rising temperature, she stared into his eyes, "Let's get our little boy and go home, okay?"

Jim smiled and pulled the handgun from his waist. He quickly checked the chamber for a round, then pulled the clip to verify it had ammunition, "Our little boy will be safe in our arms by this time tomorrow," he said, engaging the safety and placing the weapon back in his pants.

Forty

The truck pulled back onto the highway and left Jim and Carol standing alone on the rocky shoulder. No other vehicles were in sight as the two slipped into the pine forest that framed the newly paved road to Guatemala. Taking the lead, Jim moved quickly through the underbrush toward the village of Santa Apolonia. There was a small dirt track leading to the remote community, but Sergio had warned the Iverson's to stay far away from that path. Armed mercenaries, who guarded the marijuana crop, traveled the road frequently.

Jim had decided to circle to the north of the small village and approach the marijuana farm from the east. A map in Las Margaritas revealed a ridgeline that ran west from Santa Apolonia past the hidden plantation. Jim and Carol would find cover on the ridge and observe the farm below.

The driver of the produce truck informed the Iverson's that he would look for them on the highway the next morning and give them a ride all the way to San Cristobal. Jim didn't like the restraints of the timeframe he was working under, but no better plan was available.

The couple moved quietly among the tall pines of the Sierra Madre mountains. They spoke little and worried much about what they would find at the remote plantation. Sergio had warned them repeatedly about the ruthlessness of the drug runners they were about to encounter. Jim recalled hunting men much like them in the jungles of Columbia. Most were not well trained, so he planned to use that to his advantage.

Coming to a fast moving river, the Iverson's followed it downstream, looking for a safe location to cross. The village of Santa Apolonia lay less than one mile upstream, so the couple ran a high risk of stumbling across wandering peasants. Jim slowed and searched repeatedly across the river for watching eyes.

Finally, coming across a fallen tree that traversed the swift waters, Jim and Carol picked their way through the dead branches and peeling bark of the fallen spruce. Making it across without incident, they quickly disappeared into the thick cover of the woods.

With two hours of sunlight remaining, the Iverson's found the farm they were looking for. Stretching over fifty acres of the small valley floor, rows of bright green cannabis plants shimmered in the setting sun. Young workers lined the rows of marijuana, pulling weeds and harvesting the tops of mature plants while two armed guards walked among them with automatic weapons.

Jim eagerly searched the faces of the young workers through the binoculars Sergio had given him. He could not spot Taylor. Moving the glasses away from the crop, he searched a row of dilapidated shelters with barbed wire stretched around their perimeter. Nothing. Panning further down the valley, Jim slowly scrutinized the main house for signs of any other children. Only guards inhabited the immediate area around the headquarters. All the laborers appeared to be working in the field.

Frustrated, Jim searched the crops again for any sign of his blonde haired boy. Taylor was not there. Pulling the binoculars away from his face, the exasperated man handed them to Carol.

"I don't see him. Maybe you should take a look."

Carol took the glasses and panned the valley floor. Sighing loudly, she began her search again and moved slower this time, taking several seconds to look at the face of each worker in the field.

Removing the binoculars from her eyes, Carol let them drop to her lap, "He's not down there, Jim. Oh my God, what are we going to do if he's not here?" Carol leaned her head against her husband's shoulder and began to weep.

Jim rubbed his hand through Carol's hair, "He's down there, honey. The captain assured me that he brought Taylor here personally."

"What if he was lying, Jim? What if he is looking up at us from Hell and laughing at our stupidity?" Carol tightened her fists in anger and winced as her fingernails dug deeply into the soft tissue.

"The captain was not lying, sweetheart." Jim took Carol's hands and loosened her fist, "I took his last four fingers to be sure."

Carol turned her head away at the grisly memory.

Jim began to plan, "We'll take turns watching the workers until the sun sets. If Taylor doesn't show up, then tomorrow morning I'm going down there to kill as many of those bastards as I can."

Carol looked into her husband's eyes and shook her head solemnly. As the sun settled behind the mountains to the west, Taylor was still nowhere in sight.

Jim and Carol Iverson huddled closely together in the early morning chill. As the sun peeked over the mountains to the east, the couple shivered and waited for any movement on the plantation below. Jim had rested fitfully and mumbled most of the night. Carol found herself worrying about her husband's health, knowing that if he didn't receive quality medical care soon, he might become seriously ill.

"One step at a time," she told herself, "Let's get Taylor and then we will worry about Jim's infection."

The tired and frustrated woman found herself absentmindedly rubbing the small figurine of the owl *Senor* Banuelos had given to her. She had offered the carving of the Harpy Eagle to Jim earlier but he refused, saying that he now had something better.

Jim nudged his wife as one of the mercenaries walked out the door of the main house. Stretching his back and cracking his neck, the guard lit a cigarette and walked to the tree line to urinate into a pile of trash. Jim noted the Russian made AK-74 strapped to the man's back. With a thousand meter range, the weapon could easily reach the American couple on the mountainside.

Jim moved the binoculars back to the main house and watched as two other guards stepped out and walked to the laborer's shelters. Pulling barbed wire aside, the pair entered the shanties and began pushing the slave workers toward the fields for another day of monotonous chores. Jim hunted among the staggering young boys for the familiar features of his ten year old son. Twelve workers walked in a single file line toward the waiting cannabis. None of which were Taylor.

"God damn it!" Jim said under his breath. Turning to his wife, he blurted, "I'm going down there to try and capture one of the guards. I'll bring him back up here and we can question him about where Taylor is."

Carol became frantic, "Wait, Jim!" she said, "Let's think this thing through. Can you really capture a guard and bring him all the way up here without alerting his friends?"

Jim looked at Carol as he thought about his strategy, "Probably not," he finally said, "Do you have a better plan?"

"No, Jim, I don't. Let's just sit tight for an hour or so and see what happens. Maybe they have Taylor inside cooking or something."

The sun began to warm the thin mountain air and the couple found themselves nodding in and out of consciousness. Jim was shaken out of a troubled sleep by his wife.

"Something's happening," she said. "The guards just had a pow-wow and now one of them is walking away." Carol handed the glasses to Jim, "Here, take a look."

Jim brought the binoculars up to his face and quickly found the traveling mercenary. He had walked to the far side of the main house and was now kneeling at what appeared to be a door that was laying flat on the ground. He fumbled with a set of keys and worked a padlock that was securing the entry. Finally removing the lock, the guard stood and raised the door fully open, letting it slam to the earth on the opposite side in a cloud of dust. The mercenary kneeled again and reached deep into the uncovered hole before him. Straining, he lifted a young boy from the opening in the ground and stood him harshly to the side while he closed the door again.

Jim adjusted the focus on the glasses and grabbed Carol's arm. The boy that stood and sheltered his eyes from the glaring sun was Taylor Paul Iverson.

Forty-one

Taylor stood hunched, in dirty clothes and bare feet. He looked even thinner than normal, if that was possible. His hair had been shaved off and his ankles were bound together by a long piece of rope, making it easy to walk but impossible to run. Jim could not see his son's face clearly because the boy held his arms up to shield the sun from his eyes. He knew it was Taylor; there was no doubt in his mind.

Excited, Jim handed the binoculars to Carol to confirm what he was seeing. She focused the glasses quickly and found it hard to control herself.

"Oh, Jim, our baby is still alive. Look at him, honey. Thank you, God." she said.

Jim retrieved the glasses and swept the valley below. He could make out only three guards with automatic weapons. The others must still be in the house, asleep he hoped. Jim watched as the mercenary led his son to the marijuana field. The guard laughed then said something to Taylor. Jim noticed his son frowning up at the man before turning his head away and smiling.

The hole in the ground measured roughly three foot by six foot. Taylor figured that it was about the size of a grave although not quite as deep. Enough light filtered around the wooden door on top, to give the young boy a good look at his surroundings.

Three days earlier, as the sun was setting, Taylor had made a run for it. He made it to a dirt road and followed it north for almost two miles before coming across two guards, parked on a bridge in a Toyota pickup. He surrendered quickly after they pointed their large guns at him, and they brought him back to the farm and threw him in this hole. Once a day, they would raise the door and drop down a bottle of water and a corn tortilla. Yuk! Taylor was sure that he would never eat corn again.

Passing the time away in the hole had become easy. He made friends with several roly-polies, or pill-bugs as some people called them, that also inhabited the pit. Taylor couldn't remember their scientific name completely, he was sure that it had the word armadillo in it though. He named the armored bugs after his friends back in Colorado, and occupied himself by building each of them a little earthen home. They didn't like the corn tortillas either.

Taylor was unconcerned with the rope that held his ankles. As soon as he got back to the field, he would easily untie the knots at each foot and make another run for it. He had heard sounds of traffic on a nearby highway the last time he ran. This time, he would stay off the dirt road and opt instead for the safety of the trees, paralleling the rutted track as best he could.

It had been a very long time since Taylor had last seen his mother and father. He knew they must be worried sick about him. Each night, before he went to sleep, he found them in his mind and talked to them. He told them about that rotten army captain who brought him to this desolate place. The Mexican had told Taylor that his mom and dad were dead, so he now belonged to the Mexican government and he would have to work hard at this farm to earn enough money to go back to America. When Taylor asked the guards how much money he would earn each day, they had a hell of a good time laughing and smacking each other on the back. That's when he decided to run.

As the wooden door opened above him, Taylor waited for the bottled water to thump him on the head as it usually did, but instead, a pair of hands reached in and pulled him up into the sunlight. He stood, a little wobbly at first, and shielded the brightness of the day from his eyes.

The guard slammed the door shut on the earthen cell and led Taylor back to the field. Taylor couldn't help but worry about his new friends, the roly-polies, in the hole. He hoped they would be okay without him.

As the foul smelling guard walked beside Taylor toward the marijuana crop, he laughed loudly and said in very bad English, "Run next time in hole for month."

Taylor looked up at the man and frowned at his bad grammar. Looking back at the ground in front of him, Taylor thought, "You'll have to catch me first." He couldn't help but smile.

"Okay, Carol, here's what we are going to do," Jim's mind raced as he developed a workable plan to rescue his son.

"Do you see that outcropping of rocks at the foot of the hill to our left?" Jim pointed and Carol nodded her head, "Make your way down there and wait behind those rocks."

Carol began to protest, but Jim quickly cut her off, "I'll send Taylor hightailing it to those rocks as I take care of the guards. He'll run faster if he knows you are there waiting for him."

Jim brought the glasses to his eyes and surveyed an escape route, "When he gets to you, run like hell toward that tall stand of trees." Jim pointed again, "Do you see them?"

"Yes," Carol said, concentrating on her part in the rescue.

"Don't wait for me. I might be tied up for awhile, dealing with those guards and keeping them off your tail."

Carol nodded again.

"Once you reach those trees, you'll be able to see the river down below. Head straight for the river and follow it upstream until you come across the fallen tree. From there, make your way straight east until you come to the highway. Find a good hiding spot until the truck comes or I find you."

Jim looked deep into Carol's eyes, "Don't wait for me, honey, do you understand? Get our boy to safety; I'll take care of myself, okay?"

Carol blinked as she considered what Jim was telling her, "I'll do my part, baby, but you promise me right now that you will be careful. You promise me right now that the three of us are going home *together*."

Jim smiled at his wife, "I can handle these guys. I'll see you at the road."

With that said, Jim pulled the nine millimeter with its twelve rounds of ammunition from his waistband. Checking the chamber to ensure it was loaded and ready to go, he slipped into the trees and started down the mountain.

Forty-two

Jim moved silently down the wooded hillside, stopping from time to time to ensure he had not been spotted by the armed men below. He watched closely as his only son was steered toward the center of the shimmering field. The lower Jim moved on the slope, the harder it was to see Taylor among the lustrous leaves of the marijuana plants. He could make out the tops of the guard's heads which gave him adequate information as to their whereabouts. One last look toward the main house through the captain's binoculars ensured no other mercenaries were joining the party that was about to begin.

It would be tricky to slip from the forest into the uneven rows of cannabis. Jim would have to cover about seventy five feet of open ground before he reached the concealment the marijuana crop offered. One of the guards circled the field with weapon held ready, to keep the young boys from escaping. His focus was primarily on the hunched over workers. This was something Jim planned to use to his full advantage.

Waiting patiently, Jim crouched, ready to cover the distance and take the man by quiet surprise. Time ticked by slowly as the guard appeared at the north end of the field and walked his circular route. As he passed, Jim moved, covering the distance in less than ten seconds. Jim was determined to take him with as little noise as possible, so as not to alert the guards in the field.

As Jim approached, the guard turned and looked straight at him. Still ten feet away, he tripled his speed and drove the stunned Mexican to the ground. He realized how weak he had become when the young mercenary forcefully shoved him to the side and climbed onto his chest. Bracing his Russian made weapon across Jim's throat, the guard pushed hard, terminating his attacker's air supply.

Jim knew he was losing. Tearing his right hand from under the guard's left knee, he brought the nine millimeter up and shot the mercenary three times in the chest. The shots echoed loudly through the valley and all surprise was lost.

For a brief second, Jim considered picking up the AK-74. Not wanting to hurt any of the other laborers, he quickly concluded that the weapon would only be a hindrance. Struggling to his knees, he dove into the field and crawled toward Taylor's last known location. The remaining guards were calling out to their now deceased partner, and two others had stepped from the house to determine the cause of the commotion. Jim knelt quietly for a moment, planning his next move.

A slight breeze rustled the leaves of the marijuana crop. All other noises had stopped. Jim crouched lower to get a better view through the sturdy stalks. Nothing moved. On hands and knees, the former Green Beret slipped through row after row of cannabis until he caught sight of Taylor. His son was kneeling, with his back turned to the armed guard who had freed him from the pit. Jim could see that Taylor was working at untying the bonds from his ankles.

"That's my boy," he whispered to himself.

The mercenaries in the field began calling out to their friend again, unsure whether or not to abandon their posts to go find him. Jim could tell by the stress in their voices that they were quickly concluding something was wrong.

Moving over a few more rows, Jim was now in direct sight of his son. Taylor was concentrating on untying the stiff rope and didn't see his dad only fifty feet away. As Jim inched his way up the row, the guard standing behind Taylor slowly turned, surveying the outer edges of the crop field. His gaze passed over Jim and never registered the approaching danger. He was obviously focused on the expected path of the once roving mercenary.

Cussing loudly, the guard pushed Taylor aside and started up the row toward Jim. Thinking he had been spotted, Jim froze in place and watched the sandaled feet of the armed guard as he approached.

Jim had to think fast. The mercenary would see him long before he could take the man silently, but firing the handgun again would most likely bring a hail of gunfire from his friends. Too late! The man stopped and raised his automatic weapon, bringing it to bear on the crouching American. Without thinking, Jim moved to his left and brought the nine millimeter up, firing another three rounds into the Mexican's chest. Stunned, the man fingered the gaping holes slightly above his heart and sat back into the crashing stalks of marijuana.

"Taylor Paul!" Jim yelled for his son.

Taylor had taken advantage of the distracted guard and disappeared.

"Tot!" Jim yelled, knowing Taylor would respond to the familiar nickname.

"Dad!" Taylor yelled from the edge of the field, slightly behind Jim, "Where are you?"

Before he could answer, a hail of gunfire erupted from the far end of the field. Plants above Jim's head disintegrated as super heated rounds tried to find him. Crawling frantically, Jim raced for his son's excited voice. A spray of automatic fire skimmed above his head again as the mercenaries zeroed in on the flailing plants. Fearing his son might get hurt; Jim stood, turned and placed three rounds into the head of the firing guard. The spray of red was obvious against the backdrop of bright green cannabis.

"Three rounds left," Jim told himself as he moved toward Taylor. Not wanting to draw more fire, he refrained from calling out to his son.

Reaching the end of the field, Jim searched for signs of his little boy.

"Taylor!" he yelled again when he couldn't find him.

A noise from behind caught Jim's attention too late. Before he could turn, a body crashed into him and drove him to the ground.

"Dad!" Taylor yelled as he hugged his father tightly around the neck, "I knew you would come. I knew it, I knew it, I knew it!"

Jim pushed himself to his knees again with Taylor still holding tightly to his neck. He wrapped his arms around Taylor and allowed a giant sob to escape his lips.

"I love you, Tot! Now listen to me," he said, pulling Taylor away and staring him in the eyes, "Your mother is waiting for you behind those rocks," Jim pointed, "You get yourself to the tree line and run for those rocks as fast as you can, okay?"

Taylor didn't need any convincing. The mention of his mother focused him on the instructions he was receiving. Without another word, he ran with blazing speed toward the tree line then turned for the rocks.

Jim heard yelling from the direction of the main house and stood to get a better bearing on what was approaching. Bullets snapped over his head as the two remaining guards let off ill aimed bursts from their weapons. Jim immediately regretted his decision not to pick up the first guard's AK-74.

Carol waited behind the formation of giant boulders. Rocks, made from ancient red clay, reached thirty feet into the air. From her position, it was hard to see the marijuana field, but she did observe as her husband rushed from the trees toward the hidden crop. A few seconds later, she heard gunshots. From whose weapon, she wasn't sure. She listened carefully as the guards started yelling in Spanish. They were calling to a man named Geraldo. He never answered.

Wringing her hands nervously, Carol tried to peer around the boulders to catch a glimpse of her husband or son. Seeing neither, she was jolted by the sound of three more gunshots. This had to be Jim, she thought to herself. Whenever he practiced shooting at home, he always fired in three round bursts.

Carol jumped to her feet when she heard her husband and son yell to each other and was jolted again by the sounds of gunfire. An automatic rifle first, then another three round burst.

Frustrated at not being able to view what was happening, Carol left the rocks and started through the trees toward the farm. Catching herself, she bit the knuckles of her tightened fist and returned to the rock pile, "What if Taylor and Jim come from another direction and I'm not where I'm supposed to be?" she scolded herself.

"Damn it, Jim, hurry up!" she heard herself say a little too loudly.

"Mom!"

It was Taylor, running through the trees toward her. He looked scared to death and happy as hell at the same time.

Carol scooped up her son and held him tightly as she dared without crushing him. She couldn't get a word past the blubbering and running tears.

Searching the direction from which her son had arrived, Carol looked one last time for her husband before setting out for the stand of trees to the north. Jim was nowhere in sight.

Forty-three

The fourteen year old Mexican boy could barely remember his name. He had been brought to this farm over seven years ago by his father and sold to the cartel that ran it. The last time he had heard his proper name spoken was that horrible day when his father said, "Go, Antonio. These men own you now."

Antonio's mother had left for the United States to find work when he was only five. He remembered fondly the day she left with the *coyotes* she had paid to take her. She picked Antonio up and kissed him for a very long time on the forehead. He remembered her scent clearly. She smelled of rose petals and sage. Antonio smiled every time he caught a whiff of the wild roses that grew on the mountainside that bordered the marijuana farm.

His mother made it safely to America and sent word that she had found work in Santa Fe, New Mexico. She was cleaning hotel rooms and was making over five dollars per hour for her labor. Antonio remembered his father grumbling at his mother's outrageous wage. He could not earn five American dollars per day at his grueling job in the concrete plant.

His father was angry that his wife had left him to raise the four children alone. He complained constantly and when Antonio's mother would send money home each month to feed and clothe her children, his dad would take the cash and disappear for several days, leaving the siblings to fend for themselves. He would finally return, drunk and whored up, and beat the children when they asked for food.

Antonio's older brother, who was ten years old at the time, ran away. He told his younger brother that he was going to America to find their mother. He promised that he would convince her to return and take them back to the wonderful United States, where they would all be happy again. Antonio's older brother was never heard from again.

On the young boy's seventh birthday, his father loaded him and his two older sisters into their old pickup truck and drove into Tuxtla Gutierrez where he sold Antonio's *hermanas* to a brothel. From there, they drove south into the mountains of Chiapas and the young boy ended up here, where he has remained ever since.

Antonio was amazed when the blonde haired boy came to the marijuana farm. He had never seen such fair colored skin and he never knew eyes could be any color but brown. The boy was friendly and Antonio liked him from the start.

At night, they would communicate in the moonlight by drawing pictures in the dirt floor of their shelter. Antonio was excited when the boy drew a map of America and pointed to himself. He immediately blurted out the only American city he knew, "Santa Fe."

The boy responded by drawing an "X" on the map and repeating the word, "Santa Fe." Antonio was ecstatic. Santa Fe did not seem like it was very far. He could probably walk there in less than a week. For the first time in seven years, the young Mexican boy considered making a run for it. That was, until the American boy ran. He wasn't gone more than two hours when the guards brought him back and threw him in *the hole*.

Antonio had never spent time in *the hole* and he never wanted to. Some children actually died in there. The Mexican boy thought his new friend might be dead after three days down there, but was happy to see him pulled out today and brought back to the field.

He was in the process of making his way over to his American friend when the gunfire started. Dropping to his belly between the rows of cannabis, Antonio watched the drama unfold.

Jim checked his magazine to be sure he still had ammo. Two in the clip, one in the chamber.

"Damn it!" he said, "I should have conserved better."

Two men were approaching with no less than thirty rounds each. They knew exactly where he was hiding at the edge of the field because they had split up and were attempting to flank him on each side. If his aim were true and he could kill the first with only one round, that would leave two for the remaining guard. The only problem was, he would not have enough time to bring down the last mercenary before being riddled with bullets from his automatic rifle. Jim would have to pivot more than ninety degrees to take out the second man. Time was running out fast. It was now or never.

The guards spotted him as he rose from the field. Jim tried to keep both men in his line of vision as he fired at the one to his right. Because his attention was divided, his aim was not true. The one round, reserved for the first man, found its mark in the fleshy part of the guard's right shoulder. Without turning, Jim released his last two rounds and dropped the man where he stood.

The slide of the nine millimeter locked to the rear, indicating that it was empty and ready to be reloaded. Jim threw the pistol to the ground and raised his hands high in the air.

"Don't shoot, don't shoot!" he yelled, knowing full well that the guard was going to shoot.

Jim closed his eyes tight recognizing the distinct sound of the AK-74 as it unloaded a full magazine. Bracing for the impact of the rounds, he heard a thud and slowly opened his eyes, one at a time. The guard was gone.

Antonio was amazed that the guard had moved past him without stopping. As the man walked by, the young Mexican reached over and retrieved the rifle of the guard who had brought the American boy back to the field. He wasn't sure how it worked, but he had to try and help his friend escape.

Antonio stood; raising the large rifle to his shoulder, he pulled the trigger. The weapon jumped in his hands and its barrel rose skyward as the magazine quickly emptied. Thinking he had missed, Antonio fell back to the ground and covered his head. Everything remained quiet. The Mexican boy slowly raised his head and stared into the lifeless eyes of the man he had just killed.

Antonio decided to wait in the field until nightfall. If no one came to get him by then, he would head to Santa Fe to find his mother.

Jim stood, arms still raised, and turned a full circle looking for the guard who was about to kill him. Not seeing him or any other living being, he slowly lowered his arms, then ran for the cover of the trees.

Less than an hour later, Jim approached Highway 190, close to where he and Carol had been dropped off the day before. The old produce truck that had brought them here sat idling on the side of the road. Jim sat quietly behind the cover of a fallen tree and watched the road for any suspicious movement.

Jim chuckled as a thin yellow stream of urine appeared from the back of the truck on the far side. He couldn't see the individual who was emptying his bladder, but Jim instinctually knew it was his son.

Clucking his tongue against the roof of his mouth, Jim made a noise resembling that of a chattering squirrel. He smiled broadly as Taylor peeked around a crate, filled with cabbages, to catch a glimpse of the noisy rodent.

Stepping onto the road, Jim reached for Carol's hand and climbed into the back of the truck.

Forty-four

The Iverson's sat in a hotel room in San Cristobal, paid for by Dr Redding's assistant, Keith. The young man sat at the edge of the bed and fumbled through a stack of papers.

"The professor is back in Arizona, thank God. The University is working to get his visa reinstated but it doesn't look good."

The assistant dropped some of the papers to the floor and scrambled to pick them up, "He sends you his love and says that he would like to speak with all of you once you are safely back in the states."

Carol handed Keith a document that had slipped under the bed, "We have to get back to the states safely first. Did the professor offer any insight on how we might go about that?"

Keith found the paper he was looking for and handed it to Carol, "We have arranged for you to ride a chartered bus from here to Mexico City. A pharmaceutical lab brought its employees to San Cristobal for a conference and will be leaving in the morning. We will sneak you onto the bus, with the help of a lab manager who has been paid handsomely, and get you out of southern Mexico. That piece of paper has the time and location you are to meet the bus. The lab manager's name is scribbled on the back there," the assistant pointed.

Keith looked nervously at Jim, who was pale and slumped in a wicker chair, "There are warrants out for both of you to be arrested. They say that you are suspects in the disappearance of an army officer and Mr. Iverson is listed as an escaped prisoner."

Jim opened his eyes at the mention of his name. A high fever had developed overnight and his joints had begun to ache, "I didn't escape from prison, Keith, they let me out. And as far as the army officer, I'm sure he's hanging around." With a slight smile on his face, Jim closed his eyes again and tried to rest.

Taylor walked to his father with a wet washcloth and wiped his forehead and face. Jim smiled at his son's touch.

"Maybe we should take Daddy to a hospital, Mom, he doesn't look very good."

Carol stepped to the chair her husband was sitting in and felt his forehead. A deep frown crossed her face, "How do we get from Mexico City to the United States, Keith? Did the professor have any ideas?"

Keith tore his gaze away from the ailing man in the chair, "He asked that you call him once you are there. He needs a little more time to make arrangements. His phone number is on that paper as well."

Carol was slightly exasperated, "I can't read your damn handwriting, Keith. What does this say?"

The anxious assistant stood and looked at the paper in Carol's hand, "Oh, I'm sorry Mrs. Iverson. Those are ingredients I need to make dinner tonight." Slightly embarrassed, he continued, "That was the only scrap of paper available when Dr. Redding called."

Carol tore the list from the bottom of the paper and handed it to Keith. The young man's face flushed as he placed it in his pocket.

Carol grabbed a pad of paper from a desk in the room and wrote frantically. Handing the pad to the research assistant, she spoke in a serious tone, "I need you to go to the *farmacia* and purchase these items for me. Get as many oral antibiotics as you possibly can. We have to get this infection under control or Jim is in serious trouble."

Happy to have been given a task, the young man grabbed his backpack and hurried out of the room.

Taylor was watching his father breathe while he slept, "Dad's going to be okay, right, Mom?"

Carol pulled the bandage, saturated with puss and blood, from her husband's stomach. Red streaks now snaked their way from the wound up into Jim's chest hair. The rough edges of the puncture had turned dark red and in some places appeared almost black.

Pouring the last of her rubbing alcohol onto a fresh gauze bandage, Carol gently covered the wound again and secured the dressing in place. Jim opened his eyes briefly and smiled at his son.

"I'll be okay, Tot. I've been through much worse."

Early the next morning, the Iverson's rose and left the hotel to meet the chartered bus. Jim seemed much more alert with a healthy dose of antibiotics and clean bandages. He had slept fourteen hours and was a little embarrassed by his filthy condition. A shower and a cup of strong coffee rejuvenated him, although he still felt a bit feverish and had no appetite to speak of.

Climbing onto the crowded bus, Carol happily conversed in Spanish with the other passengers. She told Jim later, once they were settled into their seats, that she had informed some curious lab workers that they were shareholders in the lab and were returning to Mexico City for a tour of the facility. No one appeared to question her motives.

Settling into the air conditioned Metroliner, the Iverson's readied themselves for the twelve hour ride to Mexico City.

Forty-five

The dry desert mountains quickly gave way to civilization as the chartered bus neared the capital city of Mexico. Shanties, made from plywood and corrugated metal were tucked along the roadside as the relentless poverty of one of the world's largest cities revealed itself. Laundry hung on lines, stretched between trees, to dry in the dirty evening air. Children walked with dogs as they foraged for useful items among the trash that littered the landscape.

Taylor's mouth hung open as he witnessed, through the tinted glass of the bus, what the word poverty really means. How could so many people be so poor in such a rich nation? He would have to ask his father when he was feeling better.

Jim lay slouched in the high-backed seat, drenched in sweat and shaking from a continuous chill that caused his body to ache. A thin wool blanket covered his chest that rose and fell with his labored breathing. Carol had been feeding him mega-doses of over the counter antibiotics to no avail. Jim's condition worsened and his mind began to take him places he didn't want to go.

Jim raised the reel of telephone wire to his shoulder and set his mind for the climb ahead. His tool belt pulled at his waist; loaded with hammers, climbing hooks, and the phone set he would need to check "old man" Barber's dial-tone once the line to his remote cabin was replaced. The squirrels had done their work, chewing through a half mile of aerial wire as they sharpened their teeth on the steel strands that carried a connection to the outside world.

"Old man" Barber had been complaining for years of static and buzzing during his calls to the public officials and newspaper editors of Garfield County. Jim had repaired the line several times throughout the winter months and was happy to finally find time to eliminate this nagging problem.

Reaching the first pole on a ridgeline that led to Mr. Barber's property, Jim dropped his heavy load to the ground and fitted the climbing hooks to his boots. Slapping his hardhat to seat it snuggly on his brow, Jim gripped the pole and quickly ascended to its top. Securing his safety line, he kicked back and studied the wire he was about to remove. His gaze followed the glistening line up the ridge until it disappeared into a stand of pines at the crest of the hill. A loud sigh escaped his lungs as he contemplated the four hour job ahead.

A glint of white caught Jim's attention as he drove a fresh hook into the weathered pole. He lowered his hammer and studied the horizon to catch sight of the fluttering object again. Shielding his eyes against the morning sun, Jim scanned a meadow to the south and spotted the fleeting movement again. From this distance, it appeared to be a white bed sheet fluttering in the breeze. Its beauty, in sharp contrast to the greens and grays of the forest, called to him.

Walking silently through the twinkling branches of the Quaking Aspen, Jim approached the meadow with caution. He could hear voices as they whispered and cried from the meadow. The resonance of spirits stopped and all that could be heard was the fluttering of linen in the mountain breeze.

Jim crouched, determined to remain unseen as he advanced toward a scene that reached for his soul with a strangling grip. A bus sat disabled at the far edge of the meadow, windows shattered and sides riddled with bullet holes. Bleached white linens trembled in the mountain breeze as they fought to reveal red stains creeping through their woolen fibers. Bodies lay strewn throughout the tall grass of the lush pasture. A small boy stood from the grass and reached for the trembling man. Pink foam poured from the boy's nose and mouth as he called to Jim for help. Jim reached for the Iraqi boy, shocked by the blood that covered his own hands and the realization that he was the one who had ended the boy's life.

Jim opened his eyes as the bus accelerated up Insurgentes Avenue toward the center of Mexico City. Tall buildings lined both sides of the highway and a sign on the right welcomed visitors to Ciudad University. Brilliantly painted murals covered campus structures, depicting Mexican struggles throughout history. A beautiful oval stadium, lined with colorful flags, sat in the distance.

Not wanting to return to the visions that haunted his dreams, Jim fought the exhaustion that plagued his body. He couldn't help but smile as he watched his only son peer through the window at the vast city unfolding before him. Taylor was going to be a great man; Jim could feel it in his soul. He studied everything with unfeigned interest. His heart ached for all those in the world who suffered and he railed against injustice, always standing up for the kid at school who endured relentless teasing.

Jim wiped the moisture from his clammy palm and touched his son's stubbled hair. Taylor was going to be a great man.

Carol sat in the aisle seat and focused intently on the paralleled lines before her. Her mind poured over details of her family's appalling situation. Jim was dying, she knew it, and there was nothing she could do to stop it until they reached the safety of the United States. Checking her husband into a hospital here would all but guarantee their arrest and imprisonment. Taylor would be left alone and Carol was poised to murder again to keep that from happening. If Jim could just hold on for another day, two at most, then everything would be okay. His skin had taken on a gray pallor and his breathing had become labored. The knife wound looked ghastly on the outside but Carol suspected a deeper, systemic infection, was causing her husband's deteriorating condition.

By listening to other passenger's conversations, Carol was able to determine that the bus would deposit the group at their laboratory near a hospital in the center of Mexico City. She had decided to find a nearby hotel to settle in and wait for instructions from the professor. She trusted the man completely and knew that he would bring her family to safety. Carol would also use this opportunity to care for her husband and try to stabilize his worsening state. The antibiotics were not working and she was sure that gangrene had invaded the festering wound.

During the twelve hour trip to Mexico City, Carol had learned from Jim what had taken place in his hospital room in Villahermosa. She was astonished that her own government had turned a blind eye to their predicament. She was angered beyond belief that the Consular agent had sat and played checkers while her son was being sold to dope dealers in the highlands of Chiapas. She was incensed to have been so easily written off by the people sworn to protect her family. Carol was determined to take her husband's advice and write a book, enlightening the world to the predators that preyed on the most helpless among us. This corruption would not go unanswered.

Forty-six

The bright green taxi sped up del Taller avenue toward a
Holiday Inn in Mexico City. Taylor sat in the back with his
father and watched as marbled sculptures passed by in a blur. The
sun would soon set on the majestic high rise buildings, built over the
ruins of ancient *Tenochtitlan*.

The driver slowed for traffic, allowing Taylor to observe as
street vendors folded their brightly colored umbrellas and wrapped
flatbreads in cellophane to prepare their carts for closing. Conchero
dancers, dressed in blues and purples, swayed and skipped around
ornately carved drums as gold rays from the setting sun glimmered
among their head dresses, made from the feathers of pheasants. A
trancelike state seemed to envelop all who stood on the sidewalk and
watched. Taylor felt his heart keep rhythm with the drum as the taxi
began to move again through the sweltering heat and car exhaust.

The hotel stood large against the darkening sky. Taylor marveled
at the atrium style lobby and the rushing water of bubbling fountains.
His father held his hand gently as his mother made arrangements
for a room. Taylor could not help but reflect on the poverty he had
witnessed on the outskirts of this tremendous city. If he could, he
thought quietly, he would take all the wealth from this one building
and feed those children who were searching for scraps of food along

the busy highway. Taylor followed in silence as his parents led him
to the elevators.

Jim sat at the edge of the bed, trying to drink a bottle of water.
Dehydrated from constant sweating and chilled from the air
conditioned room, the ailing man tried to remain strong for his
family. He watched as his wife unfolded the piece of paper given to
her by the young assistant in San Cristobal. Picking up a phone on
the desk, she dialed a series of numbers and waited patiently while
her call connected. Jim accepted that she was in charge now. He
had complete confidence that Carol and the professor would get
his family safely back to America. He also knew that the clock was
ticking. The pain in his abdomen had turned to an intense burning
and the discharge from his open wound had become dark yellow.
Jim realized that a systemic infection was overwhelming his immune
system. His lymph nodes were swollen and he suspected that blood
poisoning was a probability in the near future. Jim tightened his jaw,
internally screaming at his body to fight this infection.

Carol's call connected after the fourth ring.

"Dr. Redding?" she asked, "This is Carol Iverson. We're in Mexico
City."

"Carol, thank God! I have been worried sick about you all day,"
the professor pronounced, "Were there any difficulties getting on the
chartered bus?"

"None, Dr. Redding. Thank you so much for your help." Carol let
her voice convey her deep concern, "I hope you have been successful
arranging our return to the states, Jim is very sick and needs medical
attention right away."

"Yes, Carol, everything is arranged. Let me take a moment to fill
you in on what has transpired since you left San Cristobal. Then you
will better understand the route you are forced to take to get your
family home."

Carol waited silently for the professor to continue.

"You and your husband are being sought by Mexican authorities for various transgressions. Escaping from prison, murder of a Mexican national, and the disappearance of an army officer in Chiapas. Without details, is the army officer in question a certain Captain Eduardo Marquez?"

Carol bit her bottom lip and lied, "I wouldn't know, Dr. Redding. You know that all the charges are false."

Marcus Redding stuttered slightly, "Oh, I have no doubt that your family has fallen victim to the political turmoil of southern Mexico, Mrs. Iverson. I guess that I just want you to understand why I cannot arrange for you to fly straight to Denver."

Carol finally let her frustration slip through, "I realize that you are doing everything in your power to help us, professor. Please tell me what our next step is."

"Yes, of course. I have purchased tickets for you to fly on AeroMexico to ciudad Acuna airport near the Texas border tomorrow morning. You can pick up your boarding passes at the ticket counter. Security for local flights in Mexico is insignificant, so you should have no trouble boarding the plane. Once you are there, your family will cross the border to Del Rio, Texas. Now, it is very important that you wait to cross until late in the afternoon. Air Force families from Laughlin Air Force Base usually flood the Customs and immigration checkpoint around 5:30pm, returning from a day of shopping in Mexico. Your family should fit right in and be able to slip through with little suspicion. Does this sound okay to you?"

Carol scribbled the details on her notepad and swallowed hard trying to find her voice. For the first time in weeks there was a light at the end of a very dark tunnel.

"Carol? Do you understand the plan?" the professor asked again.

"Yes!" she finally blurted out, "Thank you so much for everything you have done, Dr. Redding. We owe our lives to you."

"Nonsense!" the professor proclaimed, "Your family is under my care until you submit the final results of your study."

After a brief pause, Dr. Redding continued, "I also want to inform you that I have a meeting tomorrow with an FBI agent in Phoenix. I want to make sure an investigation is started so we can clear you and your husband of this rubbish. The information I have should warrant an official inquiry. We don't want you two being extradited back to Mexico as soon as you return home."

Carol agreed and filled the professor in on the details of the raid on the Zapatista camp and Jim's suspicion that he was used as a pawn to lead the army there. She also carefully planted a seed that Captain Marquez may have been captured by escaping rebels during the battle.

The professor was intrigued by the story and promised to include it in his report to the FBI.

Dr. Redding finally ended the call, "God bless you and your family, Carol, and please be safe."

Forty-seven

The Saab 340B twin prop aircraft readied itself for landing at ciudad Acuna airport, not two miles from Mexico's border with Texas. It was a few minutes past noon and the sun blazed at the apex of its journey across the summer sky.

During the flight, the Iverson's had discussed in depth what would take place over the next five hours. A call had been placed to Jim's parents in Phoenix the night before and arrangements were made for them meet the family at the border crossing. Jim felt that having familiar bodies on the U.S. side to greet them would raise the family's spirits and take a load off Carol's shoulders as she waited for him to recover from his life threatening illness. Jim's parents didn't blink when they were asked to drive over fourteen hours to Del Rio, Texas. Jim rarely asked for help of any kind so they knew that the situation must be serious.

Carol grabbed Taylor's hand and led him down the stairs that had been positioned outside the shimmering aircraft. The suffocating heat of the border region launched itself at the family and threatened to sap their remaining strength. Jim followed slowly and watched for any signs the authorities had been alerted to their arrival.

Carol walked quickly through the small airport and exited out the main entrance. Stepping to the curb, she hailed a taxi and climbed into the back with her son in tow. The Iverson's had decided to stay separate but close during their time in the border town of Acuna. They assumed authorities might be looking for an American family of three so they wanted to remain as inconspicuous as possible. They had agreed to cross the border in the same fashion.

Jim stepped to the curb as soon as his wife and son departed and instructed a taxi driver to follow their car. The driver eyed him in his rearview mirror and finally tried to joke with the American.

"You really tied one on last night, *si?*" the driver laughed.

Jim smiled and nodded, holding both hands to his head, "Do you mind turning your music down just a little?" he asked.

The young driver, hoping for a healthy tip, complied without question.

"Thank you," Jim said as he slouched further into the uncomfortable rear seat of the cab.

Carol paid her driver and walked behind Taylor to a storefront a short distance away. She wanted to remain within sight of her husband as he climbed from the rear of his taxi. She had suggested buying lots of items from shopkeepers to further aid their disguises as simple tourists. She desperately needed a change of clothes anyway and her boy was eyeing toy sailboats carved from balsawood.

Purchasing several bags full of worthless trinkets, Carol finally sat down at a sidewalk café and ordered Taylor and herself sodas to cool off and wait for the afternoon rush back across the border. She watched over the rim of her glass as her husband sauntered by and smiled.

Waiting for an available seat, Jim leaned toward Carol and Taylor's table and remarked under his breath, "I feel like Tom Cruise in Mission Impossible."

Carol giggled, "You are much better looking than Tom Cruise."

Jim snickered loudly, "We both wish!" he said, winking at his smiling son.

Jim straightened, trying to look inconspicuous as he followed the waiter to a distant table.

The line through the customs and immigration checkpoint snaked back almost two hundred feet from the turnstiles that counted individuals as they entered the United States of America. Border patrol agents checked identifications while customs agents questioned random citizens about their trips to Mexico. Trained dogs with their handlers, walked up and down the moving line, searching for drugs and explosives. Mexican police officers stood with arms crossed, trying to look professional to their departing guests.

Carol and Taylor, with Jim only a few individuals behind, moved quickly through the line. In busy times, customs officers were known to rely mostly on profiling possible drug smugglers and illegal aliens. The sniffing dogs showed no interest in the Iverson's and neither did the American authorities.

A Mexican police officer stared at Jim as he shuffled past. Speaking into his radio, the officer stepped forward and placed his hand on the pale man's shoulder.

"Excuse me," he said in perfect English.

Sergeant Cerenio Gonzales had been on the Acuna police force for twelve years now. It was an exciting job that offered variety, as well as good pay. Just yesterday, he and a young rookie had beaten a pedophile to death. Sergeant Gonzales had recognized the man from a photo he had seen earlier in the week.

The American thug liked to cross the border into Mexico and prey on orphaned children in the back alleys of Acuna. The American authorities had caught on and sent a profile with photo to the Acuna police department, hoping they would help capture this disgusting excuse for a man. Sergeant Gonzales was happy to oblige.

From a young age, Cerenio had taken pride in his photographic memory. He had taught himself English by memorizing the pages of American novels, then retelling the stories to his smiling parents.

Today, Sergeant Gonzales and the rookie were watching tourists as they returned home from a long day of shopping and sight seeing.

It was boring duty, but the experienced officer had become very good at picking out possible drug smugglers from the tired faces. They seemed to sweat just a little more than those who crossed the border for legitimate reasons.

Cerenio currently had his eye on a tall American man. He looked pale and was sweating profusely. This man was either very ill or he was very nervous about crossing the border. The dogs had ignored him each time they passed but that just meant he wasn't carrying drugs.

Six years ago, the ambitious officer had been instrumental in capturing a man at this very spot, who was trying to cross the border with thousands of American dollars taped around his waist. They never discovered what the money was intended for, but the Acuna police kept the windfall regardless. Cerenio received a promotion and a very nice bonus for that bust. Maybe luck was still with him.

As Carol moved closer to the agents at the turnstiles, she pulled a recently purchased cell phone from her pocket and dialed Jim's parents. Richard, Jim's father, answered and sounded relieved by Carol's voice.

"Praise the Lord," he said, "I can see you guys from where I'm standing."

Carol searched beyond the checkpoint and found her father-in-law waving, standing next to his petite wife, Linda. Carol and Taylor waved back. They were less than five feet from crossing into America.

"Carol, why is that police officer stopping my son?" Jim's dad asked through his wireless connection.

Sergeant Gonzales recognized the American as soon as he turned. Just this morning he had studied a poster with this man's face on it, as well as a blonde woman who was his accomplice in a murder and prison escape. Cerenio spotted the woman about to cross the border and radioed for help. Two more officers heeded the sergeant's call and started after the American woman.

The rookie, sensing adventure, stepped close to the escaped prisoner and pulled his newly polished nine millimeter Glock from its holster.

Jim watched as his life unraveled in slow motion. The recognition in the Mexican's face. The radio call for help. The two officers approaching his wife and son. Side arms being pulled from their holsters. Time stopped as a thousand thoughts flooded his mind. Jim would die before allowing his wife and son to be hauled off to a Mexican detention facility. Instantly, a plan was set into motion to get his family safely across the border.

Sergeant Cerenio Gonzales, sensing danger in the American's eyes, also brought the events taking place to a near standstill in his mind. He could see everything happening in slow motion as if he were watching from above. His backup was in the process of approaching the man's accomplice. The damn rookie had stepped dangerously close to the man with murder in his eyes.

Sergeant Gonzales released the tab holding his side arm securely in its holster as the American drove the palm of his hand into the rookie's nose. A call for help escaped Cerenio's mouth as he stepped backward and drew his weapon. The American had skillfully removed the nine millimeter from the rookie's hand while the unconscious trainee fell to the ground.

The officers heading for the escaping woman heard the call for help and turned to see a now armed suspect pointing his weapon at Sergeant Gonzales. Forgetting the woman, both officers pulled their side arms and crouched for a clear shot at the American.

Jim was surprised at how easy it was to disarm the young police officer. As the events unfolded around him, he briefly turned to see Carol and Taylor pushing through the turnstile and racing for his parent's open arms in the United States of America.

Sergeant Cerenio Gonzales finally had a clear shot at the armed and turning suspect. Aiming center of mass, he pulled the trigger of his semi-automatic pistol and dropped the American in his tracks.

Forty-eight

A warm breeze passed through Jim's hair as he stood on the grass covered bank of the Tigris River. The wide body of water moved past with unhurried pace. Snow colored Egrets teased the surface of the placid water, feet tucked tightly against body, necks in graceful curve. Jim watched as leaves intermittently danced in the determined current, flowing endlessly from the Garden of Eden.

A Reed boat, woven from Assyrian palm, glided effortlessly across the deep green waters, with blood red sail set firmly against breeze. The vessel turned toward shore and berthed on a sandy beach near a slight bend in the majestic river.

An Iraqi boy with dark hair, dressed in brilliant white, climbed from the woven craft and walked barefoot to where Jim was standing. A long metal rod, held loosely in hand, swept through sparkling sand, marking the boy's progress as he approached the waiting man.

Smiling, he reached for Jim's hand. The young boy would be his guide across the river.

Forty-nine

Taylor sat in the sunroom just off the kitchen, picking at an egg salad sandwich. His father's memorial service had ended a few hours before with a blazing twenty-one gun salute and a mournful trumpeted rendition of Taps. Jim's ashes, given to Carol and Taylor by the Mexican government, would be spread near Trapper's Lake in the Flat Top Wilderness of Colorado. Jim had often spoke of spending eternity there.

Taylor watched as his mother, dressed in black, said goodbye to several guests at the front door. Grandpa and Grandma Iverson, Professor Redding, and several of his father's friends from work had just left.

Taylor's Great Uncle Harry hung in the distance as his mom spoke with two agents from the Federal Bureau of Investigation. Taylor liked his Uncle Harry. He was tough and protective and never let any person guess what he was thinking. He told them directly, just to eliminate any confusion.

Reaching into his pocket, Taylor pulled out the jade carving of a jaguar warrior his father had given to him shortly before he was killed in Mexico. He rubbed the highly polished figurine pondering the events that had led to his father's death.

Carol stood at the door, facing the men in fitted black suits. They had just finished informing the widow that all charges had been dropped against her and her deceased husband. FBI agents, in cooperation with the Mexican Federal Police, had interviewed villagers in Tojolaba and discovered the lies that had been fabricated by the Mexican army.

Shortly after the missing army officer had been discovered, hanging in an abandoned church in the highlands of Chiapas, a rebel commander had walked into San Cristobal and turned himself in for the murder of Captain Eduardo Marquez. He also helped clear the Iverson's with his account of the Zapatista's plan to kidnap the American family and hold them for ransom. Sergio Salinas would spend the rest of his life in a Mexican prison.

Carol closed the door on the departing agents and turned to her uncle. He had always been a source of strength for her and she needed him now, more than ever. In the days preceding the memorial, Uncle Harry had grilled Carol for every detail of their stay in Mexico. It almost seemed that he held himself responsible for her family's state of affairs.

Finally saying goodbye, Carol closed the door and turned to her quiet son. She was amazed at how much he resembled his father.

You may contact the Author at:
HaydenNovels@q.com

Here is a preview of
Tony Hayden's 2nd novel.
Available in bookstores now

Jaded Honor

1

———▪▪ • •• ▪▪———

Leadville, Colorado

L arge flakes of snow shimmered in the streetlamp as they glided lazily to earth, adding to the fourteen inches already blanketing the abandoned streets of Leadville, Colorado. On Harrison Street, just above the red brick Scarlet Lounge, a wood framed window marked by the yellow glow of a single bulb, announced to anyone who cared to notice that the tenant of this single room apartment was still awake.

Harry Pennington rarely slept at night. On most days, as the sun began to set behind the fourteen thousand foot peaks of San Isabel National Forest, Harry would think of his wife, Beverly, lost in a tragic automobile accident seventeen years prior. A framed photo of her was the only decoration he would allow in the bleak apartment. Tonight, it sat on the table facing Harry as he took the last pull from his two-hundred dollar bottle of Herradura tequila. It was the only luxury he allowed himself.

This night, the memories were especially cruel. He imagined Beverly calling to him from the ravine she had plunged into on her way home from work that tragic night in October, 1990. At the time, Harry didn't hear her calls for help. He was on a flight to Nicaragua to monitor elections for the Central Intelligence Agency.

"Fucking Nicaragua," came the slurred speech of a haunted man, "Fuck the CIA and the Sandinistas and Samosa," Harry raised his empty bottle in mock salute, "and screw you too, Oliver North."

Mournful sounds came from deep inside Harry's chest, "And fuck the drunks..." His voice traveled off into a low murmur.

It was assumed that an impaired driver had forced Beverly from the road that night. Two sets of skid marks stained the curve in the road, but no one noticed the damaged guard rail or Beverly's car, twisted between pine and boulder at the bottom of the chasm. The beautiful woman, in her mid-forties, laid trapped in the wreckage for three days before finally succumbing to internal injuries. She had scribbled a note to her husband during the final minutes of her life.

Sweetheart, I am in a better place. I waited for you as long as I could. Please forgive me?

Harry threw the empty bottle toward a trash can at the opposite end of the room. It missed and shattered loudly on the tiled kitchen floor. Finally setting his emotions free from their dark cell deep in his soul, Harry began to cry.

"I'm so sorry, honey," he blubbered through slobber and snot, "I should have been there for you. I should have been there to save you."

A loud knock came from the first floor entrance to Harry's apartment. The drunken man sat up and wiped his face with the sleeve of his shirt. The knock came again, louder this time.

Crying once more, Harry called out to the only woman he ever loved, "I am so sorry, Beverly. Satan's demons have finally come for me."

Banging again came from the darkened stairway. This time, sounds of splintering wood accompanied the pounding.

"They know the crimes I have committed. They have seen my victims and built my chamber in Hell."

226

Creaking came from the wooden staircase that led to Harry's room.

"I'm so sorry to leave you waiting again, Beverly. I am so sorry!"

———— ■— ▪▪▪ —■ ————

Bright sunlight reflected from a pure white blanket of snow. Brilliant rays assaulted Harry's eyelids as his head rested on the table in a puddle of drool and clear vomit. An odor of strong coffee assailed his nostrils and caused him to wretch. Sounds of dishes being washed in the small sink, not six feet away, brought Harry to full alertness.

Sitting up straight and wiping the liquid from his face with his crusted shirtsleeve, Harry shielded the sun from his eyes and scowled at the back of a young man, scrubbing diligently on a large coffee mug.

"Do you ever wash dishes around here, Mr. Pennington?" the young man asked, "The mold growing in this cup could provide enough penicillin to cure syphilis in Africa."

Harry tried to clear the gravel from his throat, "Who the hell are you?"

The young man sat the stained cup back into a sink filled with steaming water and turned to his haggard host, "My name is Brian Touts, Mr. Pennington. I'm a messenger with the Agency."

Harry, embarrassed by the pool of vomit on the table, reached for a dishtowel in Brian's hand, "Mr. Touts, do you often break into old men's apartments and do their dishes?"

Brian Touts smiled and leaned against the counter, "I have been trying to reach you for several days now, Mr. Pennington. Your telephone has been off hook and you fail to answer your door when the sheriff knocks."

"Hand me that roll of paper towels, Brian, then get the hell out of my apartment."

Taking the towels from Brian's extended hand; Harry peeled one off and blew his nose into the crumpled paper. Noticing the messenger had failed to move, he offered a warning.

"Colorado has a little law we affectionately refer to as 'Make My Day'. That means, Mr. Touts, that I can shoot any cocksucker who breaks into my home."

Brian Touts chuckled, "On the advice of your supervisor, I took the liberty of securing your firearms, Mr. Pennington. Would you like a cup of coffee?"

"Yes please. Black," Harry relented, "Then you can get the hell out of my apartment."

Touts poured the dark liquid into a drying mug and set it in front of Harry, "As soon as you sign for the message I have risked my life to bring to you, I will be happy to leave you alone, sir."

Squinting out at the glaring blanket of drifted snow, Harry took note that no cars moved on the streets below his apartment. Yanking the envelope from the messenger's hand and scribbling an illegible signature on a small notepad, the CIA veteran scoffed, "Son, you don't know the first thing about risking your life."

———— • • • ————

The sealed envelope sat on the counter, unopened, as Harry Pennington showered and changed into a pair of worn blue jeans and long sleeve western shirt. Soon to retire from a career he had once cherished, Harry eyed the dispatch on the counter with dread.

"I have less than three months of service left," he muttered to himself as he fumbled with the snaps on his shirt, "and these bastards just can't leave me alone."

Tucking his shirt in as he crossed the room, Harry retrieved the envelope from the counter and ripped at the perforated seam. Unfolding a single sheet of paper, the agent shook his head as he read to himself.

STRICTLY PERSONAL AND CONFIDENTIAL
OPERATIONS ORDER

To: Harry T. Pennington
        105 Harrison Avenue
        Apt. #3
        Leadville, CO 80461

From: Paul F. Teller
        Deputy Director of Operations
        Central Intelligence Agency

Subject: Central America/Nicaragua

You are directed to meet with Chief of Station, American Embassy, Mexico City, Mexico, no later than forty eight hours after receipt of this dispatch.

Paul F. Teller
DDO/CIA

Harry folded the dispatch and placed it in a small safe under his portable television set. Spinning the tumbler several times, he stood and scratched the stubble under his chin. Harry thought about his niece, Carol Iverson, and the tragedy that engulfed her family in Mexico a year earlier.

"Very good, Mr. DDO," Harry mumbled to himself, "I have some personal business to take care of in Mexico City anyway."

2

——— •••• ———

Puerto Cabezas, Nicaragua

The platform stood just outside the Miskitu market near the center of Puerto Cabezas, Nicaragua. A backdrop of brightly painted shops with rusting metal roofs and sagging porches revealed the impoverished essence of this Caribbean fishing village. A thousand locals, mostly Miskitu Indians, had gathered to hear Gino Nunez-Esquivel speak about his vision for the Nicaraguan people. A presidential election was less than a week away and Esquivel led the conservative incumbent, Felipe Cardenas, by wide margins in every poll.

Gino stood tall among the Miskitus; his confidence was infectious, "Nicaragua does not have to suffer from a civil war long past. We have paid our dues and it is time for our people to shine in the world's spotlight." The crowd cheered.

Feedback through the microphone gave a soft howl and brought the villager's attention back to the stage, "When you elect me as your president, five and a half million people will rise out of poverty and show our neighbors the perseverance of the Nicaraguan people. We will become a union of one people, focused on the survival and successes of our brothers and sisters and we will leave no family behind." The crowd erupted again in lingering shouts and applause. Optimism was a rare commodity in this tumultuous nation.

Gino removed a bright blue cloth from his pocket and wiped his forehead. A charismatic man in his late thirties, the candidate for the Independent Liberal Party (PLI) squinted through the glaring sunlight and smiled at the crowd gathered before him.

"The Nicaraguan people will no longer serve giant corporations for pennies each day in meager wages." The crowd exploded in deafening cheer. Gino raised his hands to quiet the mass, "And we will not ask them to go away." Before the citizens could react, he continued.

"As your president, I will work with corporations to build a package of government incentives that they will be unable to refuse, and all that we will ask in return is respect and a decent wage so that Nicaragua can feed and educate her children." Gino paused for a moment, then raised his voice, "But to accomplish this feat, you must all go to the polls on Election Day and ensure that your voices are heard."

Marimba music blared from a seated band at the foot of the stage as locals embraced and danced in the streets. Gino was pulled from the stage, laughing and dancing as he traded partners and worked his way through the crowd of admirers.

———— ••• ————

The Beech King Air 300 glided effortlessly over sleeping volcanoes, bound for the capital city of Managua. Lake filled craters hypnotized those aboard the twin engine plane with diamond like glitter as sun and surface danced in the afternoon rays. The aircraft and pilots were on loan to the Esquivel campaign by a popular cola company. Gino had worked out a deal with the corporation to build a new manufacturing and bottling plant near Leon, the commercial center of Nicaragua. For a handsome incentive package that included free land, water and power, the corporation was willing to employ over one thousand civilians and pay them a decent living wage. The company had also generously offered to build and staff several schools in the areas surrounding their plant.

Gino Nunez-Esquivel had a grand dream for Nicaragua. After fighting the Sandinistas as a young man in the late 1980's, he rose to prominence among the poor as their outspoken advocate. His heart ached when he learned of children dying from cholera and other preventable diseases. He had worked tirelessly to earn grants from the World Health Organization to help train doctors and nurses to work in rural communities. Gino had fought hard for the rights of workers, organizing unions to help laborers in the sugarcane fields and textile factories. He had also tasked himself as a watchdog against government atrocities, which earned him several attempts on his life.

Gino smiled at his wife and eight year old daughter, seated across from him on the comfortable plane. His dream was finally going to come true. Nicaragua would rise from ashes and take its rightful place as a leader in Central America.

"The plane will land in twenty minutes." This came from Gino's long time assistant Alberto Sacasa, "We have a rally at Velasquez Park this evening, and then dinner with the ambassador from Venezuela. I think you should prepare yourself for a scolding regarding your flirtatious affair with capitalism."

Gino chuckled and patted Alberto on the shoulder, "President Chavez will just have to forgive Nicaragua for our transgressions," he said, "We are not conveniently sitting on the world's fifth largest oil reserve as Venezuela is."

Breaking out his rechargeable razor, Gino continued, "Invite a journalist from Reuters to join us for dinner. We need to show the world that we do not answer to Hugo Chavez. If we are going to encourage investment in Nicaragua, we must moderate our voice and tuck away our egos."

"I agree, Gino," Sacasa nodded eagerly, "In less than two weeks we are finally going to drive the conservatives from power and send them scurrying back under their rocks."

Gino began shaving the stubble from his face, "No Alberto, we are not going to do that. If Nicaragua is going to be great, we will ask the conservatives to join our government. I plan to appoint Felipe Cardenas as Foreign Minister once we win the election. It will be an invitation to his party to put away our petty differences and work together for the benefit of our nation and her people."

Alberto sat back in his seat. Conservatives and liberals had never worked together in Nicaragua. If Gino could pull this off, it would definitely be the beginning of a new era in this polarized land.

3

———— • ••• ▬ ————

Mexico City, Mexico

Harry Pennington walked past Independence Column on Paseo de la Reforma Avenue toward the American Embassy. It had been a little more than twenty-four hours since he had signed the official dispatch in his apartment back in Colorado. Bright sunlight winked from the golden *Angel of Victory* atop the marble column, which represented Mexico's triumph over Spain for independence in 1821. Harry stopped and stared at a sculpture at the base of the structure. The blatant irony of a lion being led by a child caused Harry to smile. Today, Harry was the lion, and the child he was following was about to be bitten.

The American embassy worker he was following strolled toward an outdoor café that sported brightly colored umbrellas and small tables fashioned from black iron.

"Cozy," Harry sneered quietly.

He watched as the young man snatched a menu from the hands of a distracted host and walked toward an empty table near the edge of the patio. Finally sitting, with his back to Harry, the American scoffed loudly and flipped the single page menu over for more choices on the back.

"Are we having a bad morning, Mr. Stephens?" Harry stepped around the stunned consular agent and took a seat.

"Do I know you?" the American asked with surprise.

Harry reached across the table and shook the reluctant agent's hand, "My name is Harry Pennington." Opening his wallet, he displayed his credentials before continuing, "I am an agent with the CIA, and we are looking a little further into an incident that occurred in Chiapas last year."

Harry was referring to the kidnapping of his niece, Carol Iverson, and the arrest of her husband Jim during a research study they were participating in, in southern Mexico last spring. Their ten-year old son had gone missing during that time as well. Rick Stephens had been assigned from the American Embassy to make contact with Carol's husband before he was sent to Cereso prison in Villahermosa.

"I was fully debriefed last year by your boss. I've already told him everything I know." Agent Stephens noticeably dismissed Harry and looked over his shoulder for a waiter to take his order.

Harry slid a chair over from another table and finally sat, "New information has emerged concerning the event, and Mr. Hatch has asked me to debrief you again." Harry reached across the table and snatched the menu from the consular agent's hands. Speaking in a low voice, he informed the young man, "We can do this here, nice and friendly like, or I can take you down to the basement of the Embassy and question you there."

Rick Stephens snapped his head back toward Harry. Rumors of the monstrous activities that took place in the basement of the Embassy were well circulated. Marine guards were responsible for most of the tall tales that kept the staff in a state of constant fear.

Rick couldn't help being an ass; it was just who he was, "Alright, Mr. Pennington, but since you are interrupting my lunch break, I will be leaving work an hour early today."

235

Harry shrugged and sat forward for a more intimate conversation, "What information did you have when you were dispatched to Chiapas to meet with Mr. Iverson?"

Rick Stephens relaxed a little, "Just the basic stuff. American male in custody for the murder of a Mexican citizen. I was being sent to inform him of his rights and offer to contact a lawyer for him, notify next of kin, that sort of thing."

"What information were you given about his wife and son?"

"None! That is until I reached Villahermosa. That's when your boss caught up with me at the airport and filled me in on the details of the family."

Harry sat back in his chair and squinted at the young agent, "You mean to tell me that Chief of Station of the CIA, met you in southern Mexico to 'fill you in' on the routine arrest of an American citizen?"

Stephens scoffed, "Apparently not so routine, Mr. Pennington. This poor sap's wife was giving aid and comfort to the enemy. According to your boss, she was giving a whole lot more comfort than aid, if you know what I mean." Rick snorted and smiled, apparently pleased with his witty humor.

Harry wrestled his anger back into its cage and remained calm on the outside, "Did Mr. Iverson inform you that his family had been attacked, his wife and son kidnapped?"

Stephens became serious again, "He was blubbering some bullshit about intruders or something to that effect. Mr. Hatch told me to ignore his stories and expedite his transfer to the federal prison in Villahermosa. I was happy to do so. The guy was a complete asshole. I heard they shot him at the border near Texas. Serves him right; he was a fucking traitor to his country anyway."

Harry sat back again, visibly restraining himself. Jim Iverson was not only his niece's husband; he was also Harry's friend. He could not count the times they had sat together at the barbeque pit in Jim's backyard, drinking beer and exchanging stories of heroic service to their nation. It was all Harry could do to not strangle the arrogant little prick sitting across the table from him, "I see," was all he could think to say.

Rick Stephens stood from the table, "Look, the service here really sucks. Are we finished?" Without waiting for an answer, the young man turned and made his way out of the cafe. Harry stood and followed.

Coming to a vendor's stand just down the street, Harry caught up with the consular agent as he stood in line to order a *jocho*, a Mexican adaptation of the hot dog.

Stepping next to the young man, Harry asked, "You were made aware that Mr. Iverson's wife was in fact kidnapped by Zapatista rebels and their son taken by a Mexican army officer, right, Mr. Stephens?"

The agent looked at Harry with disdain, "I read the report. It was a real tear jerker." He rolled his eyes dramatically, "If Mr. Iverson would have just kept his whore wife at home, he would probably still be alive." Stephens stepped up to the vendor's cart, "Look, this is getting very boring and I haven't eaten yet—"

A blow to Stephens' wind pipe cut his sentence short. Harry grabbed the stunned man by the hair and shoved his head into a stainless steel tub of steaming water the street vendor used to keep his hot dogs warm for customers.

As Rick Stephens thrashed and water splashed, onlookers stepped back to watch the dying *gringo*. Harry shoved harder, forcing Mr. Stephen's face to the bottom of the container. Hot dogs spilled over the sides of the cart and bubbles appeared around the consular agent's head. The thrashing finally subsided and Rick Stephens' body fell limp.

After another full minute, Harry finally raised the dead American's head from the tub and checked his carotid artery for a pulse. There was none.

Dropping the dead agent to the sidewalk, Harry pulled a wallet from his own back pocket and removed a hundred-dollar bill, "You can leave work early today, Mr. Stephens, since you didn't get lunch and all." Dropping the bill on the vendor's cart, Harry turned, winked at the crowd, then headed quickly up the sidewalk, disappearing into the busy pedestrian traffic.

Made in the USA
San Bernardino, CA
20 May 2014